TRAGEDY TRAIL

TRAGEDY TRAIL

Max Brand®

GUNSMOKE

First published in the UK by Hodder and Stoughton

This hardback edition 2009
by BBC Audiobooks Ltd
by arrangement with
Golden West Literary Agency

ISBN 978 1 405 68245 9

British Library Cataloguing in Publication Data available.

Printed and bound in Great Britain by
CPI Antony Rowe, Chippenham, Wiltshire

1

A YELLOW DIAMOND

It blazed and sparkled in her hand so that, as the strong sun poured into it and came fountaining up again, reborn in yellow brilliance, it seemed that surely the delicate palm must be burning in the flames.

"It's a lot too much to give me," he said. "I can't take it."

"But I want you to take it," she insisted. "I lay awake a long time last night and wondered what I'd give you. I want you to take it, because I love you!"

With that she held out her arms and he took her tenderly and kissed her again and again, but she was unnerved and had begun to cry.

"I'm getting you all wet," said she through her sobs.

"I don't mind," said he. "I like it. But such a wonderful present!"

"It's a y-yellow diamond," said she. "Will you always keep it?"

"I always will!"

"You won't sell it?"

"Sell it? I'll wear it next to my heart."

"Then you'll remember me?"

"I don't need yellow diamonds to help me remember you," he said gently.

She raised her head and shook the tears away.

"Charlie loves you, too," she said.

"Ruth!" cried Charlotte.

"She does! She does!" exclaimed Ruth. "She cried about you last night, because you were going away. So why don't *you* give him a diamond or something, Charlie? Blondy will forget you otherwise!"

Charlotte had grown wonderfully pink, but the nod and the sympathetic smile of Blondy, given over the curly head of Ruth, made matters a little easier for her. Then he busied himself about Ruth; for he put her back on her feet and with a vast silk bandanna he

5

dried her eyes and her rosy cheeks, sitting on his heels so that he could be her height.

"I love you, too, honey," he whispered. "And I'll never forget; and I'll always keep the yellow diamond."

He took it at last from her small fist and placed it in his upper vest pocket.

"You see? Right over my heart!"

"Dear Blondy!" said the child with a burst of generosity and joy, "I wish, I wish that you could stay!"

But she added with a frown of practical wisdom: "I know, though. You've got to go and get rich and everything; then you'll come back and marry Charlie. Will you, Blondy?"

"Of course I will," said he, "if Charlie will let me."

At this suggestion Ruth turned and stared, almost fiercely, it seemed, at her big sister.

"Who *else* would she want to have?" exclaimed Ruth. "Have you said good-bye to Rover?"

"I couldn't find him, dear."

"I know where he is and I'll get him. He's watching a badger-earth on the hill behind the barn. You just wait a minute and I'll be back with him!"

Off she went, her brown legs twinkling in the sun and Blondy and Charlotte looked after her long and steadily, partly because they loved her, and partly because they were filled with fear at being left alone and dared not meet the eyes of one another.

After that Blondy made himself busy about his horse, pretending that the cinches needed to be tightened and the pack secured, though such matters, in the hands of Blondy, were not likely to need two doings. He spent so much time over this that at last most of the pink left Charlotte's cheeks and she grew self-possessed.

"Poor little Ruth!" she said. "You won't have to keep that glass thing, Blondy, of course!"

He took it from his pocket and smiled a little as the sun flashed and burned again in the heart of the crystal.

"I'd rather have it than all the diamonds in the world," said he. Then, closing his hand over it, he made himself look straight at Charlotte. "There's only one thing that I'd rather have, Charlie!"

The flame glowed again in her face, but she looked away at a white cloud which was blowing softly over the hill, and when she glanced back again, both of them tried to pretend that they had not understood. And now Ruth came racing with Rover circling gaily about her, filling the valley with his barking. There was not much time left before the child would be on them and Charlotte took advantage of the flying seconds to hold out her hand.

"Good-bye, Blondy," she said. "There's only one thing—are you really strong enough to take the trail again?"

"I'm as sound as nails," he answered, "and if they'd punched thirty bullets through me instead of three I would have got well—you've taken such good care of me, Charlie—I—thanking you isn't much good, though!"

Her eyes began to wander swiftly from side to side.

"I'd better go in," murmured Charlotte in a trembling voice. "I left something on the stove—I—it will be burning, I'm afraid. Good-bye, Blondy——"

And she whirled away and hurried toward the house in a flurry of wind that fanned out her faded gingham apron like a wing. With a full and aching heart he watched her go; then Rover and Ruth fell upon him and beat him like a cyclone with their affection and stunned him with their noise.

Barely could he manage to get into the saddle, and turning to one side, his hat waving from one hand and his bandanna from the other, he let his horse move off on the trail. He was waving to the child and the barking dog, ostensibly, but really his eye was glancing continually toward the house for some last glimpse of Charlie.

At last she appeared at the side door, not waving, but leaning back against the wall of the house as though she were hardly strong enough to stand against the wind. From the top of the hill he had a last look of them all—the dog still racing and barking, and little Ruth frantically waving both hands, and the red-roofed house with the garden behind it, and the barns and sheds beyond, and the silver face of the brook, shadowed by groves of trees, and all the windy hills of the pleasant range dotted with colour where the cattle grazed. Last of all, he saw Charlotte throw her arm across her face and go back through the doorway.

Then he turned a resolute face to the windings of the trail before him and rode on with a frown of pain, and a faint smile of joy; and sometimes he closed his eyes altogether in order to see the pictures in the brighter light of the mind, and sometimes he took out the yellow bit of glass and stared down at it, as though it were a pool which contained all the happiness in this world.

2

AN UNWILLING HOST

HE felt almost free.

Three months before, in the last white storm of winter, bleeding, sick, with the certainty of death before him, he had looked down into the hollow and told himself that it was only the illusion of his hope and not really the light of a house which glimmered through the ravings and the volleys of the storm, but he had made toward it and fell from his horse on the threshold.

Afterwards, lying in the clean, white bed, he had watched the spring come, stared at the pattern of yellow roses on the walls, examined with patient attention the cracks on the ceiling arranged like a great river with its tributary streams, and constantly he had waited for the end. Either the door would open softly and one of them appear, gun in hand, or else a shadowy head and shoulders would slip across the window and perhaps he would see the glitter of the gun barrel before he died.

Weeks went by before hope began to appear in his breast. He had fought with all his skill and all his might, and yet he had been beaten by their numbers and their craft, beaten and almost taken, and forced to take cover where all men might find him. How marvellous it appeared that they had not discovered him! Yet, as his mind cleared and he examined all the details of that terrible night, it did not appear so strange to him. Wounded or unwounded, only luck and a rare good horse could have turned him through the tangling hills to that one valley where the one house stood.

However, time went kindly and sweetly by in that valley. He could sit up, marvelling at the leanness of his arms and the bigness of his hands and wrists; he could have his chair in the garden in the spring sun; he could sit on the back of the creek and fish; and finally he could jog his horse through the hills and begin to help Guernsey with the cattle. He thought of that hardy frontiersman as the father of the freckle-faced little hoyden, Ruth, but it was hard to imagine that Charlotte was his daughter, except that she was silent, like him, and sure and swift with her hands. In all other things she was akin to no one he had known, and she filled his thoughts as fragrance fills a garden.

Now, with the trail before him, clothed in his old strength, clothed in a greater confidence than ever because in that last and most deadly battle he had managed to break the circle, he tried to put the valley and the valley's people out of his mind so that he could give unbroken attention to his work. He could not do it; it seemed that his self was divided and one man rode through the hills along the creek, and another was here upon the outward trail.

He accepted the thing at last; he had endured enough to trust time as a healer, and the pain which made his heart small today would be less tomorrow and still less the next day, until at last it was lost in the mute throng of sorrows which are the soul of this sad life of ours.

So, with acceptance, he found relief at once, and with clearer eyes he could look around him. These were wild hills, only thinly silted over with soil, which in a thousand places was quite washed away and showed the naked strata bent and broken by some earth-labour of a million years ago. In the hollows enough detritus had gathered to give rooting to wretched, undersized trees which looked as though they were perpetually storm beaten, and on sheltered slopes and in crevices was a sparse grass just thick enough to give cattle appetite without satisfying it. It reminded him, on the whole, of the country of the upper Las Vegas where he had made his strike and for one golden week saw incredible fortune before him.

La Salle had blocked him there as he had blocked him before and as, no doubt, he would block him again; yet when he looked back on the matter he was glad that he had not taken La Salle's cash offer of ten thousand. It was better, so Blondy Graem felt, to have endured pursuit, stood battle, and escaped with three gaping bullet wounds rather than to have accepted such dictated terms. He could even look back on the thing without much bitterness, for in most of us there is a blind and unjustified belief that our acts are placed on the knees of the immortal gods for judgment, and that justice, in the end, will be done. So he told himself that one day he would have full revenge if only he could avoid a knife thrust in the dark or the tagging of an unexpected bullet in the day. This was meagre fare on which to find spiritual content but Blondy Graem had lived many a year on no richer. Hardship had hammered his body to a wrought-iron toughness, and spiritually he was not much more soft.

There are some men who must be written down as professional optimists, and they are by no means limited to those soft lovers of tomorrow who live smugly by warm firesides; most of all the ranks are filled with just such lean-ribbed adventurers as Tucker Graem, who tell themselves that they are riding to reach a goal but who, in reality, ride only for the sake of the never-ending road which winds over the deserts and tangles in the mountain wilderness of this stern and beautiful world. Fifteen years before, he had gone out on a hollow-sized mustang with a single-shot pistol for weapon and cowhide boots on his feet. For fifteen years he had ridden the long trail with courage, with growing wisdom, but without success. Only his equipment had improved, but who will invest a quarter of a lifetime for the sake of a good pair of Colts, a fine Winchester, shop-made boots, and even an excellent horse to carry him? The horse, in fact, was a little exceptional, for it was a clean-limbed bay with quarters that would have carried three hundred pounds in the saddle. One needed only a glance at him to see that his rider was not apt to be a cowpuncher; a good puncher would have dismissed the fine creature with one phrase: "A high-headed fool." And so it was—a high-headed fool, excellent for stampeding cows, but not a whit of use for calmly riding herd by day or night, and unmentionable for cutting. It merely was meant to cover miles, and therefore it was ideal in the eyes of Graem, for of course it was merest folly to try to live one's life in one circumscribed and bounded spot where the same hills stare wearily down each day and the same crow sits on the same fence post and the same cow lows from the meadow: rather one must ride on and on until, in the end, one reaches the wishing gate, and all good things come true.

It seems a childish state of mind; perhaps Graem was above all a child; and certainly he would not have understood the wisdom of the poet who declared that the greatest journeys are not made by those who roam. He would not have understood, for he was committed strongly to one way of living, and only the gentle beauty of Charlotte Guernsey had startled him with the thought of another road to happiness: for that very reason he had left her, not knowing what impelled him. If he had been asked he would have called it duty, perhaps, for that is the word quickest on the lips of self-willed men.

He did not hurry his horse on this journey; rather he rode as one conserving the strength of his mount for one priceless burst of speed. To have seen Blondy Graem looking back from every eminence; to have seen him coming warily to every skyline; to have seen him loose the girths of the horse and let it take a mouthful of water at the brook, one would have thought that he was at that moment pursued or making ready for pursuit. Neither could he keep his closest attention from the trail, and with knitted brows he considered the sign that he met, determining its age, wondering why this man had galloped so hard, driving the hoofs of his horse deep, and why that one, fully a week ago, merely had walked his mount. He was like an anxious business man, turning the sheets of a newspaper for financial news; and such, in fact, was his work, for the open trail was his journal. He could have told you from that reading tales that would have made your hair stand erect on your head!

After midday he let his horse rest and graze in a secure place, and two hours later he continued through an altered landscape. The hills were less broken; the trees grew to a kinder size; and now and again he had a glimpse of a house in the distance, with the usual clutter of a rancher's barns and sheds, and corral fences stretched about like the thin lines of a spider's web.

The trail, too, turned into a travelled road, joined by bridle paths and rough ways from either hand and gradually becoming a rutted course, which led him, at the fall of evening, to a crossroads where stood a typical crossroads hotel. It was a conglomeration of general merchandise store, blacksmith's shop, post office, and inn, a tumbled, weather-browned, broken-backed building.

He rode straight past it and put up his horse in the stable. An ancient hanger-on would have taken the bay, but Graem was in the habit of giving far more attention to his horse at night than to his own personal needs. He took off the saddle and bridle and rubbed down the gelding with wisps of straw until it was fairly dry. Then he watered it, and, taking it back to a stall, he picked over the hay in the mow until he had found what he considered the sweetest bits with which to fill the manger. There were no oats, only barley in a broken-topped bin, but the grain had a dangerously musty smell, and he refused to risk it for his present mount. Given a hard-headed mustang, and it would have been a feast for the gods, but he who wears silk must not roll in the dust.

When at last he finished and saw that the straw was bedded down deep and level enough, he unslung his pack and carried it to the front door of the hotel. Crossing the yard, he had a vague feeling that he was watched, and glanced curiously up to the windows, but all were empty, it appeared, and rapidly turning black with the approach of night.

He was compelled to knock thrice at the front door before he received an answer, and a most churlish one; for the door was opened by mere inches and a gruff voice spoke to him out of the shadows.

"We're filled up for the night, stranger. We can't put you up."

"Hold on," said the traveller. "Not put me up?"

"Filled up," repeated the other. "Sorry—can't put you up"—and he shut the door with a bang, followed by the click of the bolt as he turned the key.

Blondy Graem turned away and stood at the head of the veranda steps. There were two things to do: one was to go proudly off, not thrusting his company where it was not wanted; the other was to make trouble. On the whole, Graem was not one to make trouble when it could be avoided, for he had learned many a year before that there is enough danger to be found in this world by accident without taking risks which are thrust upon one by malice aforethought. However, when he looked across the hills from the veranda he saw the night thickening rapidly, and when he stepped down to the ground he was greeted by a small rain, blowing coldly and steadily out of the west. There is nothing so disheartening as a wind-blown mist, for a slashing downpour raises the spirit by its force and its whipping challenge, but when the wind carries a mere fog of coolness it depresses the mind.

Graem shifted from one foot to the other and momently his temper grew worse; however, he started back for the barn and would have gone straight on to it had he not passed a window at the rear of the house with light streaming through the rain-blurred panes. At the same instant he inhaled a dim fragrance of cookery—cabbage, and ham, and the delicious aroma of coffee. Then he remembered he had not eaten since morning.

Of course he had pulled his belt a notch or two tighter many a time in lieu of a meal at night, but hardships which are merely exciting at first will in time be merely monotonous, and men strive harder against boredom than against danger, if the truth be told. He decided on the spot that he would not permit himself to waken in the middle of the night with an aching head and a pain in the stomach.

The front door, as he knew, was locked; the back door, when he tried the handle tentatively, proved to be secured also, but when he tested the window at the side of the little rear porch it gave a bit at once. So he prepared himself for an effort, then jerked the sash up and jumped on to the sill, with a long-barrelled Colt balanced in case of need.

It was as well that he had prepared for action. From the little kitchen table two men sprang up, and laid their hands on their weapons as they did so, while the Negro cook grasped a pot of boiling soup and made ready to hurl it at the invader. All the three were discouraged, however, by the sight of the naked Colt, and Graem slipped his feet over the sill and rose cautiously to an upright position. Still covering the group, he pushed the window shut behind him and then stepped away until solid wall was at his back.

In the meantime he took note of the pair.

One, whom he took to be the host, was as much like a walrus as a man, small-headed, and fat, with a fleshy, puckered forehead and a pair of such sabre-shaped moustaches as were generally affected by the rougher classes in the West a generation ago, when it paid a man to look as formidable as possible. His companion looked the part of a hard-working cow-puncher, for he was very sun-browned, wide-shouldered, and even in standing his bearing was clumsy, like one who is more accustomed to the saddle than to his feet. He was a black-eyed, black-haired fellow, beginning to turn grey at the temples, and on the whole he had the appearance of intelligence and penetration; he might have been boss, for instance, on a ranch of some size. Something about him was familiar to Graem, but he put that down to a trick of fancy; very often one thinks one recognizes the individual in the mere type.

As for the cook, he was a long, lean, very black Negro with enormous hands, and feet cased in vast slippers, as though no shoes could be found to fit him. By the look of his gigantic, bony wrists, he was a Hercules.

"Well," drawled Blondy Graem, "it looks like I had to be welcome, because I see you got more chuck than you can eat, and more room at the table than you can use. Sit down, friends, but just keep your hands on top of the table, if you don't mind!"

3

"TAKE YOUR OWN HORSE"

WILLINGLY they kept their hands on top of the table; the villainous cook ladled soup into a great bowl and sprinkled some chopped new onions into it to give it flavour; he hoped that the stranger would like it. The stranger did, and even declared that better soup he had not put a lip over since he was a kid.

In the meantime his game was very much like that of the juggler who keeps several balls in the air. It might well be that mine host, the walrus, and the half-recognized man of the black hair were not ready to use actual violence; they might have decided, simply, that privacy was necessary on this evening. This was an explanation a little too simple to satisfy Graem, but at least he held it in mind; while he was willing to believe the best, he prepared himself to encounter the worst. To that end he had taken the seat at the table which put his back against the wall, and now he was busy eating, using his left hand and keeping his right beneath the table, near the handle of a revolver. The Negro cook, in serving him, accepted the rules of the game and made no effort to come too near, merely reaching across from a distance to remove a plate and substitute another, or to refill the coffee cup. No one but a juggler could have maintained this position of Graem's; he, however, was not unused to such situations and took a professional enjoyment in the scene. He set about justifying his presence, in the first place, saying to the "Walrus":

"How long have you been running this show, old son?"

"Me? Fourteen years."

"You know the ways of the land then, partner; you know that strangers have a right to a bed, if there is one, and a chance to roll down their blankets in the hall if there ain't? They got a right to have chuck, too, if there is chuck to be had. If you're the boss of this show, my friend, you know these things."

These questions were not asked in a formidable tone, but rather in polite inquiry, and the Walrus grunted most affably; he even waved the entire matter into the thinnest of horizon mists while he asked in turn:

"What are you doin' in this hundred-mile country, stranger?"

"Hundred-mile country?" echoed Graem.

"Sure. Because a cow has to walk a hundred miles to pick up a meal."

Even the cook showed his white teeth at this remark, and there was a general chuckle, except from him of the black hair, who remained lost in a heavy gloom of speculation, drawing upon the surface of the kitchen table with a fork prong elaborate designs, and studying them with intensity.

Blondy Graem finished his meal. He stood up and stretched himself against the wall.

"Do I get a bed?" he asked.

The Walrus jerked his head upward.

"Go find one, kid," he said. "You're welcome; there's a good one down at the end of the upper hall."

Mr. Graem smiled and sidled to the door.

"You better tell me what I owe you," he suggested, "in case I don't see you in the morning."

"Them that come and take it," said the Walrus, with a cheerful grin, "are welcome. You save your money for worse weather than this!"

So saying, he waved a genial, fat hand, and Graem backed deftly through the door and side-stepped a possible following bullet. After that he scratched a match and lighted himself up the stairs. They squeaked and groaned under his tread, and in the upper hall the boards rattled like a loose bridge under heavy wheels. He went straight to the end of that hall, as he had been advised, and there he found a chamber with an iron cot made up for the night. He looked around it carefully, to see how treachery could trap him here, but all seemed well. There was no window within reaching or jumping distance of his bed; the bolt of his door was strong and well stapled; and he decided that if he could not trust himself to sleep here, he could not trust sleep in any community. So he undressed, gave himself a sponge bath with a bucket of water which stood in a corner, and turned into bed. Then, just as sleep began to numb his brain, his eyes opened wide and his wits cleared.

The vaguely familiar man of the black hair—of course he remembered him now, and odd it was that he should have been in the slightest doubt about the fellow. Yonder in the Las Vegas hills when the circle was thrown around him, one man had climbed to a slender, towering rock pinnacle that overlooked his improvised little fort of rocks. The dropping fire of that marksman had driven him from his shelter—driven him with a long, terribly painful wound that raked across his shoulders. Twice he had had a clear glimpse of the La Salle hireling and seen a keen, dark face. It was this same companion of the Walrus. He had no doubt of it; it was as though a photograph was labelled.

Instead of exciting Graem, this discovery soothed his nerves at once, for it removed the mystery from the situation. He simply had been seen from the window and the La Salle man naturally wished to avoid him; the rest followed as a matter of course. He felt no malice toward the fellow of the dark eyes and hair; one does one's work, and there is an end; if the cause of La Salle was a bad cause, that had nothing to do with La Salle's hireling.

Therefore, Graem stretched his toes to the bottom of the bed and closed his eyes in sleep. He wakened on the border of night and day, for the room was still black, but the window was grey with the first ghostly light of the dawn. Ordinarily, he closed his eyes for another hour's sleep, but now he rose as if under orders, tugged on his riding boots with a groan, threw some cold water in his face, and made up his pack automatically. In five minutes he was blinking at the gloomy hall before him.

It was not a desire for stealth that controlled him, but simply a charitable wish not to disturb other sleepers that made him pick his way close to the inner wall, where there was so little give to the loose boards that he crossed them in actual silence.

On the floor below he pushed open the kitchen door cautiously, for he was afraid of that rawboned man, the cook; but the kitchen was as dark and cold as all the rest of the house, with only a ghostly glimmer of pans on the wall behind the stove. In the corner of the table he left two dollars and a half, which he considered ample for his harbourage; after that he opened the back door just in time to see his own horse led out from the stable.

By the mere sound of his step we tell a friend, but it was by an instinct that Graem recognized the man who led the gelding; and a sad twinge of pain ran through the deep muscles beneath his shoulder blades where a bullet had ploughed across on a day. It was La Salle's hired man.

Then tardy anger seized upon Graem. All things considered, he felt that he had given this fellow the best of a good deal, and he could have sworn that another would have called that hired gunman to account at once; his reward was in seeing his horse led off in the stillness of the cold, wet morning. For it was still raining, and the wind blew in mournful gusts out of the northwest, tapping rapidly on the windowpanes.

He opened the back door, took his pack in one hand by the strap and a Colt in the other, and, so equipped, he went down the steps from the rear porch. The bay was already out of sight, but as Graem hurried around the corner of the inn, he saw the black-haired fellow of the night before in the very act of swinging into the saddle.

In no act is man more helpless; and after he is fairly between cantle and pommel, he still is taking in the reins with one hand and reaching for a stirrup with one foot. Blondy Graem laid the muzzle of a revolver in the small of the stranger's back and smiled amicably as the latter jerked a startled face over his shoulder.

"Here we are again," said Blondy with the benevolence of one who wins.

The black-eyed man smiled with instant assurance.

"He looked like one that could step," he said, "so I thought I'd try him out before you were up for breakfast."

"With your pack on him, and all?" grinned Graem.

The other lost face a little at this, and he turned grey, when Blondy added sharply: "Put your hands behind you!"

"Now what's all this about?" asked the stranger, nevertheless obeying and putting his crossed hands in the small of his back.

There they were seized and a bit of rope wound skilfully around them; the protests ended; there was only one half involuntary jerk, but Blondy held his man with a grip of iron.

"Now you can get down," he suggested mildly. "I'll hold your stirrup."

It isn't easy to dismount without the use of one's hands, but the fellow managed it neatly enough.

"You're taking this all wrong," he declared, as he touched the ground.

"Two times is unlucky," replied Blondy. "You shoot me up the first time and make me scoot like a scared rabbit, but you can't expect to steal my horse the second time we meet. Now, you admit, that would be rubbing it in a little."

His companion started violently. He stared at Graem, and then without attempting to deny the charge, he glanced at the hotel.

"Suppose that I yell for help?" he suggested.

Graem glanced in the same direction. Rain and the dull morning light had turned the windows grey.

"Some sing themselves into trouble and some sing themselves out," said he. "I dunno how your luck is running this morning."

The other grew silent.

"We gotta do something about this," said he.

"We do," admitted Graem.

"You ain't gonna be a fool about it, I hope?"

"I hope not."

"Graem," said the captive, "the fact is——"

There he paused sharply, seeing that the use of that name contained in itself many admissions.

"It's all right," said Graem, "but just you come back to the barn with me and point out your horse. You might as well ride in your own saddle, it seems to me."

"Ride where?" asked the other.

"To town," said Graem.

"Town?"

"Step along," said the captor. "I got no time on my hands!"

4

"WHEN I WAS A KID"

As though the beaten man realized that words were wasted after this point, he accompanied Graem silently to the barn and there, by lantern light, he pointed to an ugly roan and a saddle on the peg behind it. This, accordingly, Graem saddled and bridled; his own pack he strapped behind the saddle, and then in front of the stable he helped the other into a seat. The horse he secured with a long lariat, running to the saddle horn of the bay, and having arranged everything in this manner, he tied the feet of his companion into the stirrups, searched him for guns, and got three revolvers and a heavy bowie knife, and then swung into his own saddle and led the way past the hotel and on to the main trail.

There was no sound behind them and the glimmer of no light; dripping and dark the hotel watched them a while from dark windows and then was lost in the thickening gusts of the rain. The captive in the meantime was whistling a cheerful tune, and when the hotel had disappeared behind them, Graem freed his hands.

"It might help you to sing," he suggested with his usual grin.

Now that his hands were free, the other used them to roll a cigarette, which he lighted with skill, in spite of wind and rain, and rode quietly along, watching the brush at the side of the trail shudder under the rising wind.

"I hope it ain't true," he said, at last. Graem waited. "I hope it ain't true that you're a fool."

"You never can tell a man till you've tried him," declared Graem.

"I seen you tried once, but I thought that you'd learned a lesson. I hope it ain't true that you'd buck against La Salle twice?"

The captor was silent.

"Because," said the other, in a louder and more anxious voice, "it don't matter about me. Not a bit! But there's a hundred more that would take up the job where I left off; they'd have to settle you first, of course. Now, you use a little sense, kid, and you'll see that I'm right."

To this Graem made no answer, but contented himself with watching the hills through which they rode. There was a limited horizon, for the full light of the day had not yet begun and the rain gathered like fog—fog that moves in heavy waves before the wind. It was hard to tell the hanging drifts of moisture from the tall trees that loomed here and there like grey ghosts.

"Graem!"

"Well, partner?"

"It's a good bluff that you throw. Only—why d'you take this direction?"

"Because it leads me to a town, and in the town there's a jail, and in the jail there's a sheriff, and that sheriff is a friend of mine, old son."

The captive laughed, but, though he made a brave effort, the sound was unmusical and untrue.

"Look here," he added huskily, "you hear me, Graem?"

"I hear you."

"I'm on an important job. I can't be stopped. I know. You remember that day on the upper Las Vegas and you want blood for blood. Well, that's a fool's way of looking at it. But lemme tell you. I got a packed wallet, kid. Look here! There's more than five hundred in that wallet. You're welcome to it. But I can't waste any more time. Understand?"

He smiled expectantly, holding out the wallet, but Graem simply regarded the rain ghosts that went past them with a wail and a swishing sound upon the brush.

"I'll tell you a yarn," he said at last, as the wind died for a moment around them, and only kept up a distant complaint among the hills. "I'll tell you how it is. When I was a kid of fifteen I was as green as grass."

"I been that age myself," said the listener with ready sympathy.

"I got into the range; I worked and made a little stake; I bought me a horse and found me a partner, and we started out to find gold. We came to a stretch of desert, y'understand? It was deep, bad going, busted up with stretches of bad rock, here and there, and my partner's horse stepped on one of those rocks and went dead lame.

"Well, we were a long stretch from a water hole, but I stayed with him, of course, and we took turns on horseback, and that night we made a dry camp. You know what a dry camp on the desert means, partner?"

The other found occasion to rub his throat.

"I know," said he.

"What's your name?"

"Jerry. They all call me Jerry."

"When I woke up in the morning," said Graem, "it was still dark, Jerry, and I looked around for my partner and hollered that it was time to break camp and start on."

Here he paused as though to give his imagination time to conjure up that moment out of the past.

"My partner was gone," said Graem. "Faded out complete. Mind you, he was an older and a stronger man than me, and a lot wiser than I ever could be, and he knew that I was a tenderfoot and a greenhorn.

"'Great Scott!' says I to myself, 'he's taken his lame horse and gone away; he wouldn't be a burden to me!' But I was wrong, Jerry. When I looked at the horse that was left, I seen that it was the lame one!"

Here Graem laughed a little.

"I started on," said he, "leading the lame cayuse. We went for thirty-six hours. Twice the mustang lay down and I kicked him up. Once I lay down and he stood over me and gave me his shadow, if you know what I mean! Anyway, at the end of the thirty-six hours of going blind, he took me to water where no water was supposed to be. We both lived, and a week later we got out of the desert."

"He was a skunk, the hound that double-crossed you there," declared Jerry with extreme heat.

"His name was La Salle," answered Graem, and Jerry bit his lip.

"Well," drawled Blondy, "I dunno how it is, but ever since that day I've hated a hoss thief. Times has changed; the desert ain't as wicked as it used to be, and there ain't any desert right around here; but still I can't help hating a hoss thief!"

"And you're right," said Jerry hotly. "A low sneakin' useless lot they surely are——"

But here Graem turned a quiet glance upon him and his voice died away. It came again in excited stammering protest: "Look here, Graem, you don't think that I'm one of 'em! You wouldn't class me as a—a——"

"I recollect when I was a kid," said Graem, breaking in without violence, "that in our block in town there was a dog-gone mangy cur that wasn't any colour, but mostly scabs and pink flesh. He would stand around shiverin' in the wind with his tail between his legs and lookin' like nothin' at all, and his ribs was always stickin' out, because he didn't have no home, if you know what I mean. Well, sir, every new dog that come to town no sooner seen that caricature than he went for him to shake the bones out of that mangy sack of hide, though he looked so bad that you would never expect that a decent, upstandin', self-respectin' dog would even want to bite him, he was that low! However, when the fight began, it was wonderful to see old Pinkie, as we used to call him, pull himself together. Once he got started, he never finished until he'd quietly got a grip on the throat of the other dog, and then he closed his eyes and wiggled and chawed, and chawed and wiggled, until he'd eaten the life right out of the new dog. Now, I'll tell you the reason why. You never would've taken him for anything but a mongrel hound, but the fact of the matter was that he was a white un, in spite of the pink look of him. That was a white bull terrier, and he was clean bred back as far as Adam, and he had the heart of a giant locked up inside of his mangy skin. So I learned from that dog that you never can take things for what they seem to me. To take a look at you, *I'd* say that you were a straight-shootin' puncher and a decent sort, if yo' understand what I mean. But I've seen you fighting for La Salle in his gang of hired cut-throats, and I've seen you riding out on my horse on this here wet morning, Jerry; and so I let the looks go by and I say: you're a low-down, worthless, sneakin', man-killin' horse thief, Jerry, and I'll never leave you till I get you inside of that jail; and if the boys want to lynch you for what you are, I ain't going to take the stump and speak against what they want. Now, Jerry, maybe you and me understand each other better, and we won't have to waste no more words. Because, to tell you the truth, it hurts me, Jerry, and it near breaks my heart to have to yarn with a yaller-bellied fish like you!"

When this long speech was ended, Graem looked up to the sky and yawned to see a rift in the clouds and a slit of blue beyond it. Silence as a matter of course followed; the rift grew wider; the clouds began to tumble down from the vault of the heavens as though rolling with their own iron weight, beating out a sound of thunder from the invisible bridges of the sky. Presently the low eastern sun was shining; it flashed incredibly bright on wet bushes and on thin ponds standing on the fields. By degrees, as its strength increased, steam rose from the hills and the bogs of wetness, so that trees and valleys were walled away behind transparent silver and only just above their heads was the sky richly blue.

Through all of these changes of atmosphere, the captive said nothing, offered no further persuasion, suggested no ameliorating explanation of his crime, until they came to a crossroads, or rather a dim crosstrail, and Graem turned to the left.

At that, as though wrung out by agony, the voice of Jerry cried: "Why that way, Graem? Why that way?"

"This is Loomis way," explained Graem.

"But it's twice as far as Chandlerville!" exclaimed the prisoner. "And its jail ain't half as big or as strong. Why d'you want Loomis, Graem?"

"Because the sheriff there is a friend of mine," said Graem, and he added softly: "Once he had a little job put up on him the same as me; and ever since that day he's nacherally hated hoss thieves. He's gone out after 'em like trout fishers go after trout, and salmon and perch won't tempt 'em. That's why you're gonna go to Loomis."

Then he began to frown and stare attentively at his captive, for the latter had taken on the appearance of a very sick man, grey of face, hollow of eye. He attempted to speak at that instant, but no words came, and his mouth sagged open, and his dull eyes looked blankly across the steaming hills where Loomis lay in wait.

5

INTO THE STORM

EVEN in fear there may be control; even when blank panic seizes upon the spirit there may be a restraint opposed to its sway. So it was with Jerry, who journeyed on through the day like a man in a dream, or like a condemned criminal who realized that all chance of appeal had vanished. It seemed to make no difference to him that they skipped lunch—having had no breakfast—and he even descended to small talk in a sort of numb and hopeless manner, as one on board a sinking ship might admire a sunset, as the deck beneath him staggered to the grave.

Blondy Graem, not being a man utterly without heart, took notice of this attitude and eventually asked some questions. For one cannot take so much as a cricket from a million of its kind, for the purpose, say, of a scientific experiment, without wondering if the chosen victim has not some claim to be considered different from the rest of its fellows. So he asked about the past life of his companion, where he was born, where he had lived in the meantime, what was his family, had he wife or children, what was his ambition, and what was his hope?

Mechanically Jerry answered, his hollow voice sounding without passion, and without hope that, in his answers, he might waken some sympathy in the breast of his captor, for the little story of the horse theft in the desert had not been told in vain.

He was born in Louisville; he had gone to New York with his father, as a boy, and there he had become apprenticed to a blacksmith. Having reached early manhood, he had qualified as a member of the trade, only to succumb at once to the yearning for the free West which had been born into his blood. So he had gone West, and there he had followed all the usual trades, from punching cattle to driving mules, and had come, at last, within the sphere of La Salle's influence.

It was strange to hear that gloomy, hopeless voice narrate the incident which first brought him to the notice of La Salle, master criminal, master of men. He told how one "Nashville Jack," filled with pride and folly, had attempted to terrorize a little border town, and had succeeded very well, though watched by one handsome, slender, dark-faced man with curiosity rather than with anger—and how Nashville Jack, at the last, had collided with Jerry. There had been a brief interchange of words, then the crash of guns, and as the smoke cleared, Jack lay on his face, clutching a newspaper in one hand and a gun in the other, while Jerry stood over him, still frightened, but still determined.

"That handsome gent with the brown eyes, he took me aside afterwards: 'I think I could use you,' he says to me, 'and perhaps I could be useful to you.'

"'How come?' I says.

"'For one thing, I can tell you that Nashville Jack is the blood brother of the sheriff of this county.'

"It scared my wits out," admitted Jerry. "I asked him what I could do.

"'You leave it to me,' said he, 'if you want to pay my price for the thing.'

"'What price?' says I.

"'You'll be my man, kid,' says he.

"'How long?' says I.

"'So long as you live,' says he. 'At good wages,' he adds.

"Well, who minds being somebody's man so long as he lives—at good wages? I thought it over; I looked him in the eye, or tried to. But the job was hard.

"'What's my proof that you can do what you say—save me from the sheriff and then give me a steady job?'

"'My name is my proof,' says he.

"'And what's your name, partner?'

"'My name is La Salle!'

"Of course I'd heard of him. Who hadn't? I knew that he'd done more crooked things than any man living on the border, but I knew that his word was stronger than iron. I looked him over again and then I held out my hand.

"'You take me in,' said I, 'and I'll never double-cross you. I'm your man, La Salle.'

"It was a one-horse dump, that town," continued Jerry. "I hardly know where it was standing, because the prairie rose up and swallowed the place one day. A fire in the fall, and the next spring the grass was jumping up right over the foundations of the town. Anyway, that day when we walked out in front of the hotel things looked full of life, and I remember that the anvil in the blacksmith's shop was clanging and banging, and the hammers was clattering on a couple of shacks that was being run up across the street. It looked like this place was just a sample of the whole West—everything growing—a man couldn't take on any job without making good at it.

"Then I thought of La Salle. He was young, hardly older than me, but he'd made his name."

"As a horse thief, and such?" suggested Blondy Graem gently.

The narrator ran on over this interruption: "I felt that I hardly cared where I threw my dice, because in that country I couldn't lose. Besides, an honest man gets a sort of a thrill out of working for a crook, letting go all holds, trusting to chance, letting the crooked brains work for him. So I worked for La Salle. And I never knew a time when my pocket wasn't full of money. I'll tell you what I've done. I've gone to La Salle, and I've said: 'Henry, I'm tired of this game. I want to quit, and I want a stake to quit on.' I was mad drunk at the time. I was wild with booze. I would've fought if he'd turned me off with a shrug. Well, he knew that, but it wasn't fear that made him answer."

"No," agreed Graem, with something between a sigh and a groan. "fear never made him talk."

"He gave me five thousand," said the other, with a touch of awe which almost overcame his hopelessness.

"'You come back whenever you want to,' says the chief.

"'I'll be hanged if I ever come back,' says I. 'I'm gonna buy a farm and settle down to a white man's life.'

"'I hope you do,' says La Salle, 'and I'll help you out whenever I can!'

"He did too. I started a ranch, and he bought my grain and cows at top prices. Fire and Indians cleaned me out. I went back to him after three years. 'I'm coming back,' says I.

"'You've had hard luck,' says La Salle. 'Work a while and make a stake and I'll be glad to see you start for yourself again.'

"So I went back to work for him, and there I've been working ever since—until the other day—until the other day——"

The voice of Jerry died away, and he looked dismally before him into the horizon mist, while Graem reconsidered the picture. The cunning of La Salle, admittedly, surpassed the ways of human understanding; for he was quite capable of setting up a valued assistant in independent life, in order to buy his gratitude, and then ruining him in order to bring him back into the number of his hired men.

"Who started the fire that cleaned you out?" asked Graem.

The other turned to him with a smile and a snarl.

"I know what you mean. It might have been La Salle. Perhaps it was. I dunno. He could do anything. Anything!"

And he relapsed into his hopeless silence again.

They had been climbing a range of hills all the afternoon, and now from the summit they looked down at Loomis town itself, and at the grey expanse of the desert beyond and below it. For Loomis stood at the mouth of a shallow valley that stretched back into the lumber and mining regions of the upper mountains, and at its portals the wagon trails converged from the desert and the bridle paths wound to its threshold. It was a halting place for those bound south to the hot desert and for those bound north to the iron mountains, and the value of that halt made its existence. They could see it clearly, though it was thirty miles away, for the rain mists had cleared, the air was dry, and nothing lay between them, except the descending ranks of the brown hills, unbroken by a tree, hardly spotted by a bush. It was not a hot day; a slight breeze out of the north tempered the air, and even the spirit of the captive rose a little, though he was looking down upon the town which he dreaded to approach.

"I remember once," he began, "I had a stake from La Salle, and I was in Loomis, and I had a pal along——"

His voice trailed away and he looked curiously at his companion, not as at an enemy, but as at an overmastering fate; his tale died unspoken.

Descending the winding trail from the upper hills, they came in sight of a rising wall of purple in the south, and the northern wind had died away.

"It looks like a blow," suggested Graem. Jerry said nothing, but draped his slicker around his shoulders.

In half an hour the first gust reached them—a hot oven breath with force enough to stop the horses in their tracks. Heaven alone could tell what an inferno raged on the desert beneath the hills, but even upon that height the force of it snatched the breath from the nostrils. At first there was a brown haze of finest dust which sifted at once down the neck, and through the protecting layer of silk bandanna into mouth and nose and ears. Then came the sand itself, cutting the skin, and making the horses whirl around—driven to face the sandstorm by the compelling spurs, and turned away from it by the cutting force of the blast itself.

The horizon was narrowed to a twenty-foot vision through a mist of grey and brown; the sun was a blood-red circle pressing down through the smoky atmosphere; and the hills were utterly lost to view.

Bowing their heads, they straightened their horses down the trail.

"There's thirty miles of this!" shouted the captive, and his voice came in a faint and far-away whisper to Graem.

For a weary, stifling hour they beat on their way, losing the trail again and again and fumbling for it with infinite difficulty. Then a building loomed like a shadow at their right, and they both turned instinctively toward it. They rode straight up beneath the wall, and found raw, unpainted boards rising above them.

The house shut some of the roar of the wind away from them.

"We stay here for the night," yelled Graem, and the other, cupping his hand behind his ear, heard and understood with gratitude.

6

MINE EASE IN MINE INN

IT was a new inn which they had stumbled on by lucky chance. The discovery saved them from the necessity of halting on the lee side of a hill, digging in, and lying face downward on the leeward of their horses, with silk handkerchiefs tied over nose and mouth, fighting for every breath, and so remaining for miserable hours.

In the barn behind the inn, where they left their horses, the atmosphere was a dusty brown, and the horses coughed heavily in the unnatural twilight; even in the house itself the sandstorm had penetrated and made a false dusk so that the lamps had to be lighted, and shone with a brown halo around them, for the fine dust had penetrated everywhere through the cracks in the ill-built structure.

It had been erected by a hardy old pioneer who, having washed a little gold on the desert and saved a bit from riding herd, had moved to the happier hills on which he had looked longingly many a time from the hot flat beneath them, envying their cool mist of blue that filled all the hollows on the hottest of August days. He had gone to Loomis, first of all, trusting that he could build there, but the sight of the many people discouraged him; he had been accustomed to the desert silences for too long to endure the noise of many noises day and night. Therefore, he came up through the hills and settled not at a crossroad, but merely where two trails joined. Already he had been here a year. His guests were few, but they paid well, and often they remained for many days together. What induced them to stay there would have been hard to guess in other countries, but here Graem understood that there were many men who would not relish the curiosity and the many eyes of a prying town. For such as these, the host was a perfect man. He asked no questions; neither did he look for trouble; he did not even raise his shaggy brows when he saw Graem enter with Jerry lashed to his left wrist. But without a question, as though this were the ordinary manner in which people entered his hostelry, he showed them to a room, brought them hot water—with a film of settled dust on the top of the pail—and then, as the night began, he served them with a meal of fried mutton, stale homemade bread, and coffee.

Afterwards they sat about and listened to the dying scream of the wind which diminished until the host could open doors and windows and let the fresh, pure air blow in through the house, sweeping whirlpools and eddies of the dust before it. At length, they could sit on the front veranda and watch the luminous faces of the kind stars that shone on mountain and desert alike.

Gladly the host would have talked, but since his guests offered no leaders, he asked no questions, and contented himself with speaking gently of his own life on the great sun-dried plains below, maundering on from point to point. He spoke of the days when the great herds were driven up from the southwest to the cattle marts which roared with guns and brief prosperity in the early days. He spoke of brief fierce tyrannies of cattle kings and bandits, of wars between sheep-herders and squatters on the one hand, and the lords of the cow range on the other. The sense of trailing years seemed to seep through him; the past was mirrored in him as the stars are mirrored in a calm pool, or as a wild storm hangs quiet as a picture in the broad, calm surface of water. He was a part of all that he had seen, but divorced from it by the wisdom that comes of long experience. One might have thought that he was talking now with children of his house to whom he could unbosom himself quietly and freely, rather than to strangers who were lashed to the wrists of one another and for one of whom, beyond doubt, some savage fate lay in wait. No doubt, upon this situation the host pondered with all the intense cleverness of one accustomed to puzzling out complicated, dim trails upon the desert; but he did not allow this preoccupation to prevent him from fulfilling the duties of a perfect host.

Up the trail from Loomis came a solitary horseman, shadowy and faint of outline against the blacker, distant hills. Past the three glowing cigarette stubs on the veranda he jogged his horse, then turned sharply.

"This here is Crocker's place, ain't it?" he asked.

"I allow it is," answered Crocker.

"Well, so long, boys!"

And the stranger jogged off up the wind, and presently appeared against the stars, a big, long-legged man who made the mustang that carried him appear no larger than a burro. He dipped over the next ridge to the east, and the talk of Crocker's went on where it had left off and flowed smoothly forward into the tale of how Billy, "the Kid," spent his last night on earth, how he came toward the house of his friend, carrying a steak in his hand, how he covered one of his enemies in the yard of the midnight house, but allowed the man to go, by some freak of mercy or of doubt——

"Crocker!" broke in the sharp voice of Jerry.

"Aye, partner?"

"Is there a lower trail running back toward Loomis?"

"Aye, there is," murmured Crocker. "Why?"

He allowed himself the luxury of this question because the sudden remark of Jerry had startled him out of his customary self-control.

"Listen, listen!" gasped Jerry.

He raised his free hand; they grew quiet; in the intensity of the stillness all senses were sharpened and they could notice distinctly the sour savour of the alkali dust, not yet settled since the last rider went by. Presently they heard also the rattle of hoofs from lower down the hillside, a sound instantly muffled by sand and grass, but barking out at them again over a stretch of rocks and gravel.

"Somebody's streaking it," said Crocker. "There ain't anything funny about that. If you're in a dead hurry, you take the lower trail; if you're hunting for comfort and good going, you take the upper way."

"Oh, damn all the fools!" groaned Jerry. "Will you listen again, I say? Will you listen?"

They became silent again, but far more strained, for the terror and the hard breathing of Jerry made a pulse of fear in all their hearts.

"D'you hear?" murmured Jerry.

"He's still legging it," answered Tucker Graem.

"Lame in a foreleg," exclaimed Jerry. "That hoss is lame in a foreleg. You see what that means? Him that rode by here a minute ago, he had a hoss that was lame in a foreleg, too. He's ducked back for Loomis when he passed. He's gone to tell. He's one of them. Graem, for Heaven's sake, lemme go, will you? Damn you, will you lemme go?"

His voice broke, as a child's voice breaks when it is overwhelmed by emotion; and like a child he flung himself at Graem with his free hand, as though he had forgotten for the moment that his captor was armed and could drive a ·45 calibre bullet through his body at any moment. He put home no blow. Inside the lifted, flailing arm of Jerry, Graem hit hard and short, like a snake that strikes without preliminary coilings. There was a dull, chopping sound and Jerry fell inert. Graem stood up with the senseless body in his arms.

"I guess it's bedtime, partner," said Graeme. "You mind showing me where we bunk in? We'll need a couple of beds in one room, if you can manage that; otherwise we'll just thank you for mattresses and sleep on the floor."

Up the stairs ahead of Graem went Crocker, carrying a lamp and giving the uncertain flame the additional shelter of his hand; after the outdoors, all within the house was close and hot and filled with an alkaline pungency from the sandstorm; a thin mist still hung in the air and stung their eyes. Down the hall above, Crocker led to a rear room. Walls, ceiling, and floor were bare, unpainted boards.

"Open the window, Crocker."

It was done, and Graem stood at it, breathing deeply of the purer air of the outer night. He took note that there was no break beneath the window, but a sheer fall to the ground of twenty feet; two casements were below, but each was considerably to the side.

After that he looked up, but the eaves were high above, raised over another storey and an attic; overhead also there was no window in line with his room. When he had made sure of this, he nodded with satisfaction and turned from the casement, still holding the burden of Jerry as lightly as ever a mother held a child. "You got a good layout here," said he.

Mr. Crocker lifted his lamp a little and lifted his eyes also beneath their bushy brows so that for a moment he stared at his guest with almost a fierce interest.

"I thought that you'd like it," said he. "I kind of thought that this was the only room in the house that you'd like at all." And he smiled faintly. Then he added: "You want anything for him?"

Graem laid his victim on the bed and undid the lashing which bound their wrists together; after that he tied one foot of Jerry to the foot of the bed and one hand to the top of it; still Jerry lay in a deep trance. A dark purple mark was rising on the side of his chin.

"The button," remarked Crocker with interest, leaning to watch the spread of the spot. Then he glanced curiously at Graem's wrist, arm, and shoulder. "It's in knowing how," smiled Crocker. "It's in knowing how and where, even in the dark."

He favoured his guest with another rather grim smile, and then retired and shut the door softly behind him. This admiration had been so peculiarly flavoured that Graem followed and listened at the threshold with keen attention; his own step was of a catlike softness, and that of the host was equally silent, for no squeak or groan of the new flooring attested his passage down the stairs or through the hall. So Graem finally turned away, rubbing his knuckles over his chin; turned to find his captive at last recovered and working with a stealthy and frantic haste at the knot that fastened his hand to the head of the bed.

7

A SCREECH OWL?

WHEN the captive saw that his efforts were observed, he ceased them and lay staring at Graem with gloomy, wide eyes. The latter sat on the edge of the bed and observed quietly: "You'll have no luck working on those knots, old-timer. If you had both hands and daylight to help you, it'd still be only luck that'd show you how to loose 'em. So I advise you to sleep quiet through the night. It's the best way; it'll rest you up for what's coming."

Jerry closed his eyes. A gust of night wind at the same moment tossed the flame in the lamp, and perhaps it was this wave of light that made the features of the captive seem to twist into a convulsion of agony. But he said not a word while Blondy Graem tossed off his clothes, gave his riding boots a careful rubbing, then put out the lamp, and stretched himself on the second cot with his good-night cigarette between his lips.

"Are you smokin', Jerry?" he asked courteously.

Jerry responded with a sigh. At length his voice, made as soft as possible as though to guard against eavesdropping, murmured: "Blondy, what d'you want out of me?"

"What the law gives me," said the other calmly. "I'm not a pig, I'll take what the law gives. Three or four years in the pen for you is all that I hope for."

"If you could get more?"

"Five would do for me. I dunno that I hold the shooting against you, old-timer. It's only the horse stealing."

"So—so—so," murmured Jerry to himself, and made another pause before he sighed again.

Then he remarked: "Lemme tell you something."

"I'm listening."

"You'll never get me on the inside of a jail."

"You're a doggone bright optimist, Jerry. You don't know the way the folks feel about horse stealing in Loomis."

"You'll never get me to Loomis."

"Thanks," chuckled Graem. "I like the way you put it, but no matter how many partners you got working for you, I'll lay a bet with you that I pull you through to Loomis."

"You got no chance at all," said the prisoner with grave

deliberation. "I been laying here and thinking it over; you got no chance at all. I've worked it out. You can add up the chances each way, and I've added them up."

"Go on," said the captor. "You sound like a story, old son. Go right on."

"You got everything," said Jerry. "You got the fast hand and the straight eye, and you got the brain in your head; but you ain't got the numbers, and you ain't got La Salle behind you. You can never get me there."

"It's a good bluff that you throw," admitted Graem honestly.

"Bluff?" cried the other, growing hot. "Bluff? Do dead men bluff?"

"You're dead, are you?"

"I'm a dead man," said Jerry.

"But still able to say your piece?"

"I dunno how it'll hit me," said Jerry thoughtfully. "Poison, a knife, a bullet, or maybe a rope tossed over my head from the window, yonder, and pulled tight—they got different ways of working, and all of them are good; but I know that I'm a dead man lyin' on this here bed, and neither you nor anybody else can ever get me alive through that door, or through that window."

Graem tossed his cigarette through the window; it vanished in a thin, red arc.

"I think you mean what you say," he muttered.

"I can smell my own death," said Jerry with emotion, "as clear as you can smell the sod that's been turned up out of a new grave. I tell you, this here room is a coffin, and I'm chokin' for breath in it!"

These were hysterical words, but the dull and quiet voice of Jerry gave them a different significance. Here Graem slipped from his bed, glided to the door, and flung it open. Straight down the hallway he looked; through the window at the farther end he could see the horizon stars, but not a sign of anything stirring against them. So he closed the door softly and went back to his bed.

"I thought I heard something," he explained, "but I was wrong."

"You were right," answered Jerry, "Aw, they're here, all right, by this time!"

"You mean what?"

"La Salle's men—his nighthawks, his damned sneaking murderers and crooks," said the prisoner in the same quiet voice.

"You been running away from him?"

"I have."

"But by your own account, there ain't any use in trying to run from him."

"I was a fool," said the prisoner heavily. "I was a terrible fool. But when I seen the chance, it looked to me like it was worth even defying La Salle for the sake of it. Who wouldn't want to be rich— even if you got to die tomorrow for it?"

Then he added savagely: "And maybe I could have beat him, after all. I had a long start and a running start, and I was a good lead ahead when I smashed into you—— Ah, damn you and your black heart, Graem!"

"Good," said Graem. "Now you're warmin' up. But, look here, kid, d'you think that I'll listen to you rambling on with no facts in your pockets? Talk solid facts, or else shut up and let me sleep. I'm ready to snore, and I know that you're bluffin'. I know that."

"You're a fathead and a fool," answered Jerry with some calmness. "Why shouldn't I tell you? Because if you know it, they'll get you, too."

"That's logical. They got an ear listening to what you say, of course?"

"Sure they have."

"Then why do you whisper?"

Jerry's bed creaked as he turned as much to one side as possible. "Graem!"

"I hear you."

"Will you talk soft?"

"Sure," whispered Graem, and he began to grow tense; there was reality in the trembling murmur of Jerry.

"If I convince you—do you give me a chance to break loose from here? Maybe they haven't come—maybe there's a ghost of a show— I—Blondy, what do you say?"

"You tell me a yarn that looks likely," said Graem after consideration, "and one that I can't punch any holes through, and maybe I'll do what you say. But I'm critical. Now, go ahead and shoot."

Sometimes Tucker Graem hardly could hear the murmur of the man on the bed as the narrative began; sometimes it was a mere hissing; but presently Graem had turned on his side as close to the prisoner as the bed would let him come. He raised himself upon one elbow and drank in every word, for such words were worth hearing.

"It was only a few days back; I dunno how long—time don't count in hell and heaven—I come in from a job in Montana——"

"What does La Salle do in Montana?" asked Graem.

"He does something everywhere. D'you know his range?"

"He's a gambling shark; that's how he made his start—that and horse stealing," said Graem with a bitter hardness of voice. "He's a counterfeiter and a pusher of the queer; he smuggles opium and what not across the Rio; he's taken his hand at cattle stealing when a big deal offered; besides that, his boys have blown a few banks for him, and it's said that you can buy a man's head from La Salle. That's a few of the things that I *know* about him. Is there anything more?"

The other man laughed softly in the darkness and the laughter was not a pleasant sound.

"*Amigo! Amigo mio!*" he murmured. "And you think that you know La Salle? You dunno even the chapter titles—not even the chapter titles. You don't know nothing—and you one that knew La Salle when he was making his start."

He halted here and then muttered: "Nobody would believe! Nobody would believe!"

Graem waited, but he was no longer in a doubting humour. With taut muscles and clenched fist he leaned in the darkness and drank in the tale as it came slowly from his companion.

"I was back from Montana. It had been a long trip and a hard one, with lying out at night, and watching by day, and sneaking from one place to another. I tell you, for two thousand miles I never come up to a skyline ridge without figuring that I'd have my head blowed off when I dipped over to the far side. I never passed a clump of trees without figuring that they was waiting for me in the shadows. A hundred times I felt something like death shoot through me—and it was only the sparkle of the sun on some poplar leaves. Well, kid, I went for five months like that. Twenty times I thought I was done. Twenty times I give up hope. Once I was clean surrounded——"

He gasped and then added: "Anyway, what I mean to tell you is that I was played out, and when I come back I lay flat on my back for two days in the shack. La Salle had sent up a Chink to wait for me there, and the Chink took care of me like a baby. I needed that kind of care, lemme tell you! Then La Salle come himself and took a look at me.

"'How much did we bargain for?' says he.

"'Twenty-five hundred,' says I.

"'You can count this pack of bills after I leave. I guess you'll find it right. Stay here and get some flesh on your bones. Then you come down and have a talk with me.' With that he went out of the shack and——"

Here, from the dark of the night, a long, deep, mournful cry sounded, and there was a hysterical gasp of fear from the prisoner.

"What's wrong?" asked Graem harshly. "That was only a screech owl tuning up."

"How can you tell?" breathed the prisoner. "It may be one of *them!*"

8

A SECRET MISSION

THIS suggestion was received by Graem with a positive snort of indignant disgust.

"Now what you been reading, Jerry?" he asked. "You're full of ghosts and bunk. I never heard nothing like it. Lemme hear the man that can imitate the screech of an owl so's I can't tell the difference. Now go on, Jerry, and cut it short, will you?"

There was only a submissive sigh from Jerry, as of a man whose heart has been subdued but whose nerves are still at loose ends. However, he was no sooner speaking than his narrative carried him away.

"I counted that wad," said he, "and lemme ask you how much was in it?"

"Thirty-five hundred," suggested Graem. "He's not the sort to short-change a good worker."

"You got the idea," said the other, "and you got the tune, but you miss on the words. Ten—thousand—iron—men."

"He gave you ten thousand?" echoed Graem, stunned at the mere naming of such a sum.

"He gave me ten thousand—dollars—hard cash—coin of the realm—real spending. Gave it all—to me. What a man!"

That emotion of awe was shared by Blondy Graem; softly they cursed in unison.

"The sight of it," continued Jerry, "was a two-week rest to me; it was two weeks of high life, and chicken and cream, and 'lemme take your hat, sir,' and 'will the parlour do you?' and 'have another because the drinks are all on the house.' I only counted the money forty or fifty times to make sure of it. Then I cleaned my gun and lay on the floor in the door of that shack, waiting for the gent that came to take the wad away. But nobody came. I cooked up a fine feed with the help of the Chink, and then I went back into the horse shed behind the shack, and there I found three horses as good as anybody ever threw a leg over. Blood, hot blood, in all of 'em. You see the idea?"

"Left by orders of La Salle. You take your pick."

"Yes, take my pick or take all three. I spent a whole half-day fearing that I'd select the wrong one. He's like that—La Salle, I mean. He knew which was the best, and if I picked the wrong horse he'd always have felt a little contempt for me; he judges his boys by the little things even more than the big. 'Any fool can be a hero,' says La Salle, 'but it takes a wise man to be a coward, now and then.'"

"Like pinching the horse of a partner and leaving him with a cripple to starve in the desert?" suggested Graem quietly.

"I loaded down that horse—he was a grey with all dark points— and I headed for La Salle. I took it easy. Five days of loafing along; four meals a day; and a pound a meal put on my ribs, I suppose. Then one day I come to La Salle's place——"

"What is it like?"

"Ask somebody else," snapped the prisoner, as though the old habit of loyalty to such a lion-hearted master still controlled him. "Anyway, I seen La Salle setting in the shade under a tree, all alone."

"I thought he was never alone."

"No more he is. But he can seem more alone than anybody in the world, and some fools have tried to play him for being alone. One whistle brings ten old-time gun fighters buzzing down the wind at you with their guns turning red-hot in their hands. Well, I sashayed up to La Salle and swung out of the saddle.

"'I didn't figure on you till tomorrow,' says he. And I laughed when I heard him. Mind you, a week before, I'd lay on my back shakin' like a girl with the hysterics; then he'd met me and told me to take a long rest and get fat before I saw him again. But, all the same, he knew when I'd come. Mind reading! Oh, trust him; he can do that fine!

"'I had some good literature to read,' says I, 'so I thought that I'd come here and see if you had the continuation of the story.'

"He grinned a little; then he looked off at the hills as if the outline of them didn't please him a lot—as though he was going to change it, maybe.

"'You left a couple of good horses behind you,' says he.

"'I did,' says I, wondering, if I'd picked wrong.

"'The chestnut,' says he, 'is an outstanding horse.'

"'It is,' said I, 'but a little too much chest on him, I thought.'

"'The bay,' says he, 'has four legs to stand on.'

"'I never seen better,' says I, 'but I liked the grey.'

"'And why?' says he.

"'For no reasons,' says I, 'except it seemed the kind that would bend but not break.'

"He frowned at the hills again.

"'It ought to,' says he. 'It's by Spindrift out of Her Grace.'

"I could remember those names, not clear and easy, but the way that you remember something that you saw in a newspaper six months before and then forgot, and it comes back to you. Spindrift and Her Grace had won stake races, handicaps, that sort of thing; I picked the clean-bred champion of the three when I nailed the grey. I was satisfied, and I could see that La Salle was satisfied too; something that he had been holding back from until he'd seen me and weighed me now cleared up in his mind's eye, and he looked at me in a different fashion.

"'D'you know what Napoleon said about one of his marshals?' he batted out to me after a minute.

"'I dunno,' says I.

"'He said: "I found him a pygmy and I left him a giant."'

"'I don't see the drift of that,' says I, wonderingly.

"He began to rub his hands together, like he had a way of doing even on the middle of a day in August down in the Arizona desert, so's you would think that he couldn't get any warmth into his skin. Then he stopped to watch a lizard that had come out from a tree and was aiming to skin across the open and go up the trunk of the next tree like a flicker of a whiplash. He gave me a grin and a nod. Something told me what he meant, and when the lizard made his dive, I pulled my gun and cut loose. A lizard ain't a standing bull's-eye, and he's no thicker than a ray of light; besides, he travels crooked. I bashed up the ground in front of that running streak; I tore away the ground behind him; but finally I blasted the dirt right under his feet, and the kick of the gravel tossed him into the air. By the time he came down, rolling on his back, I had the bead, and the fourth shot blew him to bits.

"'You don't get four shots at a man,' says La Salle, looking at me very cold.

"Well, when I looked at him, so beautiful and so young-looking— ten years less than his years—it sort of scared me, because all at once I knew that here was a man that would likely balance my failure to hit a running lizard against my long Montana job and the way that I had picked the right horse, and a thousand other things. I felt that La Salle was partly brains and cold, hard thinking, but the other part was the thing that's in a gambler—that makes him keep putting his money on the red five times in a row, makes me feel that the hunch is a certain number at roulette—you know what I mean. So here was La Salle thinking over his hunch about me.

"Finally he says slowly: 'It's knowing how and where, even in the dark.'"

There was a stifled exclamation from Blondy Graem. He swung to his feet and stared down through the darkness at the place where the other must be lost in greater blackness than night.

"Who said that?" he exclaimed hoarsely.

"Why, Adam, maybe," answered Jerry. "It's an old saw, I guess. What about it?"

"Old saw? Maybe it is. Maybe it is," said Graem, but he settled very slowly back on the bed, full of thought.

"'However,' went on La Salle, 'you killed it at last, and that's the trick that counts. Look here. Take this—read the direction and burn the paper. Then take this envelope and ride like fury. Take that grey of yours. Burn him up. I want you to leave him dead at the end of three days, and I want you to be there at the end of three days. You hear me?'

"I listened to him; I took the paper and read the directions four times over, half hypnotized—but that's the way things sink in the deepest sometimes. I read them over and I touched a match to the paper.

"'Recite!' says La Salle.

"I spieled those directions off by heart, and La Salle grinned.

"'I think that you'll get there,' said he. 'Mind you, youngster, this isn't important. It's a test for you. But if you do it right, then I'll know that you'll be fit to tackle something big. Now get out of here and ride for it. Feed him leather, let him go.'

"I got out of there, of course, and gave the grey a taste of my quirt, but after that I didn't have a chance to touch him up again, because it was as if I'd whacked a thunderbolt; he smoked across the hills and gave me a new horizon before I'd fair settled the old one in my mind. I only had one glimpse behind me, and that showed me La Salle tilted back in his chair, smiling, but not at me—down at his cigarette that he was making, if you know what I mean. Say, Blondy, ain't the door open?"

"No," said Graem, "but the wind's rising a little, maybe. Go on. You're afraid of your own shadow."

"I had to aim backward," said Jerry, "sighting over my shoulder at a pair of mountains that looked like a couple of lopsided donkey ears, with a bump in between them. I steered by them for three days, and all the way I was thinking. La Salle had lied, of course, when he said that this job wasn't important—that it was only a trial. La Salle was always lying; and yet you never could be sure when he meant what he said, and Heaven help the man that didn't take him at his word! Anyway, the idea got hold of me that I'd sure like to have a look inside of that envelope, and yet I knew that I'd never have the nerve to unfasten it.

"The morning of the third day I came across a little, measly run of water that the grey could have jumped and laughed at, but I jogged him through it, and in the middle he plopped into a bog hole and soaked me to the neck. He floundered out, and the first thing that I thought of was the envelope. I pulled it out; it looked safe enough, but the water had softened the mucilage and the flap was fairly asking to be raised."

9

STILETTO!

"THEN you remembered all at once that La Salle was your boss," suggested Graem dryly. "You remembered that, and you just shoved the envelope into your pocket."

It seemed that the other did not hear.

"I touched the flap, and it opened as if it were working on a spring. I looked in, and there I found a scrap of paper that I took out and give a look at it. There were only five words scribbled on it."

"Remember them?"

"Remember them?" murmured the captive. "I remember them perfect; I can't remember anything else. The first word was——"

Here the voice stopped abruptly as though the immensity of the secret which Jerry was about to impart overwhelmed him; so Graem waited for moments in silence, unwilling to force his companion ahead with the strange confession which had started so fluently.

"All right," said Blondy Graem at last. "Let it drop, it's your business, Jerry. I'm not begging to know."

There was no answer to this.

"If that's the end," said Graem testily, "I'll go to sleep."

He composed himself with a grunt and a roll on his bed, but now he felt a chill breath of night wind on his face, followed by a long, sighing sound that passed down the corridor.

Unquestionably the door was now open, though Blondy was certain that when he last closed it the latch had worked and held it firmly shut. His first surmise was that Jerry might have been working covertly, while he talked, at the knots that held his hand and foot; that he had loosed them and finally had slipped noiselessly from his cot and vanished down the hall. So Graem threw out his hand to the other bed and instantly touched his companion; touched him and found his coat wet, which he thought odd—a sticky wetness which clung strangely to the tips of his fingers.

He scratched a match. The flame flared and died; by that instant of illumination he saw only the dark, open doorway and wide, staring haunted eyes watching him from the adjoining bed. It brought Graem to his feet, braced and alert for some desperate danger, he hardly knew what; he was almost afraid to light a second match, but this one burned steadily, and, forgetting the open door, he regarded only the white face, the staring eyes, and the unchangeable and horrid grin of Jerry. It seemed a smile of mockery; again it seemed a grimace of horror and of pain. He stepped closer—the whole breast of Jerry was flooded with dark crimson. "Jerry!" he called, but the eyes were unwinking, the grin never varied, and as the flame touched his fingers and the match dropped to the floor, leaving him again in darkness, he knew that the renegade from La Salle had been murdered at his side.

Blondy lit the lamp with trembling hands; a loathing of the dark possessed him, and so nervous was his grasp that the chimney of the lamp tottered and chattered as he carried it to the table beside the bed where the dead man lay. The open door of darkness seemed to yawn upon him with many watching eyes; yet he had to turn his back to it to continue his examination.

Jerry had been thrust through the heart, and the instrument of his death projected slightly above a double fold of his coat. The handle of it was not more than two and a half inches in length, hollowed at

the butt as though to make place for the grip of a thumb. Graem
drew it forth. The blade was six inches in length, of finest steel, as
shimmering and thin as the gleam of an icicle perishing in the sun.
And it doubled the horror, for it seemed to Graem that no Western
mind could have conceived such a weapon, no Western hand could
have used it; rather had an occult and Oriental viciousness slid
silently through the doorway, lain listening on the floor, and then,
as the cobra raises its hooded head, so this assassin had raised and
poised his hand in the darkness, ending the tale of Jerry.

Now that the thing was done, the cold sweat stood upon Graem's
forehead, considering his own mad folly; for Jerry had known when
the door was opened and when the danger had entered. He knew,
too, that his death was predetermined in this house—had felt the
coffin-like shadow of this very room. But Graem had held him
there—if there had been a death, was not Graem more than doubly
guilty?

All this shot through the mind of Blondy Graem in the mere instant during which he leaned above the body and drew forth the
glimmering little instrument of death. Then he turned to the door,
gun in hand, and leaped out into the hall. But pursuit in that direction would be expected; he ran back to the window, dropped
through it, and, hanging for an instant by his fingertips, let himself
fall. The sand was soft and broken beneath; nevertheless, it was a
staggering shock that he received. He leaned for a moment against
the wall, weaving the gun through a semicircle before him until his
head cleared a little.

There was nothing above him except the chilly beauty of the stars,
and nothing before him save the dark heads of the rolling hills,
splotched with shrubbery; certainly there was no moving form, and
certainly there was no sound of sand whispering around a human
footfall or the muffled pounding of the hoofs of a horse. To make
surety more sure, the wind had fallen away at this moment to an
utter end of sound. Ears could serve better than eyes, but ears said
nothing.

He slipped to the corner of the hotel and ran to the back of the
building. The black rooms of sheds and barns were etched against
the stars; it was a painted scene, and from this quarter, also, came
not a whisper to disturb him. Then with a savage burst of exultation
came the hope that the secret murderer might still be within the
house. He closed his eyes and set his teeth—if luck would only give
him one glimpse of the assassin!

The back kitchen door shattered his hope, for the rusty hinges screamed as he pushed it cautiously open, and, furthermore, after the open and the starlight this interior seemed buried in a black fog; somehow, the stale and homely smell of cookery seemed to make it impossible that he should find the destroyer in this house.

He fumbled on into the lower hall, and, as he stepped through the doorway, a blinding shaft of light fell on him; he leaped back through the door, gun ready, but the light had flashed out as suddenly as it came.

"Who's there?" called the voice of old Crocker from the stairs.

"Is it you?" gasped Graem, and swore with relief and surprise.

"Well," said Crocker, unhooding the lantern fully, "did you get hungry in the middle of the night?"

Graem mounted the stairs and confronted him.

"What are you doing?" he asked. "What are you doing wandering around with a bull's eye this time of the night?"

Crocker regarded him patiently.

"When I hear my door opened," he said, "am I gonna lie still like a scared kid?"

"Give me that lantern," commanded Graem.

"Excited, youngster, ain't you?" remarked Crocker, surrendering the light without further protest.

"Maybe I am. Now hold out your hands."

"I'd rather do that than hold them up," answered the host, and chuckled as he obeyed.

Crooked from long toil with drill and single jack, padded with hard calluses within, and wrinkled without, never were seen hands of more honest toil, and there was no sign of bloodstain on them. Still, blood may be washed away, and Graem felt the fingers to see whether they had been softened by recent moisture; the calluses were dry as paper under his touch.

"If you ain't a bit nutty," said the proprietor, "d'you mind telling me what this is about?"

"Turn around and walk ahead of me, and go down the hall into my room," said Graem, and Crocker, as one who recognizes an emergency even if he cannot understand it, obeyed. He marched down the hall and, entering the guest room, stood by the bedside of the dead man, over whom fell soft waves of light, for the draught was tossing the lamp flame up and down in the chimney; it seemed more than ever that Jerry was alive, grinning in mockery, as the lights changed in his open eyes.

Graem closed those eyes forever, closed the grinning mouth, and stretched the arms of the dead man along his sides. All this he did without removing his attention for more than an instant from his host. Then he faced the latter sternly.

"He knew that it was his finish in this here house," said Graem. "He knew that he was gunna die in this room. Now, I want to understand—what did *you* know about it?"

And, turning the bull's-eye, he flashed its strong ray full in the face of Crocker. The latter endured the search unwinkingly.

"When I was a kid," said Crocker, in his quiet voice of narrative, "if I stole a berry pie from the pantry, I always used to act as though my big brother must've done it."

"Now, what might you mean by that?" asked Graem.

A half-crooked forefinger was raised and pointed at him. The innkeeper took a step toward him.

"You bring in a gent tied to your arm; you bash him in the jaw when he tries to get free; you tie him hand and foot to a bed in the same room with you, and, pretty soon, I hear something in the night; I come into that same room; I find your man still tied, and I find him dead and you asking questions. All I say is, maybe you'd better answer some questions yourself."

The words were blunt enough, but the voice was as calm as ever, and, in spite of his excitement, Graem felt a touch of admiration for this fellow of iron nerves.

From the coat of Jerry, gingerly, with the tips of his fingers, he raised the stiletto.

"I know what you mean, Crocker," said he, "but I ask you—if I'd wanted to get rid of Jerry, would I have brought him in here to the hotel to do the killing instead of using some of the handy places out yonder in the hills? And, if it came to killing, would I use a hairpin like this?"

The horribly wet handle slipped through his fingers as he spoke, and the stiletto, falling suddenly, buried its point deep in the tough floor and hung there, humming like a bumblebee. Even the steady nerves of the old miner gave way a little at this, and he shuddered, avoiding the searching eyes of his guest.

"Not you—not me—nobody else in the house—it looks snaky, partner," said he.

10

FACING THE MOON

THE eye of Graem returned to the dead man; when he lifted it, Crocker had gone, and his footfall was creaking on the floor of the hall at some distance. There was no purpose in recalling him, so Graem sat down to consider, and he needed such a period of reflection, because his mind was drawn in three ways by this tragedy. He felt that he carried a burden of guilt because of his own share in rendering the victim helpless; he was filled with a quite unrelated fear because this crime, as Crocker immediately had suggested, might be imputed to him; but, most powerfully of all, he was forced on curiously toward the adventure of Jerry which was now brought to an end. With all his soul, for instance, he yearned to know two things: what was the nature of the wealth with which poor Jerry had fled from the ubiquitous La Salle, and what were the five words which he had found written on the slip of paper? No doubt the wealth was some secret which Jerry had spied upon, and, having once trodden forbidden ground, he had fled with his knowledge and died here obscurely in a wayside tavern with all his hopes dead about him.

It occurred to Graem that there might be some clue to these secrets about the dead man, and he reached his hand into the inside pocket from which Jerry had produced his wallet earlier in the day. The wallet was not there, and when he searched hurriedly through the rest of the pockets he found every one of them empty. Jerry had already been completely searched.

At that, Graem sat back, biting his lip, and then retreated to a corner of the room to think the matter over, so that he would be out of range either of the window or the door; for still he had the uncanny feeling that he was being watched, as though eyes were set into the wall. That sense of danger formed itself naturally into the slender figure and the handsome face of La Salle, that face which time could not touch but left invincibly boyish and beautiful.

One thing Graem was sure of: no matter with what uncanny silence the murderer of Jerry worked, he could not well have rifled the pockets of his victim without disturbing the man on the next bed—a man, moreover, who was listening hard, and with not the dullest ears in the world. This meant that, after Graem started on his hunt for some sight or sound of the criminal, the man had boldly returned to the room and made his search.

Fear had been rising in Graem for some time, and now it mastered him so that he wanted only one thing in the world, and that was immediate freedom from that inauspicious room, that unlucky house, and a chance to ride beneath the stars. He gathered his pack together, slung it over his shoulder, and went softly from the room. In the hallway, his heart almost failed him; for from behind, the glimmering doorway of the death chamber seemed to yawn threateningly, and before him were shadows at the end of the hall, and deeper pools of shadow in the well of the stairs. Twice he paused on those stairs and listened, but he knew that the frightful beating of his heart must be loud enough to cover stealthy sounds.

Once on the lower level of the place, he breathed more freely; but when he pushed open the kitchen door his heart was well-nigh stopped again, for a slender silver dagger seemed hung in the centre of the blackness of the room. His eyes cleared instantly, as he stared; it was no more than the upper rim of the rising moon, which now broadened as it lifted over the edge of the eastern hills. It was shedding a faint but growing light everywhere when he passed through the rear door, childishly glad that he did not have to make those dreadful hinges scream again.

Now he stood under the wall of the house, breathing freely at last and rubbing an uncertain hand across his forehead; he could thank God for the open face of the heavens, now, as he had never given thanks before. As he lingered a moment, he saw Crocker—distinct enough in the moonshine—bring a mustang to the door of the horse shed, swing into the saddle, and gallop away around the corner of the building toward the north. He was so amazed by this sight that he rubbed his eyes and looked again at the spot where the apparition had been. Crocker had gone; Crocker, the blunt and honest and labour worn, had slipped away into the night. No doubt, however, this was no sign of guilt, but simply a proof that the old fellow wanted to see justice done. Fearful of being seen or heard from the house, he had ridden north, but would circle back and so come again to the Loomis trail and speed on to let the sheriff know of the horrid murder which had been done that night in his hostelry.

There was still another exciting possibility, however, and the thought of this stirred the heart of Graem with a bound. He remembered the booklike thickness of the wallet from which Jerry had proffered five hundred dollars so freely. What if Crocker, going to search the dead man while Graem was away from the house, had come upon that same treasure which induced the dead man to venture the wrath of La Salle and flee?

At any rate, Graem made up his mind that he would follow Crocker if he could; he ran first to the corner of the barn and, shading his eyes from the almost level moonbeams, and looking down into the hollow, he saw the rider dimly in the pool of darkness, and saw him swing, as he had expected, toward Loomis.

That settled the course of Graem. He snatched a saddle from the wall behind his horse, flung it on the bay, and instantly was on its back and away. He did not follow the exact line of Crocker's flight; what need was there for that, if the man were indeed heading toward the town? Instead, he rushed his gelding past the silent hostelry and, as he gained the front, looked up with indescribable horror at the one dimly lighted window. And it seemed to Graem that he would go half mad unless he could banish from his mind the picture of the corpse lying on the bed, for he could not see the closed eyes and the composed face; to his imagination Jerry lay as at first, with a dead grin of mockery turned toward Blondy Graem.

Neither did he take the main road toward town, as it wound leisurely past the front of the inn. Beyond was a rougher but shorter path, and down to this he spurred his bay. It was only a dim trail, but it had been blazed, not by meandering cattle, but by hard-riding horsemen such as he was on that night. It bent aside only a little to climb sharp slopes, and it drove like a swooping bird from the heights into the hollows.

At last its course ended with two hours of frantic riding; they had come into the main trail to Loomis, and Loomis itself lay not half a mile before him, uncheered by a single yellow lamp, but with its roofs gilded and its chimneys aflash with the silver of the moon.

There was a little grove of lodge-pole pines near the trail, too scattered to serve as covert in the day, almost too thin to serve for that purpose on such a night as this, but he tethered the bay on the side of the grove farthest from the trail and then ran at full speed back to the edge of the woods, for he was in terror lest Crocker should have slipped by him. First, as he broke from cover, he glanced toward the town and saw that the trail wound and dipped all empty into Loomis; to the east the moon hung smaller and higher in the sky, and a coyote from the north and a coyote from the south were crying at it in querulous tones, but that way the trail was empty, also, twisting beside shrubs, past gilded, gleaming rocks.

He sat down in the shelter on a raw-edged stump from whose rim little sprouts were beginning to rise again, heroically. Fifty years hence one of them might be another tree, as tall and as stout as the ancestor from which it had sprung. Graem thought of this; he even fingered some mouldering chips now rotting where they had fallen—how many years before?—when this old tree was felled. So with small things he filled half his mind, but the other half was back there in the distance with the dead man in the lighted room—and he hoped with an odd fervency that the lamp would not go out and leave Jerry in darkness before the dawn began.

In the meantime, there was no sign of Crocker. Now that he was in the distance, Graem wished with all his soul that he had secured the innkeeper or grilled him more closely, for the man seemed too wise, too much like a fox! Then, dimly, growing louder by degrees, shut off entirely, coming again with a burst near by, he heard the pulsating hoofbeat of a loping horse and rose to one knee in the attitude of a sprinter ready for the starter's gun.

Over the brow of the next rise from the east came Crocker—indubitably Crocker, because of the breadth of the shoulders and the little stoop such as elderly men have in the saddle unless they have been trained into rigidity of spine. Very thin arose a curtain of dust behind the bobbing form of the horse, thinner than a ghost in the moonshine, and the face of the rider was black with shadow.

Then Graem arose with a rifle at his shoulder and took a careful bead. He did not speak; there was no need of speech, for the rider tossed his hands instantly above his head and stopped his mustang with a single word.

"All right, partner," he drawled without the slightest perturbation. "You're a fast rider, it seems."

"I was afraid that an old chap like you," explained Graem, "would be catching a cold, out at night in the mountains. Or else you might lose your way."

"Thanks," chuckled Crocker.

His good humour and the steadiness of his nerves were amazing to Graem. But, after all, Crocker had not had a man stabbed to death by his side that night.

"I got sort of leery," explained Crocker. "Thought I'd just sashay down to Loomis and put up with one of my friends. Sleeping out the night in a big barn of a place like that with a dead man for company—it ain't the comfortablest thing in the world, is it?"

"You had me there," suggested Graem.

"I didn't think I'd have you for long," said the host, "and you see, I was right."

"All right," said Graem. "Just ease yourself out of the saddle and then face the moon."

"Certain," nodded the other, and did exactly as he was told, moving with ostentatious slowness, as though he had been in such positions before and knew that a rapid movement might be his last.

So he stood with his hands above his head while Graem fanned his victim from head to foot. But all that this search produced was a small tangle of twine, a pocket knife of formidable dimensions, one ancient, single-action Colt, and a plug of tobacco. There was not a trace of the wallet of Jerry.

11

A DANGEROUS WALLET

"IT eases me," remarked Graem; "doggone me if it doesn't ease me a lot to see that you ain't a thief, Crocker."

"You suspected that?" asked the veteran, with wonder in his tones.

"Someone went through every pocket of Jerry's," said Graem. "When I saw you sashay away from the house, I kind of thought it might be you, but—just put your hands behind you, Crocker, if you don't mind."

It was done, and with Crocker's own stout twine Graem lashed the wrists together.

"It's a mite cold," suggested the old fellow, but without the tone of complaint.

"It is," said the other readily enough. "But I just want to think a while. The point is how you left the house. Suppose you said to me: 'I ain't going to stay here. Ghosts. I'm going to go to town.' Why, supposing that you'd said that, I would never have stopped you. But you sneak out and start by a back way——"

"I was afraid of you, son," admitted the old man readily. "I saw you handle Jerry, as you call him. I was plain scared, that was all."

"Ah?" murmured Graem.

"Yes, sir. It gave me a chill to see how easy you handled a strong young buck like him; suppose that you laid hands on me, I'd break like kindling wood."

"Now," answered Graem, without venom but without courtesy, "you're lying. There's no more fear in you than there is in a bull terrier."

"Thanks," chuckled Crocker. "I wouldn't mind that on my head-board, when they have the planting of me."

"Keep quiet a minute," muttered Graem. "I want to think."

When in doubt, go slow; he had learned that long ago on the trail of game and humans, and the fastest tracker is he who makes sure of every step. He rolled a cigarette now, and began to walk up and down meditating. He thought of all he knew of Crocker, and it seemed a straight enough story, except for the singular craft he had used in departing from the hotel. This could be explained as Crocker explained it, through funk; but fear attached hardly more easily to the character of the old fellow than water does to a duck's back. Something was wrong; where, Graem could not see, so he dragged out the minutes until his cigarette was finished.

Most men walk straight back and forth when they are in thought, but Graem varied from one direction to another as stopping points came in his thoughts, and so he went deep into the brush and back to the road, viciously kicking twigs and pebbles before him as he found them. Now he flung the cigarette to a distance and gloomily followed its fall with his glance. It dropped near a stone, but a very odd stone it appeared to be, being perfectly rectangular and glimmering softly in the moonlight.

Idle men follow idle fancies, and so do abstracted ones; Graem went to the bright little stone, and picked up—Jerry's pocket-worn wallet of durable pigskin, thick as a book with its solidly packed contents.

Then he returned to his prisoner.

"What were you going to do with it?" he asked, presenting it to the eye of the other.

"Give it to the sheriff," said Crocker without hesitation. "There was enough in that wallet to scare me."

"Scared again," muttered Graem angrily. "Crocker, I ain't a baby. I know the sort of stuff you old sourdoughs are made of. Scared?"

He sniffed with disgust, and then opened the wallet in the moonlight.

He saw a thickly packed sheaf of papers; when he fanned the edges with his thumb, they appeared an incalculable number, almost; and when he picked off the top one a little shudder went with electric speed from the heart of Graem to his toes and back again to his heart. For it was a five-hundred-dollar note, good United States currency, crisp and sweet to the touch.

He tried to restore the bank note; the sheaf was too tight to admit of this, so he folded it and stuffed it into another compartment of the wallet.

"Scared you, old son?" asked Graem dryly.

Crocker, as though unwilling to maintain any new pretence, shrugged his shoulders.

"You do what you please," he said.

"I ought to take you to the sheriff," said Graem, "and tell him about the dead man in your hotel tonight, and the reasons I got for suspecting you."

"Tell him about the wallet, too," said the other, "and let him have it for luck."

Graem swallowed hard.

In all his days, never once had he come under the suspicious eye of the law, except once or twice in his earlier youth for breaking the peace and the jaws of quarrelsome drinking companions. Certainly it was his duty now to give into the hands of the sheriff, until claimed by a rightful owner, the fortune which apparently was stuffed into this wallet, a fortune so great that he well could understand how Jerry had been tempted to defy even the omniscient La Salle. In another case not a thousand times this wealth, whatever it was, could have induced him to break the letter of the law; but he felt now that he could be sure of one thing, at least, concerning the treasure—that it had originated with La Salle, and whatever came from the hands of La Salle might rightly pass into the hands of Tucker Graem, partly because of the bitter wrongs he had sustained at the hands of that master criminal, and largely because the cash value of the stolen mine might well have equalled even such a sum as this one appeared to be.

So Blondy Graem paused and bit his lip.

The rough, calm voice of old Crocker broke in on him: "Keep to the straight and narrow, kid. It pays in the long run."

"You damned pocket picker!" exclaimed Graem in a sudden rage which washed away his lack of determination in a single flood. "You damned old snake in the grass! If a man could take a look at the way you made your pile, I got an idea that they'd find you paid for your winnings with more than one dead man. Tell me, Crocker, have I hit it right?"

And he stepped closer, in a very savage humour indeed.

There was no flinching on the part of the other. He merely replied with the utmost calmness: "You'll wind up with murdering me, I suppose."

"I'm going to tie you to a tree, here," said Graem. "And you'll have your chance to get loose when the morning comes, and somebody takes to the trail. Walk on ahead of me. I'll tell you when to stop."

To be lashed to a tree in that lonely place seemed terrible enough to have unnerved other men, but old Crocker walked straight on as he was commanded; he sat down in front of the designated tree and, without protest, permitted himself to be lashed securely to it. His own slicker and saddle blanket were wrapped around him.

"Are you gonna turn numb? Are the ropes tight enough for that?" asked Graem, a touch of pity coming to him as he considered the years of his prisoner.

"Thanks," said Crocker. "I can stand this fine."

"You're close enough to the road to holler and get attention from the first man that rides down the road."

"I mark that, son. Thanks again."

"Now, one thing more. You may be straight. I dunno. But by the kind of trouble, if any, that comes my way after to-night, I'll know what you've had to do with it; and Heaven help you, old or young, if you get under my eye afterwards. Is that straight with you?"

"I understand it fine," said Crocker. "You might cut me off a chew of tobacco before you go, will you?"

A faint oath from Graem was the comment upon this iron-nerved request; he cut the required bit, dropped the plug on the lap of the bound man, and then went to find his horse. Returning to the main trail, a touch of his quirt sent Crocker's grazing mustang at a full lope toward the east, and Graem made sure that the horse would keep on until it reached the inn where the dead man lay.

Then he pointed the bay toward Loomis and jogged the fine animal softly down the slope into the main street, where the hoofbeats were lost in the deeply muffling dust. The village slept soundly, not even a dog was awake to bay the moon, and Graem smiled a little grimly as he remembered other days when Loomis never had slept at all, except during the blazing noon of a mid-August day. Sheriff Lew Bergen could claim the glory for the transformation.

Straight toward Bergen's house Graem made his way; he had

made up his mind that, no matter how great the treasure might be, he would surrender it into the hands of the officer of the law and so wash his conscience clean. If it were vast wealth—a hundred thousand dollars, say—nevertheless, to Lew Bergen's safe it should go until the proper owner could prove his right to it, even if that owner were La Salle himself.

He found the house set back from the road behind a little garden, and, throwing the reins of his horse, he passed through the gate. It swung to, squeaking loudly, behind him, and even that small cause made the sweat spring on to the forehead of Graem. It started a dog barking, too, and presently a woolly collie darted around the corner of the house to guard the premises of his master.

"Shep, you old fool!" muttered Graem, and the wise dog came to a sliding stop and stood at watch, ready to resent a suspicious move, but recognizing a vaguely familiar voice.

So he allowed Graem to knock at the front door until a window was pushed up.

"Who's there?" asked the voice of the sheriff's wife.

"I want Lew," said Graem from the shadows. "Is he here?"

"Who is it?"

"I'll tell your husband that, Mrs. Bergen."

"Lew's away; he's driving in from Coronal; he won't be here for an hour at the earliest. Who are you?"

"Talk low and come to the door. I'm Tucker Graem."

12

WHAT DOES IT MEAN?

WAITING by the door, he heard the stifled cry of Mrs. Bergen and then the shuffle and patter of hasty feet as she came down to him. When she opened the door, with one hand she shielded herself from the light and cupped it upon her visitor, but he could see her glistening eyes and tousled hair and a man's slipper on one foot, a slender pink one on the other.

"Blondy—Blondy!" said she, and reached out and drew him in. "We all thought you—— Go in there and set yourself down!"

He was shown into a little parlour with an upright piano in a corner, a carpet covered with vast roses and intricately interwoven green vines, a hair-cloth sofa, and plush-seated chairs. On the walls were enlarged photographs from which the pale eyes of ancestors looked forth upon them.

Molly Bergen, putting down the lamp, was beginning to giggle with excitement while she patted at her dishevelled hair and drew her bath robe tighter around her. She looked very pretty with her face flushed partly by sleep and partly by pleasure, so that Graem looked back almost with envy to the time when he had been the man for Molly; that was before he left for his year's cruise into northern parts of the range, before the time Lew Bergen rode forth and became famous by killing Jack Doyle and bringing terrible Larry Doyle back a prisoner. So Graem came south again to find that his girl had married. She had cried a little on the occasion of that meeting, but Graem held no malice; he could tell her honestly that he approved of her choice, and he gave Lew Bergen his horse and left Loomis on a picked-up mustang. After that, he had been the family friend, and only the year before he had ridden four hundred miles through wind and snow to stand as godfather for the baby, which was named Tucker, duly.

"Is it all right," asked Graem, "for me to be here alone in the house with you, Molly, seeing that it's night?"

Molly tapped her knuckles on the back of a chair.

"Those that have bad thoughts about me can choke on 'em, for all I care," said she. "Lew would never have a question. But I want to know; we thought—I mean everybody thought—that we'd never see you again, Blondy."

"I been lying up in the hills," said Graem calmly. "Been lying up and resting. I thought I deserved a vacation."

"Did you get *that* on your vacation?" asked the girl, and pointed to a broad line of purple which began at the side of his jaw and disappeared backward and downward into his collar.

"Just a scratch," he answered. "You thought I'd snuffed out?"

"We heard that you'd sold a mine for about a million to La Salle, and that robbers held you up and murdered you——"

"I didn't sell a mine," answered he. "I wasn't held up for money, and you can see that I wasn't murdered. Now, you run along upstairs and go to bed again."

"I won't," she protested. "You're hungry, too. And you always can drink coffee."

"Are your neighbours deaf, Molly?" he asked her. "Do you regularly have many callers around midnight?"

That suggestion weakened her, and finally he sent her off, though she lingered in the doorway to smile back at him with such a gentle kindness that, after she had gone, he remained for some moments in a muse over women and married life; but in his reflections the face that had smiled at him altered deftly to another picture, so that it almost seemed as though Charlotte had been yonder in the doorway and Charlotte's soft voice had been sounding.

The sense of his true situation returned to him; he lifted his head out of the dream and took the wallet from his pocket. All good caution warned him that it was safest to keep his eyes from the contents, but the thing clamoured to be opened, as it were, and presently it lay unfolded in his hands.

Once more he viewed that compact sheaf of notes, deep and tight as the compressed pages of a book, weighty, and thick. He fanned them with his thumb—to the very bottom of the pile it was currency. He flicked the corners more slowly this time, and past his blurring eyes ran a swift succession of big numbers—very few hundreds and nothing smaller—nearly all were thousands and five-hundred-dollar bills!

He counted. There were five hundred bills. He separated the three denominations, and found three hundred five-hundred-dollar bills, fifty hundred-dollar bills, and a hundred and fifty thousand-dollar bills. A hundred and fifty thousand, and five thousand, and again a hundred and fifty thousand. Answer: three hundred and five thousand dollars in cold cash, coin of the realm, ready for circulation. Not even the trouble of negotiating good securities.

Automatically he packed the notes together and thrust them back into the compartment which had contained them. All at once he wished with all his might that he had allowed Molly to make some coffee for him, or that the sheriff would come back. He felt his face, and it was moist and cold, and a pulse was throbbing rapidly in his temples.

Thoughts and pictures slid through his mind like a moving picture when the reel is allowed to spin at treble speed; but above all he was seeing the "House on the Hill," as everyone had called it at Chisholm, where he was born and raised. In Chisholm, he had learned to ride, to rope, to trail, to shoot; and during all the years when he was completing his education the House on the Hill had been to his thoughts like the sum of all good, the end of fairy trails. If a palace appeared in a story, it took on the form of the House on the Hill; and if a millionaire were mentioned, he visualized the broad, kind face of John Hanley, who owned the house and all the good acres of hill and valley that lay in the range behind. John Hanley had died, and his widow sold the place, the land, the livestock, the barns and sheds, the big House on the Hill, the three pianos, the rugs on the floors, the pictures on the walls, the long and heavy curtains, the wonderful sofas, the deep, luxurious chairs—and she had received a hundred and fifty thousand dollars altogether.

How imagine double that sum? How imagine the two Houses on the Hill, acres twice as extensive, two rivers instead of one, two villages to lie in worship and wonder at the foot of two such mansions?

The heart of Graem swelled big, and he jammed the wallet into his pocket. For it was his. It came from La Salle. La Salle had stolen the mine. This was indirect payment, put in his hands by the just fate which watches over foolish punchers and keeps them from the deepest pits of their folly.

But almost instantly he had the wallet in his hands again. He shifted his position so that neither the window nor the door bore upon him and the treasure; but, instead of examining it again, he went through the other compartments of the wallet. In one he found a partly written letter, produced with infinite apparent effort:

Dear Olive: Yours of the twenty-fifth to hand. I was sure glad to hear from you. I got back from the North a while ago; had a hard time, which you said I would. Have got a surprise for you which is going to be no engagement ring, but——

Whatever the surprise, it was never to be revealed to Olive, for here the letter ended, and the hand and heart which composed it were stilled for ever. Graem, suddenly grown chilled in spirit, refolded the letter, hesitated, and then restored it to the compartment from which he had taken it.

He searched again, but nothing remained in the wallet except a fold of paper on which was written either balderdash or at least the strangest jargon that the eye of Graem ever had looked upon. It was in the same hand which had written the letter—Jerry's, therefore, beyond a doubt—and it proceeded as follows:

Nompah perug kakhoo ag kemah kakhoo nompah perug namary mah hannah ta tuck a auga mah hannah mah hannah nompah perug namary kakhoo namary ta tuck a mah hannah aga mah pa ta tuck a mah hannah nompah perug mah hannah auga mah hannah ag kak hoo auga tohpa nompah perug namary mah hannah ta tucka nompah perug mah hannah ag kemah mah hannah ta tucka.

Over this he brooded with a frown. That Jerry, to whom writing was plainly a bitter labour, should have wasted so many letters in the endeavour to compose ridiculous nonsense was, of course, out of the question; there was a meaning in this, and, considering Jerry's powers with the pen, probably there was a meaning of the greatest importance. Language, he felt, it hardly could be, because language does not consist of such rapid repetitions, and there were so many "mah hannahs" and so many "nompah perugs" and "ta tuck as" in this brief series of words that the bewilderment of Graem grew apace. Had it been the writing of another, he would have abandoned it without further thought; but the dead writer of this episode held a claim upon him, as he felt. Moreover, to the very cockles of his heart he was warmed with curiosity.

Graem tried reading the thing aloud, and when he did so it struck him as having a sound vaguely like that of an Indian language, but none which he ever had heard. In his day, he had spent much time among the Sioux and could speak and write their language; this, on the whole, was totally different from the Sioux dialect, and yet there was something about the run of the sounds that made him feel the thing might be Indian.

He had reached that conclusion when he heard the rattle of hoofs in the street and then the loud jingle of harness and the snorting of a horse as a team turned in from the street and jogged down the alleyway beside the sheriff's house. It was Bergen returned, beyond a doubt, and Graem stood up with the wallet pinched hard between his fingers, while he turned the matter back and forth in an agonized brain. Whatever was due to him from La Salle, this particular sum was not his; neither did he have sheer proof that it ever had come from that arch-criminal.

And all the weight of his honest years of living now suddenly swept him out of the house and made him hurry back into the yard to give the wallet to the sheriff. As he strode into the corral he saw the sheriff, with a lantern, at the watering trough with a span of horses.

"Hey, Lew!" he called.

"Hello, Blondy."

"I got something for you, here."

"Keep away, will you?" answered the sheriff. "This roan will kick your head off. Wait till I get them put up."

And Blondy stood idly, the precious wallet swinging a dead weight from his hand.

13

TOO MUCH MONEY

THE sheriff hurried his horses into the barn; he came out again, the lantern swinging in his hand, the shadows of his legs sweeping gigantically back and forth across the oak trees that fringed the corral.

"Where are you, Blondy? Where are you, old son?" he was calling.

"Keep your voice down, Lew!" said Blondy Graem.

They found each other and gripped hands mightily. They were of one age, one heart, one life; they had rolled in the dust of the Chisholm streets as infants; they had fished and hunted and studied and fought together in Chisholm schooldays; they had ridden a hundred trails together thereafter; and they were to one another all that the word "man" stands for in the West.

"What have you got for me, Blondy? Some contraption for the kid, I suppose?"

"I got nothing for the kid; I got nothing for Molly; I got nothing but trouble on my hands."

"Ah—ah," murmured the sheriff. "You've killed a man that *didn't* need killing. Is that it, Blondy?"

"No."

"It's the only foolishness that you might slip into," said the sheriff instantly. "What's wrong? La Salle?"

"It's always La Salle. Now something else. There's a dead man in Crocker's hotel, Lew. It's a man I brought there living, and I found him dead a yard away from me, a while after, in my room."

Lew Bergen swung the lantern idly. He looked a grotesque figure in that alternating light and shadow, for he was immensely tall, vast of hand and foot, and had a face of starving ugliness. He closed his eyes in pain as he heard the rest of the story. It began at the point at which Graem had refused to sell his claim to La Salle; it skipped lightly through Charlie and her people; it carried rapidly down to Jerry, his captivity, and the strangeness of his death; it detailed, also, the dealings with Crocker. And there it stopped. No word of the wallet was mentioned by Graem.

After this, the sheriff laid his great bony hand on the shoulder of his friend and maintained a silence which he broke at last by saying: "It's La Salle, I suppose?"

"I suppose so."

"We'd better go in and have some coffee."

"I'll do without coffee. You don't stop to enjoy your coffee when you're on a trail with La Salle behind you."

"Now, gimme strength," said the sheriff's tremendous bass voice in a fervour of devotion, "and I'll find La Salle and something that'll hang him. But if ever you disappear, old son, I go straight for him and shoot him with no questions."

"I wanted to tell you, Lew. They'll come foaming in to you. They'll swear that I done the murder. Well—I'm riding west."

The vast hand patted his shoulder.

"I'll go south, son. Will you come in and see Molly?"

"I had a word with her and sent her to bed."

"You better come in for a minute; otherwise, she'll be mourning for you for months, Blondy."

"I got to go. Get me some bacon and coffee and such truck out of your kitchen, and some salt. You know what I need. I'll be waiting out in front with my horse."

The sheriff disappeared on the run toward the rear of his house, and presently he came out with a load and met Graem by the hitching rack.

"Let me strap it on," said the sheriff. "You never had no more idea than a Chinaman about making a pack. Look where you got your slicker! Blondy, you'll never grow up or know nothing."

"I want to know one thing. Is there a man anywhere about that knows a lot of Indian lingo?"

"I know a good deal, and so do you."

"Not half what I want now."

"Old Chris Meeker, he could talk five tongues, in his day. And out in the desert by Old Cliff there's a professor something from Washington that's studying the doggone footsteps of dead Injuns. He could tell you anything."

"I know Chris Meeker. He ain't apt to understand what I want. By Old Cliff?"

"I went by there last week. It's two days' riding on a good horse. Have you got a good horse here, son?"

"The best you ever dug a spur into."

"You're going now, Blondy?"

"I'm going."

The sheriff raised his lantern and let the light fall full on the face of Graem. Then he lowered it and let it swing idly from his finger-tips.

"Have a good time, Blondy."

"Same to you, Lew. Tell Molly I'm sorry I couldn't stay."

The bay moved off, struck a jog trot, and so drifted down the street, and still everything slept on either side. At the first turning, Graem swung about in the saddle and saw that the lantern still burned in front of the sheriff's house. At that, weakness went like water through the veins of Graem, and he was on the verge of hurrying back; he would lay the wallet in the hands of Lew Bergen, confess his fault, and beg for protection against the long arm of La Salle.

But the bay jogged on, the corner was turned, the light of the lantern shut away, and in Graem all willpower seemed to have vanished. They came to the end of the town, where a wooden bridge stretched over a creek and a tall and graceful poplar stood on either side as if set there by conscious intention. Hollow and mournful sounded the echoes beneath as the horse trod on the planks, and so Graem faced the open country once more.

The weakness was gone, and yet he felt that he had left a part of his strength behind him. In all the years of his life, never had the suspicion of a lie passed between him and Lew Bergen; but the lie had been told now by mere omission, and it left Graem sick at heart. He wished mightily that he had said to the sheriff: "I've left some black pages in this story I tell you; I've done one bad thing; how bad, I don't know. Lew, I'm no longer straight!"

Well, he had not said it. He made his teeth come together hard, and, so rousing his spirits, he entered upon the tossing sea of hills. Before him, he knew, was great danger, but how great he could not tell. There would be the sinister intelligence and the many hands of La Salle against him, for one thing. There would be the law, also, but how rapidly the law would work he could not guess. Certainly, if the hunt were put in the hands of the sheriff, as it really must be in this country, he would lead it far astray to the south; and with the law counted out for a few days and with only La Salle to encounter —why, he had faced that dangerous fellow before, and he was still alive to talk about it.

In a sort of bad lands, a region split with a thousand sharp-sided little ravines, he halted at dawn, made a bed of shrubbery, and stretched himself on it. By mid-morning the sun wakened him, so he mounted again and went on. The bay was still fresh. Not in vain had he picked that animal from a great herd, and now it went forward with eager eyes and a restless pressure on the bit.

About a mile from the start of this day's ride, he tried a flying shot at a rabbit that started up by chance on the side of a steep ravine with a brook brawling down the midst of it. The bay plunged to the side and unbalanced his rider so that, to save himself, Graem dropped his revolver and reached for the mane. He kept from a fall, but with chagrin he saw the gun bounce down from rock to rock and fall in the midst of a white cataract.

He hunted for it with scrupulous care; it was an old and favourite weapon, shooting a hair's breadth high to the right, but accurate enough when revolvers are apt to be needed. Nevertheless, he had to abandon the search. No doubt it was being rolled along in the tumble of stones at the bottom of the narrow water, so he leaped the bay across the stream and journeyed on with a deeper foreboding than before. Certainly this was an unlucky start for his adventure.

Just at noon he sighted a little village which he had never seen before, the reason being apparent at first glance, for the small houses were composed of raw, unpainted boards. What had inspired the building of the community in such a location appeared difficult for Graem to understand, but cities are like people in the West, and many a one is built upon a careless whim.

At any rate, he knew two things: that in yonder town he could buy a new revolver and a solid meal, and both would be vastly welcome to him. This was probably his margin of grace and after today he would not dare to venture into any town, however small. The hounds of the law would be on his traces. Even now, perhaps, the news had sped before him into the new village; that chance, he decided, he would risk.

So he entered the town in the full heat of the midday, the sun burning through the shoulders of his coat and fairly scorching the skin beneath, a sun so fierce that it seemed to beat down the few rising columns of smoke. Heat of the sun, however, was not what he feared, and as he jogged the bay ahead he kept a sharp lookout to either side from the corners of his eyes, and found cause to bend and examine his saddle pocket so that he could glance down the sun-drenched street.

There was no sign of activity beside him or before; as the village slept when he entered it, so it slept in the sun now. At the general merchandise store, therefore, he dismounted, threw the reins, and entered. At the gun rack he paused to make his selection.

The manufacturers will tell you that every weapon is like every other they produce, but not a puncher on the range agrees with that viewpoint. So he fiddled with gun after gun until he found a Colt which, he told himself, balanced a little more truly, fitted his palm more kindly. That he bought, and paid for it with one of the new hundred-dollars bills from the wallet of the dead man. Nervously he paid, and waited with compressed lips until the change was brought, the clerk chuckling:

"What part of the range you been riding, partner, where they pay you with hundred-dollar bills?"

"Did you ever play poker?" asked Graem, and with that he left the store.

14

WHAT THE SHERIFF KNEW

GRAEM began to feel safe now, and particularly when he found that the interest of the town was gathered around the arrival of a sixteen-mule team, hauling two wagons into the village. The driver was one of those leathery fellows, with many wrinkles and few words, such as one finds most often on the desert; he was pointed out to Graem as "the biggest man·in our town, and a deputy sheriff, if you want to know—that's Sam Loren." Mr. Loren was the centre of all attention, but Graem moved past him and into the hotel, where he found the long dining-room table laid out with a score of enamelled-iron plates and great cups of the same ware standing without saucers. A quarter given to the tired Negro waiter was sufficient to earn for Graem an early meal, and he was deep in his mutton and 'pone before the rest of the crowd poured in. They sat down with loud scrapings, waving of dusty hands, shouts of greeting; they kept their hats on, but pushed them back as they leaned over their food, allowing long and ragged forelocks to drop down across their eyes.

They were such men as Graem knew; he was of them; and yet he felt a difference which had kept him at a distance from such people all the days of his life, so that he had many acquaintances but few friends. Perhaps it was because he had ridden on so many lonely trails; perhaps it was an instinctive horror of the crowd that rose in him, but at any rate he felt a strong disgust for the noise and the company of these people. There was much freedom, much courage in their hearts, as he knew; but, also, there was apt to be ignorance, un-cleanliness of mind and body, and a self-conscious satisfaction in their virtues and their vices, because each man felt himself a hero. For their turbulence, for their oaths, for their display of many guns, Graem felt the contempt of the true fighting man.

He hurried to finish his meal, and he had come to the last of it—a great wedge of pie made from dried apples—when he felt the flick of a curious eye upon him. Those who have been both hunter and hunted are delicately sensitive to observation; litmus paper does not change colour more readily in the presence of acid than the man of the lonely trails changes under a curious or a hostile eye.

Quietly, with gradual glances to the side, Graem surveyed his companions, slipped hastily over the lantern-jawed youth opposite and the noisy fat man who was his neighbour, and arrived at a young, handsome, and brutal face, full fleshed around the jowls and signed with the mark of the beast. It was "Bud" Crogan, suspected widely of rustling and horse stealing, known to be a henchman of La Salle. Now that his attention was drawn to the man, Graem was keenly aware of the next glance of Crogan, which bore suddenly upon him and clung to him with the interest of a man reading a page of print.

It troubled Graem. He told himself that if Crogan had been sent to ferret out his trail, the man would not have shown himself so openly; but the ways of La Salle were strange, and he worked so often by opposites that one never could be sure of his intention or his method. That close scrutiny might also have been inspired by other reasons; it might be that Crogan had been one of those who made the ring around the nest of rocks that day on the upper Las Vegas, and if Graem had reasons to remember that encounter he suspected that the besieging party had other reasons almost equally strong. Three of them he knew he had hit, and one, at least, had gone to the last accounting; so Crogan might well be examining his former enemy with the curiosity of one who has felt the fire.

The wedge of apple pie, reduced to the rear rim of crust, was abandoned; the last swallow of coffee poured down; and, leaving a coin for payment and tip, Graem rose and idled toward the door. There he paused, turned a little, and pretended to be absorbed in the rolling of a cigarette; as a matter of fact he was studying Crogan from the corner of his eye and noticing that the latter was bolting the remnant of his meal with odd haste.

This was more than significant, it appeared to him, and he was about to go to his horse when Sam Loren came smiling up the veranda steps.

"You're the hundred-dollar fellow, ain't you?" asked Loren.

"I dunno," said Graem.

"The hundred-dollar poker man, I mean?" went on the other.

Graem smiled and nodded in turn.

"Sometimes you go by the name of Tucker Graem, don't you?"

The latter grew annoyed; it was distinctly off the books, this manner of firing questions point-blank; decidedly it should not be done west of the Mississippi.

So he shrugged his shoulders to end the conversation, deliberately raised his glance over the head of little Sam Loren, and studied a cumulus cloud which was swelling up rapidly in the south.

"Maybe we better go along and talk in my office," suggested Loren, and when Graem looked at him again he discovered that a short-nosed revolver was covering his heart.

"Maybe we better," agreed Graem.

Mr. Loren thrust the gun into his coat pocket, but kept its nose obviously thrust out toward his companion.

"I don't want to make no scene, Graem," he said. "I know about you; I know you're straight, mostly; but I just want to ask you some questions. You walk along beside me and a little ahead; I got to warn you that I'm covering you all the time, partner."

These directions Graem obeyed in silence, for he felt the danger ahead and resolved to meet it warily and with apparent submission. Besides, if Sam Loren were the biggest man in this village, it appeared that he was also fit to be the biggest man in a much larger place. He went about this work of arrest with the smooth technique of a man at a familiar practice.

"You're arresting me?" said Graem, as they sauntered up the street.

"You might call it that."

"You need a warrant for that, Loren."

"I got one," said the little man instantly.

"I'll have a flash at it, if you don't mind."

"You've already had a flash at it, partner."

Then Graem understood. Whatever the crime that he was suspected of, it had not yet been entirely proved, and now he was to be examined. He promised himself with a resolute click of his teeth that it would go hard if any damaging admission came from his own lips. Now they came to a house that was no better than a shed, and he was directed to push open the door, which admitted them to a single-roomed shack—bedroom, kitchen, dining room, living room, in one.

"Set down and rest your feet," invited Loren, pointing with his left hand to an upturned apple box.

When that invitation had been accepted, the captor continued in his usual quiet voice:

"I want to find out that you've done nothing wrong, Graem, because I know Lew Bergen; but I got to act like you would be dangerous to me if you had a chance, and I know that the kind of danger you can furnish is man-sized. So, if you don't mind——"

He brought the revolver out of his pocket, and, sitting on a homemade stool, he covered Graem steadily with the weapon.

"Now, I want to know about that hundred-dollar bill," he said. "Where did you get it?"

"Now I want to know," echoed Graem, his heart beating very fast, "what business it is of anybody's?"

"It's the business of every police officer in these here States," replied the deputy, "and every treasury officer, and it's the business of the president, too. That's how important it is to us. You understand what I mean?"

"I don't," said Graem.

"Before you get a chance to understand better," said Loren. "I want to advise you to put your cards on the table. Have you got any more bills like that?"

Graem shrugged his shoulders.

Then: "You can see my wallet if you want," said he, and reached his hand toward the inside of his coat.

"Steady!" snapped Loren. "Understand me, Graem, I want to like you fine, but if you try another funny move like that, I'll shoot you dead. Stick your hands up and I'll get that wallet for myself!"

The hands of Graem were thrust slowly above his head; this affair was taking on an odd importance, for Loren was obviously not the man to make much of a little thing, and this matter he was treating very like a murder case.

And the picture from Crocker's place darted back upon the mind's eye of Graem—Jerry grinning with mockery in his death, so that it seemed, now, as though he were promising that Graem would follow him on the last trail before very long.

There was plenty of nerve in Blondy Graem, but now he began to sweat profusely. The blunt-nosed revolver was thrust beneath his chin, and the slender left hand of the deputy sheriff began to reach into his pockets. Presently it found the wallet and drew it forth. After that, he stepped back, pinching the pocket-book.

"It's thick with the same stuff, I suppose," he said with a gathering sternness. "This looks like it's gunna be hard on you, Graem—though I hope not. I ask you again: where did you get that hundred-dollar bill?"

He said it crisply and sharply, jabbing the muzzle of his gun a little toward Graem as he spoke.

"Don't take time to work up a lie for me!" he added with hot energy as the glance of Graem wandered toward the open door.

It was not under the pressure of invention, however, that Graem looked in that direction, but because young Bud Crogan at that instant had stepped into view with a tarpaulin in one hand and a naked revolver in the other. He made to Graem a slight motion as though to signify that he came as a friend, and at the same time he began a stealthy advance toward the deputy.

"Talk up, youngster," went on Sam Loren, "and if you need to have your tongue loosened a little, I'll tell you something that we know—this here hundred is counterfeit money, Graem!"

15

FROM BEHIND

It was like the winking out of a light for Graem, so completely did this announcement alter all his ideas. No doubt, if the bill were counterfeit, then all the rest of the package of money was false, and poor Jerry had fled from La Salle, and thrown away his life, for the sake of a treasure which was of no more value than dead leaves.

He closed his eyes and tried to summon up the picture of that unlucky bill, but still it seemed to him to have been perfect.

The deputy sheriff continued: "It was a mighty good job, and the best that I ever seen; the marshal will say that, too, when he has a look at it. Only by good luck I had a hundred-dollar bill in my own pocket, and a magnifying glass that showed the difference. But to the naked eye—I'd defy anybody to read the crookedness into that money."

He spoke half in admiration and half in horror.

And Graem looked again toward the stalking form of Crogan, going forward with a desperate face and stealthy steps.

"I don't know a thing about any counterfeiting," said Graem honestly enough.

"Then tell us where you picked up this stuff. That's what I want to know."

Graem sighed. It was like being forced back upon the path of virtue, and still he could not help regretting bitterly the great fortune which had been in his hands. Now the house on the hill was wiped away for ever, before his hands had set their grip securely on the mere means of purchasing it. Like a pretender abdicating his hopes to the throne, Graem sighed.

"Where I got it——" began Graem, and did not reach the next word, for Crogan made the rest of his distance with a single bound and struck downward with the barrel of the revolver. Little Sam Loren gasped, staggered, and would have fallen on his face had not Crogan seized him, throwing the tarpaulin over his head; and then, kneeling on the back of the fallen deputy, he tied the hands of Loren behind the small of his back, secured the head covering so that it could not be removed, and lashed his feet to the foot of the stove.

Graem, still more than half stunned by the news which Loren had given him, scooped up the wallet, and replaced it in his pocket, not that it had a value for him now in the stack of counterfeit it contained, but because it also held the piece of paper on which the dead man had written down his strange jumble of unrelated syllables.

Now, his work of securing the fallen man completed, Crogan stood up and stretched out his hand.

"I'll take the wallet, Graem; hand it over, will you? We got to get out of here!"

"We'll get out first," suggested Graem. "Go up the street and head out of the place north. I'll go south. We'll double around and meet on the west trail."

Crogan flushed with sullen anger.

"Have I earned that wallet?" he asked. "What good is the queer to you? And I've kept you out of the pen for about a twenty-year stretch, Graem!"

"I'm not dodging you," said Graem. "I say that I'll meet you on the west trail. You can see two hills three mile out from town, and I'll wait for you between 'em."

Crogan started to speak, changed his mind, and hurried from the shack; and a moment later Graem was drifting his horse south down a narrow and twisting cattle path. When he had a hill shoulder between him and the town, he turned straight west and let the bay fly, for something told him that it might be very wise to come to the trysting place before Crogan arrived there. Up hill and down dale the bay went, and so he swept up to the little pass in time to see Crogan flying toward him on a lathered horse, frantic with the torture of the spur.

It gave Graem time to dismount and loosen the girths; he even had a cigarette rolled by the time that Crogan, lifting his bowed head, swept in between the hills.

"Well!" snarled Crogan, and glared with most evil intent upon the other.

"Almost like brothers, ain't we?" remarked Graem. "Shoulder to shoulder—against all enemies—doggone if it doesn't stir me all up, Crogan."

Crogan let his lips writhe over words that made no sound.

"You come busting up here to double cross me," he suggested.

"I came busting up here to keep you from double crossing me, Crogan. I was here first. If I wanted to get you off my trail, I could have picked you off as neat as pie, Crogan, from the minute that you got over that hummock yonder."

Crogan snapped a glance behind him and then shivered a little.

"But you," continued Graem, "would have stuck me up the minute that you had a bead on me. Now, old son, we understand each other."

"All right," said Crogan, and held out his left hand. "I'll take the wallet, Graem. Mind you, I know what's in it to a penny. Everything: I'll take the wallet; just fork it over."

Graem smiled, and Crogan grew almost tearful with honest indignation. There is nothing so unnerving as self-pity.

"You sit there with little Loren's teeth in you, not able to move— a twenty-year stretch at hard labour ahead of you—and then you want to beat out a gent that's saved you from that! Why, Graem, you got the reputation of bein' white!"

"What would La Salle pay for this wallet?" asked Graem, taking it out, but with his left hand.

Crogan started violently in his saddle.

"Who said La Salle?" he barked. "I never said nothing about La Salle!"

Graem chuckled.

"You did me a good turn a few minutes ago," he admitted. "And because of that I won't try to take out on you what I might take out."

"I dunno how you're drifting," growled Crogan.

"Were you ever on the upper Las Vegas?" asked Graem suddenly.

And he had the sinister pleasure of seeing the other whiten under the blow.

"Now we know each other," said Graem. "Be off with you, Crogan. If I had a wiser head on my shoulders, I'd say that the trick you served Loren only half paid off the dirty work on the Las Vegas. I'd pull a gun on you and leave myself with a quiet trail; and, by gravy, I'm more'n half minded to do it!"

Crogan, paler than ever, nevertheless thrust out a great, square jaw.

"I got one chance in three against you," he said, admitting his inferiority frankly enough, "but maybe the luck would be with me. However, the main point is that it wouldn't quiet your trail, Graem. I'm not the only man. There's a dozen working for the chief to get you!"

"That's news, too," Graem nodded. "Now get out, Crogan. I know you; don't ride across me again."

Crogan, with no further argument, turned his horse. Only when he reached the farther end of the cleft between the hills he turned and shouted back: "You poor fool, Graem, you're a goner!"

Then he galloped off to the north.

West and south rode Graem, until he came to a loftier range of hills. On the crest of one of these he lay down with a strong glass at his eye and swept the country. He could pick up Crogan easily enough because the man was riding a black horse, which showed like a dark shadow marked with silver-bright high-lights. He had gone well to the north, by this time, and the last Graem saw of him was as the black horse paused uncertainly at the verge of a ravine and then was swallowed in the darkness of the canyon.

So much for Crogan, who doubtless was heading straight to make his report to La Salle; perhaps fresh swarms of wasps would issue to string the life out of Graem. In the meantime, what of the town?

It, also, was plainly in sight through the crystal clarity of the mountain air, and, when the glass was turned upon it, it came up as large as life under the eyes of the observer. There was presently much activity—a swirl of horsemen in the streets, and then they drifted from the town and disappeared over the southern slope. And that meant they had taken up the trail of Graem!

He looked anxiously at the bay, but that long-legged speedster was grazing in perfect content, with an eye as bright and filled with courage as though he had been freshly taken from a stall. If they worked up close, he would give those hard riders a bellyful of work, even if little Sam Loren led the procession.

Now the hunters came into view again, swinging up the grade steadily until they came to the two hills; there they disappeared for a few minutes, and when they came in sight once more, they were stretching away to the north. They had changed trails there, as Graem hoped they might, and when he had observed this, he mounted again and let the bay resume the journey at a steady and effortless jog-trot.

He had an odd feeling now that his work was much simplified by that meeting with Loren and what had followed it. Doubtless, he was under the shadow of the law as a passer of counterfeit, and as an assailant of an officer of the law, and, eventually, he would be charged by Crocker with the murder of Jerry. Nevertheless, his own conscience would be cleared the moment he mailed a hundred dollars in honest money to the General Merchandise Store which had changed the false note.

La Salle, of course, was at the bottom of the attack on Loren, and the reason was that the criminal did not wish the counterfeit treasure to pass into the hands of the law. Crogan had been sent out with two instructions, doubtless: one was to get rid of Graem, but the other was above all to gain possession of the wallet for the sake of the cunning forgeries which it contained—and perhaps, also, because of that same little piece of paper on which Jerry had written down the strange words.

At any rate, Old Cliff was his destination now, and he settled his course steadily toward it, bearing well south as he went until the hills dropped away before him, the sun grew hotter, and he entered the misty, stifling atmosphere of the desert. He looked back as he drew rein at the entrance to this oven and on the last slope from the hill he saw three horsemen hurrying straight toward him, bowed low over their saddle bows and jockeying their mounts to great speed.

16

ALL IN THE GAME

HE let the bay run, and like a swallow in full flight before the wind that noble animal responded; but five brief minutes told Graem that his horse did not run well enough, for behind him the pursuers first held even, and then they began to draw up a little. The mounts undoubtedly were fresher; they could not be of much better quality than the bay.

On the desert one horseman cannot avoid a fleeter enemy. It was for that reason that the Comanches, above all the Indian tribes, prized speed and endurance in their saddle stock. Now, Graem, glancing repeatedly behind him and skilfully judging the ground that he was losing, became desperate. There was a sheer plain around him of reddish sand, with a stretch of greasewood in the distance like a low roll of smoke across the level. No cover was there, and hardly shelter for a rabbit was in sight except in the distance where a tall butte rose like the prow of a ship.

The sun was now westering close to the horizon and its pale face was broadening to crimson and gold, which gilded the butte, in turn, and covered the sky with a coloured mist. What help lay in the butte Graem could not guess, but he turned toward it in despair, for at least it was better than the open waste. There, in some nest among the rocks, he might try to hold off the three pursuers until water failed them, or until he himself went mad with thirst. He went forward, not in actual hope but rather in despair, and the closer he drew the greater became his gloom, for both sides of the butte which he could see rose like the polished steel plates of a battleship, smooth, hardly broken by a joint. He would need wings to climb up such a fortress height.

Certainly his pursuers were not worried by his course, but as though they understood that nothing was to be gained by him in this direction, they kept their mounts to an even pace and indeed allowed him to gain a little upon them when he gave the bay its head more fully.

Press a horse beyond a certain point and one mile kills it quicker than five at a reasonable clip; the bay had given up a great store of power in the past forty-eight hours, and though he responded willingly enough to this last call, still it was plain to Graem that there was little left in the reservoir of the gelding's strength. His head was no longer straightened out, his tail no longer arched, and the fore legs flung out with a pound. He changed twice in a single mile; in half an hour the three pursuers would have him in their pockets, so to speak.

Now the butte rose loftier before him; it lost its character of a ship and seemed rather a cliff with a turreted and half-ruined castle on top. Such a fortress could have defied all the armies of the days of spears and bows. It had lost its glory of golden fire at the same time that the sky altered rapidly from flame to mists of lavender, and now Graem swung around the prow, where the tumbled rocks looked like a frozen spray curling away from the cut-water. Down the side of the eminence he kept the bay at a hand gallop, feeling the heaving sides of the good horse under his knees and anxiously looking over the wall of rock. It was by no means a polished entity as it had seemed from a distance; it might even be climbed; but such a feat would have taken weary hours, clinging by toe and finger, and in the meanwhile, the pursuit would rush upon him and take him at its will.

Straight down the sheer flank of the cliff, therefore, he galloped, and turned the corner into a heap of scattered boulders and a number of ruinous shacks, while the dark mouth of a tunnel yawned like a natural cavern in the base of the rock. Just before that circle of darkness sat a ragged fellow smoking a pipe and bending low over a tattered magazine. But the heart of Graem rejoiced; he felt that never had he seen a picture more beautiful.

So he rushed upon the stranger, drew rein, and pointed stiffly down the tunnel.

"Old-timer, if I ride into that cave there, could you tell the three gents that come behind me that I've rode straight on? Straight down that draw, d'you hear?"

He fumbled in his pocket for the change which he had received for the hundred-dollar note. That bundle of silver and paper he pressed into the hand of the other, who stood up and revealed himself as a tall, slender, stoop-shouldered man, his face shaggy with unshaven whiskers, his eyes at once keen as the eyes of a fox and lazy as the eyes of a pet dog.

"You sashay right along after me," said he. "I'll show you where to hide."

"Then hurry, for Heaven's sake!"

The mine-keeper, if that were his job, broke into a shambling run, plunged straight into the tunnel, and immediately turned to the right.

Here he jerked open a heavy wooden door that covered a long passage whose termination the last of the daylight refused to reveal to Graem.

"Get in there—you and your horse. We could hide a thousand right here in the old mine!"

And he chuckled with perfect confidence, as it appeared, while Graem eagerly led in the horse. The door was swung shut behind him with a screech, and closed with a great rattling, after which he could hear the trailing, lazy feet of the mine-keeper moving off toward the mouth of the tunnel.

It seemed hardly a moment after this before the sharp rattle of hoofs sounded, and then the voices of the hunters. That outward fanning mouth of the tunnel gathered the sounds which then were reflected down the smaller heart of the shaft, and Graem heard with perfect clarity every word of the conversation that followed.

The three stormed at the keeper with a first flurry of questions: Had he seen a single rider on a beaten horse? Had he gone this way? Had he tried to dodge into the mouth of the mine?

The response was according to the plan: "Down that draw was where he ran. He wouldn't want to be cornered in a hole in the ground, would he?"

An exclamation of satisfaction answered; off went the volley of hoofbeats, and Graem, with a rising heart, heard the sand swishing, then silence. The keeper began to whistle "Annie Laurie," sadly out of tune; but this attempt at sang-froid ended suddenly, followed by the return of the horses.

"You been lying, you old desert-rat!" shouted a voice.

The keeper protested gravely.

"Search him, Charlie and Ed," commanded the apparent leader. "And make it lively."

"Appears to me, if we got him bottled in there, he'll have to stay put."

"I tell you, he's a rat that will gnaw his way through ten feet of solid rock. He'll be through our fingers!"

There was a little pause, followed by: "Where did you get this money?"

"That's my last month's pay," answered the keeper.

"What pay d'you get?"

"Forty-five."

"Now you lie. Nobody but a fool would pay forty-five to a spindle-shanked old goat like you."

"Nobody but a fool owns this here mine," answered the keeper with a calm indifference.

"There's fifty-one dollars here," said another.

"He threw in six dollars," said the keeper smoothly, "because he'd been short with me the month before."

"He gave you fifty-one dollars and you didn't spend a cent in town?"

"I had something left from the month before."

"Old son," said the leader with quick decision, "you never had a pay day in your life that you didn't blow in every penny over the bar or for moonshine. Is that the truth?"

"It's likely the truth for young bloods like you," said the shambling fellow, with no sign of fear in his voice. "But I got my first touch of rheumatism a while back, and that made me decide to start saving."

"You lie faster than a clock ticks. Here, Charlie, spread him out on that rock and we'll get the truth out of him with my quirt."

"This'll be like old days before the mast," rejoined the keeper, with undaunted nerve.

"Hello!" broke in the leader. "You a sailor? Now I take another look at you, you're Tom Wolf. Answer up!"

"I don't say that ain't my name," answered the keeper.

"You're Tom Wolf," declared the other, "and you were in on the Mendoza job."

"It's a lie!" exclaimed Wolf. "I never was within twenty mile of Mendoza when——"

"Aw, shut up, will you?" demanded the leader. "You're among friends, Tom. We're all in the know. We're all in the game, old boy. Now you listen to me——"

His voice fell away to a murmur which even the perfect sounding board of the tunnel did not reflect to the ear of the prisoner. Then he heard the keeper exclaim: "La Salle!" in such a tone of fear and surprise that Graem's heart sank at once. He foreboded at once what the end would be.

Therefore, he was not surprised when, after a short, murmured consultation, the whole party of four came clattering down the shaft and stopped in front of the wooden door.

"Graem! Hey, Blondy!" called the leader's voice.

There was no use in silence.

"Well?" he answered.

"We got him, by George!" said the other. Then he added: "The game's finished. You gave us a good ride, old-timer. Just walk out here, and walk with your hands up, will you?"

"Thanks," said Graem. "I'll stay put."

"It's a good bluff," said the leader. "I give you credit. But we ain't here to waste time. We'll smoke you out, old son. And if we have to do that, when you come, we'll tag you with lead. Now make up your mind."

"I'd like a few minutes to think," said the refugee.

"You've had your minutes."

"What do I get?"

"A safe ride to the chief."

"I'll take the kind of safety that I get here," replied Graem. "Start your fireworks, boys, and luck help the fool that lets me have a shot at him!"

17

A FOUR-HORSE MAN

THERE was no reason behind this defiance, but there is no place for logic in such a position; the logical man surrenders like Mack at Ulm and the rest of the world derides him for ever. So it was with Graem, who felt that he was hopelessly lost, yet who could not surrender without some sort of a struggle for freedom.

He struck a match. The flame rose steadily in the still air and showed him the pricked ears and the shining eyes of the bay gelding, keenly alert and very frightened, so that it shouldered up to its master and seemed to look to him for protection. Graem laid his hand between those glistening eyes and spoke softly; and he had a sudden thought of mounting the horse and rushing out when the flames had eaten through the door. But he knew well that such an action would be folly; the men whom La Salle hired were not the sort to miss a flame-lit target at close range.

With another match he examined the shaft. It was not only lofty enough for a horse to walk through it here, but even in the dark distance it still had sufficient dimensions. He looked gloomily at the pick strokes, at the rotten and sagging woodwork, and then there was a heavy crashing and a faint gust of wind reached him. Already they had beaten in the door; in another moment the air was acrid with smoke. But of course they were furnished with plenty of wood from the shacks near the mouth of the mine, and weeds thrown on the flame would furnish a source for the smoke.

The bay snorted, coughed, and, crowding closer to his master, shuddered as he watched the leap of the fire. Graem, in a blind fury, snatched out a revolver and poured out three shots in rapid succession; loud laughter answered him; then the fire was depressed with a burden of weeds, and a heavy, stifling smoke rolled up the passage, as if a wind were blowing it.

Graem started erect. As if a wind were blowing it! For indeed, why should the smoke move so freely?

"All right, Graem," called the voice of the leader of the La Salle men. "You see what'll happen. We give you a chance to come out now—a last chance, mind you!"

"Oh, be damned to you," he shouted savagely in answer, yet there was a thrill of hope in his tones.

For it had occurred to him that, since there was no wind to blow in that smoke, it must be drawn from the end of the passage, and that meant that the shaft was to some extent open to the outer air at the far end. He turned, therefore, and with the frightened horse crowding at his heels, stumbled forward, lighting match after match as he went.

The shaft dipped, veered to the right, dipped again, and he had to walk up to the knees in black water, crusted over with a heavy scum. On the farther side, he slipped and struck his head heavily against the side of the passage; a warm trickle of blood ran down his face, but he hardly noticed it. There was hot, eager hope in him, for the smoke still followed, as fast as he walked, pungent wisps of it being drawn out ahead of him. He could see it by the matchlight, like crawling arms of mist.

The shaft diminished. He came to a place where one of the great cross-timbers had broken down and a heap of débris made it barely possible for him to wriggle through, leaving the horse behind. But he could not leave it behind; at such a moment the poor animal was more than a horse—it was a companion in distress. Feverishly, therefore, he worked, pulling the fallen crossbeam away, and tugging at the rocks and stone splinters. It was hopeless to attempt to free the place to such a degree that the bay could walk through erect, but when he had widened the space as much as possible, the gelding came frantically after him, crouching low, scraping and struggling like a dog; and at last it was erect beside him, snorting with fear and trembling.

He hurried on, with the shaft as wide and spacious as ever, until he came to a solid wall of stone that ended the passage. No, not a solid wall. As he lighted a fresh match, he saw that it was composed of rudely squared stones with many a gap between them. Starting at the top, he dislodged a ponderous fragment, and instantly the desert air touched his face, and he saw before him a dim cluster of horizon stars.

The nearness of freedom gave him a mad strength. He picked up the massive boulders as though they had been dried wood, and heaved them to this side and to that. Rapidly the opening widened. Already, it was ample for him, but still he laboured frantically for the sake of the horse until, in the end, he led the bay out under the sky, with a cloud of smoke issuing about them. It was like the fabled exit of some demigod from the fiery nether regions.

Then into the saddle, dizzy with joy, leaped Graem, and spurred madly across the sands. He put a half-mile behind him, and then checked the gelding and sat to think. This was avoiding his pursuers, but not checking them for long. They would find the cause of his escape unless he returned and built up the wall again; so he turned back with a groan of impatience and once more approached the lofty and solemn shadow of the butte.

However, as he turned back, his spirit rose; he who attacks has thrice the courage of the defender, and now that his face was turned toward the enemy he thought rather of harassing him than of covering his own trail.

Fate willing, the three still were in the heart of the main shaft, working at their fire, half stifled at their work, but certain that every moment was choking their victim in the dark heart of the shaft.

He dismounted and threw the reins a short distance from the mine entrance; then he crept carefully up behind the nearest shed. A steady smoke was curling up from the shaft mouth, and between him and that point stood the three horses. By one glance at them he could tell why they had pressed the bay so hard this evening, for they were animals of the finest quality, long-reined, long-legged, with a girth about the cinches that told of wind and heart. Even as he crouched to watch, the fire-builders stumbled out of the smoky mouth of the shaft and he heard them gasping for breath.

"You, Harry, go back and keep watch there," commanded one.

"I'll be damned if I do," coughed Harry. "If I was half choked, he must be all choked. He ain't a salamander, is he?"

"He's a hard one, Harry. He's harder than chilled steel and

meaner; easier for a dog to kill a badger than it is for a man to kill Graem even with smoke and fire."

"Wait till I get a breath. I'll go in again."

Never had Graem heard sweeter words than this praise from his enemies. It gave him fresh power and fresh surety, so that he slipped at once from his shelter, and stepped in among the horses. He gathered up the reins of two easily enough, but the third, a black beauty, reared and snorted.

"What's that?" shouted a voice. "Harry, there's somebody in there with the horses."

"Don't be a fool."

"I tell you, I see—hey!"

And with a shout the man started running—a shadowy form in the dim desert starlight. Luckily the black was in hand by this time and, slipping into the saddle on that restless horse, Graem cantered him around the shed and led the two others behind him, so putting the small building between himself and the torrent of yells and curses that broke from the three. A shout to the bay, as they swept past, made the good gelding toss its head and gallop on in the lead; guns began to crash behind them, but in a moment they were hopelessly out of range and Graem stopped his course to indulge in a fierce laughter of rejoicing. So far as stinging revenge was concerned, how much more perfect to have baffled and beaten these men and taken their horses from them than even to have laid them dead behind him! They would be ashamed almost to madness by this misfortune, and every camp up and down the course of the range would laugh at the story and envy the luck and the prowess of Blondy Graem.

So, when he had secured his prizes and strung them out on the lead-rope, he rode on across the desert, the very happiest man that those dim stars looked down upon, in spite of the shadow of the law that lay on him darker than the night, in spite of the hostile power of La Salle.

His spirit was rising for another reason, which was no reason at all, for he told himself that luck was working for him, and, like a gambler with the feeling that the tide had turned for him, he was ready to wager high. In the meantime, instead of one very tired and failing horse, he had four beauties to choose from, and no immediate danger of pursuit behind him. He rode on for a scant hour at a brisk pace—certainly the three could not trail him until the morning, at their best—and then he paused, with the stars glimmering on the face of a water hole. An owl rose from the edge of the water and slanted with a hushing whisper to the west, and then there was no sound except the plopping hoofs of the horses as they waded down through mud to the edge of the water and drank deep.

Here he made his camp, for there was plenty of grazing for the horses and water for himself, and good dead brush to make his fire. He built it recklessly large and by the edge of the water, so that the long, yellow images licked rapidly across the black pool, and afterwards, while he lay at ease with his cigarette, the red coals gleamed like eyes from the heart of the tank.

So he took stock of his affairs, as he wrapped himself in his blanket and used his saddle for a pillow. And as a miser counts and fingers in imagination the coins in his hidden chest, so this son of the West counted and fingered and literally rejoiced in the difficulties and the dangers before him, estimating them, planning against them, and feeling his strength and his courage rise to meet the burden.

Sleep descended gradually upon him; but he was unwilling to close his eyes, and fought for a long time to keep them open to taste still the confusion of La Salle's outflung forces and relish the desert stars that burned over his head.

In the morning, he took the way toward Old Cliff, aiming his course by the position of the rising sun and the northern hills, and above all by the latent instinct which kept a map of the country in his mind. That night, if all went well, he should reach his goal unless the law or La Salle managed to catch him again, and he would have wagered heavily against the chance of either.

18

FINDING A TARTAR

HE studied the horses as they moved across the red desert. They were four of a kind, but when he shifted from one to the other he felt that two stood out from the rest—the black and his own bay. The two he would keep—the others he would dispose of as he could; in the meantime, let who would heave above the horizon to give chase, now that his saddle was on one horse, and his pack on another, with four splendid animals to change to. Graem felt rich indeed: the richness of an Indian of the desert.

The deadly desert heat began, and there was no shelter from it. Softened by long residence in the northern mountains, the sweat now poured steadily from Graem's body; his hands slipped on the reins. Then, after midday, with the horses dropping and stumbling, great fortune brought him to a little shack with standing water beside it in a "tank." In front of the shack sat an old man with a pipe who lifted his hand in a sort of silent Indian greeting and went on with his deliberate smoking.

The horses were watered and left to pick at the grasses beside the water; then Graem turned into the shack.

"Chuck, partner?" he asked.

The old man pointed a thumb over his shoulder.

"Pone and cold fried bacon," he said. "The fire's out."

The fire was distinctly out, and there was no wood to kindle it again; plainly this hermit of the desert never stirred until the evening coolness began. Then perhaps he would wander out to gather mesquite for fuel, or look at his snares for rabbits, or try to knock over larger game with his rifle. One fire a day would do his cooking; fifty dollars a year would supply his wants amply; for as the desert plants live with little substance of moisture or of good soil to nourish them, so the desert men grow lean and dry and hard and light.

The cold food was duly found—not cold, really, but lukewarm in the even temperature of the house. Graem ate, and came back to squat on the doorstep and smoke a cigarette.

"You got some horses," said the old man at last.

"Four," said Graem obviously.

"The bay and the black," said the hermit, "might be worth buying even."

"Aye, they might, but they ain't to be sold," said Graem.

The other clucked and refilled his pipe. He seemed only mildly interested in his companion, in the heat of the sun, in the horses, in life itself; all was removed behind a veil for him.

"The other two could be picked up pretty cheap," said the hermit.

"Could they?" said Graem, irritated by this calm assumption of absolute knowledge.

"Yes," said the hermit, "they could be bought dirt cheap."

At this, Graem scratched his chin; his temper was rising as it should not have done in the presence of an old man who was also his host. But there was about this veteran desert-bird something so extremely irritating that his gorge rose. It was not merely age and arrogant self-confidence; it was also something unhuman, removed, distant from the ordinary courses of kind, warm-hearted creatures of the flesh. Every second that he sat beside the man his emotion deepened and grew more hot. He had felt that La Salle was of all men the worst, but suddenly, without real proof offered, with a sort of profound, instinctive reaction, he shrank from the desert-dweller as the most evil of all creatures.

He stood up.

"I'll be going on," he said.

"Naw, you'll stay awhile," answered the veteran.

"I will?"

"I ain't through talkin' to you," said the hermit. "That's the main reason."

This malevolent self-assurance so far shook Graem that he even glanced rapidly over his shoulders to see if there were not allies of the old satyr creeping up on him from behind.

"There ain't anybody else," snarled this grim mind-reader. "There's nobody but me to be afraid of, sonny."

"Afraid?" echoed Graem, more angry than ever, because fear had been mixed with that emotion.

"Afraid," said the old man with conviction. "But, speaking about the two horses, I'd take those two off your hands, son."

"How much?" asked Graem with the glittering eye of a disbeliever.

"Say fifty for the pair," offered the other.

Graem compressed his lips.

"I see how it is," said he. "You're sort of shortsighted. You take them for a pair of thick-legged, hump-backed, wall-eyed, ewe-necked mustangs. Ain't that it, old-timer?"

"I take 'em," said the strange old man, "for a pair of high-blooded, high-headed, high-priced racers. Am I wrong?"

"Ah," said Graem satirically, "so you're offering a bang-up price for that pair of racers, ain't you?"

"Things depend," said the other. "Things depend a lot on circumstances."

For the first time he turned his gaze from weather and horses and his own reflections and favoured Graem with his full attention, and under the filmed, moveless stare the cow-puncher stirred uneasily.

"What price a glass of water?" said the hermit. "Why, it's free. Nobody would never have the nerve to charge for a glass of water, except under circumstances. Like, say, you was out in the desert doing a forced march with your canteens empty and a mangy gang of Apaches heaving up in sight—then, what price for a glass of water, sonny?"

"As high as you please," agreed the puncher. "You been in a tight hole like that?"

"I been," announced the other, "where just thinkin' about it would curl up the hair of the youngsters of these days, or maybe burn their hair right off their heads."

"Humph!" said Graem.

"Grunting don't change the truth, and the truth is what I've spoke," said the hermit. "Now, to get back to horses——"

"What might your name be?" asked Graem.

"By name of Martin—Martin Larribee—maybe you've heard about that name?"

And his old eyes glimmered with a light of eager vanity as they searched the face of Graem.

"No," said the latter with a merciless satisfaction. "I never heard of that name before."

The eyes turned dark again.

"Ignorance!" exclaimed Martin Larribee. "Ignorance is what the young folks of these here days is raised into. Doggone me if it don't make me sick to think about the school taxes that is paid to eddicate them. What eddication has they got, you ask? None, I answer. Not even they don't speak the language right; not even they don't know the history of the country that they're livin' in. But there was a time, young man, when the name of Martin Larribee was known from the Rockies to the Mississippi and back again! Now, to get back to those horses——"

"There's no good getting back to them. You've never seen enough money in your days to buy that pair off of me."

"No? Well, if you had a right to sell 'em in the first place——"

He paused and let the pause fill in the place of words.

"I haven't the right to sell 'em?" asked Graem, partly alarmed and partly angered again.

Under his eyes the other opened a wallet and revealed an amazing sheaf of notes. From these he selected several, studied them in his hand, and then replaced them after some hunting with still more finger-worn specimens.

"Here," said he, "is a hundred dollars. You take it and gimme the horses and the saddles and the bridles. And I won't ask you nothing back for luck."

"Those two saddles alone," suggested Graem, beginning to be amused, "are worth a lot more than the money you offer."

"Sure," said the other, "and the guns in the saddle holsters are worth more than the money I offer, too. But I'll get the whole lot for the price that I'm showing you. Don't lemme get my arm tired holding this coin out to you!"

No young man can endure the dry absoluteness of an elderly companion without some touch of nervous irritation, and so it was with Graem at this moment. Nevertheless, he chuckled.

"Larribee," he said, "I'd hate to say that you're a fool—you being older than me."

"A fool?" shouted the old man, his voice raised for the first time.

"You've showed me enough money to make me put a gun at your head—if I was like a good many fellows on this range."

"Aye, if you was like them—if you had the sense that they have," said the old tartar. "But you ain't like them a bit. You ain't got the wits that they have, so I could show you a million—and you'd never touch it!"

At this implied scorn and mingled compliment, Graem stepped back a little and regarded his host more critically.

"You know me pretty well, I take it," said he. "You've known me for about a half-hour, I suppose."

"There is men that runs in streaks like pay dirt," said the veteran. "And there is men that's like jewels, none like another. Now, take me—you've never met my like before, and you'll never meet it again; but take you—I've seen tons of men like you. Army officers and such —they're like you. I've seen tons of 'em lying and rotting after the Indians got through with 'em. Fools—high-headed fools like those hosses, yonder. Talking about honour, mostly. Acting as though the world always was worrying about them and watching them and afraid that they'd do something that would disgrace it. I've known tons and mountains of men like you, your stamp and cut, but better, mostly!"

He finished this tirade with another snarl of scorn.

"All right," said Graem quietly, for he began to feel that Larribee was a mixture of equal parts of vitriol, meanness, and cunning, "I'll be going along."

"You fool," said the hermit, "if you don't sell me those horses, where else would you be selling 'em?"

"To the first right-headed man that I meet."

"Right-headed, did you say?"

"I said that."

At this, Larribee leaned forward a little and his smile grew absolutely devilish. "And who," said he, "would be right-headed if he bought a stolen pair of horses from the murderer, Graem?"

19

AN UNWORRIED WIZARD

HE put in this shot with glee and watchfulness, drinking in its effects upon Graem; he actually began to nod his head and rub his hands as he saw the younger man change colour and glance with frightened eyes across the burning plain where the heat-waves danced and shimmered, almost as bright as the waters of the tank nearby.

"You," said Graem a little huskily, "are the devil!"

"I am," admitted the other gleefully. "I'm the devil and the devil's daddy. You begin to understand me. Now you understand what I mean when I offer you a hundred. Fifty would really be enough, except that you're the kind that would rather rot than sell for such a price. Howsomever, sell you must and sell you shall. What else have you got, young feller? What else have you got to buy your way, except you begin to sell your guns? And money is what you'll need. Not every county is run by a Sheriff Bergen—the fool! The soft-headed, blear-eyed fool!"

"I'm kind of tired," said the fugitive, "of hearing you rattle away. Mostly it makes me tired to hear vermin like you name a man like Bergen."

"Spoke like a man," responded Larribee, with a cant of his head and a nod, like one hearing familiar music. "Spoke like a man of the old days—all honour—all glory—all friendship—all courage—all fertilizer for the prairie grass, finally. Doggone me, but it makes me feel young to hear such a lingo! Bergen's your friend. Bergen's a saint. You don't have to talk, kid, because I know what you'd say."

The name which Graem had applied to this withered old fellow now began to seem more than apt, for he seemed to have the omniscient knowledge of the fiend. He could not help drawing back a little from Larribee.

Then he exclaimed frankly: "You scare me, Larribee, Doggoned if you don't scare me! It's like you'd been my shadow."

Larribee rolled from side to side, chuckling and nodding.

"You ain't the first that I've scared," said he. "But we've talked enough nonsense. I want to finish this here business. Are you going to take this hundred, or are you going to try to cash another of that wad of bad money that you got in your wallet?"

Graem had been shocked too often in the last few minutes to be startled greatly again; it was as though his person and his past stood revealed by a sort of X-ray eye.

"You know everything," he admitted simply. "Perhaps you're right, and I couldn't sell those two horses; they're not mine. But I suppose that makes no difference to you?"

"Not a bit."

"You got ways of using 'borrowed' horses?" smiled Graem.

"I got ways," said the other, more kind now that there was an air of submission in the youth.

"Then take the pair of them," said Graem, "and give me the money."

The hundred was promptly placed in his hand. He kept it extended for a moment, adding: "Before I take this coin, Larribee, I might as well tell you that the three men that I took the horses from are apt to be along this way, and if they see the horses—they won't stop to ask your price for 'em!"

"Larson and Moon will never see these hosses again," said the veteran, "and as for Lowndes, you'll be riding his black."

"By George!" exclaimed young Graem, "you even know *their* names."

"Even *their* names!" mocked Larribee, but in increasingly good-humoured tones. "And their chief was a fool to send out three like them after one like you. Three buzzards can't kill a hawk, and three hawks can't kill an eagle. He ought to have taken the trail himself."

"Who?" asked Graem, curious to hear the most important name of all.

"But he, havin' the trouble of all folks that spread out their interests too wide, he's got to use the hands and the heads of too many other folks. Like Napoleon. Napoleon was never beat. It was his second-hand imitations that was cleaned up—his thick-headed marshals, and such. Same with La Salle. Everything that he tries by himself is done perfect. There's no smarter man on earth than what La Salle is; he's even overreached me. But now he's spread out too wide. Think of a man like him letting a poor, sneakin' hound like Jerry Tyndal get around him! Think of that!"

"Jerry Tyndal?" exclaimed Graem.

"Aye," said the other, "the man you murdered."

"You lie, there! I didn't murder him."

"No? Anyway, what are you gunna call it when you tie a man down helpless and let somebody else run a knife into him? Ain't that next door to murder, if it ain't actual murder itself?"

Graem sat down suddenly.

"If you know everything," said the puncher, "tell me about poor Jerry."

"Jerry," said the oracle, "was a half-breed. His mother was a Sioux. He wasn't all raised in the tribe, though. He was took hold of and give a good rearing by a man by the name of Furness that was out studying Indians. He made Jerry learn 'em. Ever hear Jerry chatter?"

"No."

"He could talk pretty near everything Indian, and even some of the old lingoes that had died out. But he got to know more'n he could hold. He left Furness and took some of the household goods along with him, together with the old man's purse. After that he punched cattle when he couldn't rustle them, and he worked for money with his hands when he couldn't work for it with a gun. Finally he hooked up with La Salle. Then he met you and was polished off. That's Jerry."

A thumbnail biography, but sufficiently complete; Jerry was born, raised, and buried in one minute's time. A little shudder went through Graem.

"You know them all," he sighed, "and yet you're not a part of 'em."

"You can't be a part of a thing that you know," snapped the old man. "You got to stand back a hundred miles to see a whole mountain range. Now, you better be travelling, son. Those hosses have got enough in their bellies."

"You're not worried about the three?"

"Them? Me?" Larribee laughed aloud in a most evil tone. "I ain't worried about them," he declared with quiet complacence.

"So long, then, Larribee."

"So long! Well, what you hanging on for?"

There was a sigh from Graem; his eyes had become partly wistful, partly ashamed.

"It's no use asking. Even you, Larribee, can't know everything. But there is a farmer back up in the hills—I stayed with him——"

"You mean Guernsey?"

Graem drew a long breath.

"You know even that? Then you *are* the devil. But tell me, Larribee, what——"

He paused.

"I dunno about La Salle," speculated the old man. "How he's taking that, I can't tell. That's one mind that I can't read, but I dunno that he ever forgave anybody for ever helping an enemy of his. Especially an old hand of his."

"You don't mean that Guernsey ever was one of La Salle's—I don't believe it!" exclaimed Graem.

"No," said the hermit, "you wouldn't be likely to believe that. You take an honest man, he's always a fool. Thinks every friend is honest, too. But now, a quiet man like Guernsey, you never can tell. Not even me, I can't always tell; not even La Salle, he couldn't always tell. What Guernsey's done he's paid for, he thinks. But maybe he'll start in paying all over again."

He paused to chuckle, and his expression grew absolutely devilish —the exultation of an evil spirit in pain for the sake of pain.

As for Graem, he was thunderstruck and numb with these tidings.

"But Guernsey never knew and never could have guessed that I had been shot up by La Salle's men. He——"

"He knew," answered old Larribee.

That calm assurance left Graem without power to deny the speech, and it cast, suddenly, a new and frightfully keen light upon the past. He saw again in his mind's eye the grave, quiet, and gentle face of Guernsey, which was yet capable of hardening into unexpected resolution. He had been gradually growing, in the memory of Graem, into the ideal of the calm and brave spirit; but he also had seemed the stainless soul, the fit father of Charlie. Ah, well, there would be some explanation of that slip in the past. In the meantime, he would keep his faith intact.

But it stirred the very heart of Graem to know, now, that Guernsey never had been deceived, that from the first he had understood that the helplessly wounded man in his house was hunted by La Salle, that he himself would be damned by that criminal for having given this shelter. Never by so much as a darkening of the eye, or a hardening of the voice, had he allowed his guest to suspect his knowledge, but he had taken his cross and borne it; in his charity, assuredly, he had not allowed the right hand to know what the left hand was doing.

"Aye," admitted Larribee suddenly, "Guernsey played the white man with you. He played the white man. But he's likely to die like an Indian. And nothing you can do!"

He actually chuckled at the thought!

"Nothing you can do, for if you ride north to help Guernsey, it'll simply concentrate La Salle on the two of you. All you can do is to keep on running and hope that all the pack will finally take after you!"

This consideration made him grin like a withered little ghoul, and there was something in his eyes as though at that very moment he was wondering how death would come on Graem, how the hounds would pull him down, by night or by day.

There was no heart in the fugitive to bid farewell to his strange host. But he waved his hand and started off. The bay, perhaps, was still over-wearied, so he swung into the saddle on the black and was about to ride on when he saw Larribee beckon, and turned grudgingly back toward the little wizard.

Larribee suddenly pointed a finger at him.

"I'm a soft-hearted fool to tell you," he said, "but this trail that you're on is a blank. Jerry didn't tell you enough. Mind you—he didn't tell you enough!"

20

FIVE WORDS

It did not occur to Graem to doubt this terrible old man who had turned all the secrets of his mind inside out in the last few minutes; but now he felt a sort of despair sweep over him. There was no trail in his mind other than this toward Old Cliff, which, as it seemed, Larribee proclaimed to be a futile effort. Or did he simply mean that the whole effort to penetrate the mystery of Jerry Tyndal was pre-doomed to failure?

Nevertheless, he let his horses drift forward across the red desert south and west; in the distance he turned and looked back and saw that the old man was still discernible in front of the cabin, letting the sun wash fiercely over him. Yes, La Salle himself could not be more terrible than this withered creature!

When man and shack had sunk from sight at last, the spirit of Graem rose again; for no matter what the prophecy of Larribee, he could tell himself that the affairs with which he had to deal were human affairs, and no human action was altogether impenetrable to the wit of man. Furthermore, when he regarded the plenitude of weapons and fine horseflesh with which he now was equipped, he could not help lifting his head and smiling at the hot world which was spread before him.

In mid-afternoon he changed from the black to the bay and pressed steadily forward. It was not necessary to urge these horses; each was well up on the bit every moment, and the miles drifted rapidly behind them.

He had not expected to make Old Cliff until the dusk, but the sun was still more than an hour high when he sighted the group of tall buttes which rose suddenly and hugely at the end of a gradually sloping train of hills, which, in turn, melted off to the north among the loftier mountains there, now more than half lost in the heat mists.

He found a mule-skinner with a string of twelve and a single high-wheeled wagon breaking away from the buttes, and of him he made inquiry for the professor.

"You mean old Furness?" asked the teamster. "Sure. He's yonder. You go up the south face of Old Cliff. He's up on top with his men working like a gang of prairie dogs."

The south face of Old Cliff was broken away to a series of terraces up which an easy road wound, and up this slope rode Blondy Graem, very ill at ease, for since he had found such detailed knowledge in the possession of Larribee in the middle of the desert, he felt as though the entire world must know about him. Perhaps there was a price on his head, by this time, as murderer and passer of counterfeit money! Perhaps this interview with the professor would be his last on earth.

In the meantime, he remembered that Furness was the name Larribee had given to the foster father of Jerry Tyndal, and his interest increased.

When he reached the top of the butte he found a stretch of some ten acres, closely littered with the remains of stone houses built by Indians uncounted years before. There was a large gang of Negroes at work digging out the detritus from the base of a well, and overseeing their labours was a slender, bowed old man wearing a cork helmet with a handkerchief suspended from the back of its spreading brim. He was smoking a cigarette, in an extremely long holder, and he walked restlessly back and forth. As Graem rode up, the old fellow spied something in the growing hole of the excavation and, leaping down into it, he struggled back to the top with a flat-faced stone clutched under his arm. He squatted upon his heels to clean it and then examined it carefully with the naked eye, and then with a strong glass. The result was disappointing, for he sprang up with a youthful agility and flung the stone away from him.

Not until then did he face Graem. He was Hamilton Furness, he admitted with a snap; and he would have nothing to say to newspaper correspondents.

"I'm not working for a newspaper," said Graem.

"Magazines are worse," cried the irate old man. "Sensation—pictures—nonsense—every statement garbled—I detest 'em! Young man, I'll have nothing more to say to you!"

"I'm not from no magazine," declared Graem.

"There! There!" exclaimed the other, shaking a finger at Graem. "They send out men that can't speak grammatically; then how in the name of common sense can they write grammatically? Young man, go back to school and learn—learn—learn before you come out here to interview me."

"I've come a long way," said Graem, "but I'll start back if I have to."

"Hold on," said the scientist. "There's the cook's tent. Hey, Andy, give this man something to eat! I need a cup of coffee myself. Come along with me."

He took the arm of Graem as though time pressed terribly and an extra moment stolen from his diggings might mean the loss of incredible treasures. He rushed the young man to the cook's tent, where a Negro with a face shining with moisture set beans and brown bread before Graem, and coffee for both.

Since it was impossible to ask direct questions of this irate wasp of a man, Graem took out the crumpled sheet of paper and laid it on the board which served as a table. Furness raised both hands, shut his eyes, and turned his head away, exclaiming: "I know these written questions! Worse than spoken ones. All garbled, changed, distorted they are."

He glanced at the paper almost against his will, then leaned to peer, then snatched it up.

"Mandan!" said he.

He dropped the paper to the table.

"Phonographic!" he shouted. "Why do you bring me phonographic writing? Nonsense! Roots lost—everything gone—no progress with such stuff. No ties!"

His voice changed a little and he looked at Graem with new eyes.

"Did you write this, my lad? Can you speak Mandan? Well, well——"

"I only——" began Graem.

"Nothing but numbers," broke in Furness. "What about this? A puzzle? What is it? Where did you find it? *You* never wrote this," he exclaimed in an accusing tone.

"Got no idea about it at all," admitted Graem. "That's why I came to you, because you know these lingoes. Will you tell me what that paper says?"

"Nothing but numbers—nothing but numbers," said Hamilton Furness. "But—Mandan. Well, well, well—the old tongues are not yet forgotten. Write them down, then. Twenty, five, sixteen, five, twenty-three, one, eight, eleven, one, twenty-three, five, three, eight, one, nineteen, eight, one, twenty-three, one, eleven, fifteen, fourteen, twenty-three, one, eight, twenty, one, sixteen, one, eight. And there you are. And now where are you, young friend?"

Graem rubbed his hard knuckles across his chin.

"One step farther ahead," said he, "but where it'll lead me, I don't know."

"And what have you to do with Mandan?"

"Nothing," admitted Graem. "It meant nothing to me before to-day. Don't think that I ever heard the word before—except once."

"No," said Furness gloomily. "All the American past is nothing to the people who live in our country. Nations rose and fell, dwindled, died out like the Mandans. Culture lost. Nothing left except a few notes by an ignorant amateur like Catlin. Ah, well, who cares? Who cares?"

He left his coffee half finished and hurried back toward the excavation, filled with a new preoccupation.

The cook leaned over the table and grinned broadly.

"There ain't another like him, mistah," said the cook. "All bark and no bite, sir. But jus' as kind as your own mammy."

He added that all comers were made welcome except adventurous newspaper correspondents, and that if Graem wished to feed his horses, both grain and hay could be had at a ruined building which was used as a storehouse and barn. Accordingly, Graem fed the bay and the black, and then retired in the settled dusk to pore over the paper.

This chain of figures certainly could not represent a mere sum; it had some other meaning, and to decipher it seemed totally beyond his power. However, he had some experience with conundrums of various sorts. On long winter evenings in bunkhouses from Montana to Chihuahua many a puncher killed the time with cogitations over puzzles of all sorts. And the simplest of all, of course, are those in which the letters of the alphabet are represented by numbers, variously disguised.

For that purpose, therefore, Graem wrote out and numbered the letters of the alphabet, and then he began to make his substitutions of letters for numbers.

The result was certainly neither English nor Spanish, for the letters succeeded one another as follows:

"Tepewahkawechashawakonwahtapah."

He puzzled hopelessly over this jumble, staring at the paper, repeating the syllables over and over to himself as a man in despair will do, until the first four chimed again in the ear of his mind.

"Te-pe-wah-ka." He had heard that somewhere. Sioux, of course! Council house was what it meant.

The heart of Graem leaped. "Council house!" There was the beginning. And then, as he stared at the remaining letters, the jumble cleared itself with a magic speed.

"Council house mystery man river."

There it stood at last before his eyes, and there could be no doubt that he had solved the mystery. "Council house mystery man river."

And then his exultation subsided a little. What in the world could those words mean?

Before he had time to grow too downhearted, his spirits were raised again by remembering that when Jerry Tyndal took the slip of paper from La Salle's envelope he had seen upon it, as he said, five words.

Not instantly to be deciphered, no doubt, but this same conglomeration of apparently unrelated syllables which he, accordingly, had restored to the envelope after copying them. When Graem studied them, the knowledge which he had gained from his own ancestry and from old Hamilton Furness had given him the key to the mystery. He had resolved the puzzle to five words. And, therefore, it meant the clue to the trail which poor Jerry had followed to vast wealth, as he thought, but in reality only to a hoard of counterfeit riches. But whatever else it might mean, it was the trail to one of the crimes of La Salle, and for that reason it was worthy to be followed.

21

ASHES

CAUTION told him, of course, that he should leave this camp and go off by himself, now that he and his horses had been fed and refreshed; but he was too filled with his problem, and, therefore, he determined to risk an overnight stay at the butte.

He slept like a man with fever, waking again and again with a start while the tangle of words rushed brightly across his mind:

"Council house mystery man river."

Those might, of course, be mere code words, having meaning for the initiates but no meaning whatever for an outsider who lacked the key. Jerry himself might well have had the key, seeing that Jerry was deep in the confidence of La Salle. And that thought reduced Graem to despair.

Yet he knew that he had advanced far; somehow he might be able to pick up the trail again.

There was another way to go about it. For had not Jerry spoken of riding until he came in line with two mountains like the ears of a donkey, and a lump between them like the curve of a donkey's head? That was something to be hunted for, and then follow the line south and south for three days of hard riding—such riding as would kill a good horse. And though it might be difficult to locate the start of the trail, yet it was something to be done.

He was down from the butte before even the cook was stirring, and he started at once across the level lands toward the north. It was his hope to work through the hills towards Guernsey's house, buried in its almost lost valley, and thence to strike across the range, zigzagging back and forth until, by good luck, or by hard labour, he should be able to find the two peaks like the ears of a donkey. He closed his eyes and tried to visualize them, tall, slender mountains, leaning a little away from one another, curving up to sharp points—but he felt that never had he seen such summits before, and he could hardly believe that he would see them now.

He avoided the long tongue of hills which, sloping into the flat, ended in the abrupt and lofty heights of the buttes where Old Cliff stood; his course lay north and east from them, but still he was sorely tempted to sacrifice time in order to gain the shelter of the brush and the trees which crowned the lower hills and thickened toward the mountains.

It was a hard march, with only one water hole to refresh him and the horses; but at night he had reached the foothills and camped on the edge of a little stream which ran bubbling down a minute valley and sank for ever in the broad sweep of the desert sands.

Above his camp, the hills ran rapidly into the main range, and, as they turned from brown to blue in the evening, he studied them with care to pick out the most favourable trail for the ascent of the morrow. He knew well enough that the deep indentations of the water courses should be avoided, for those apparent natural ladders to the heights were in reality illusions and snares which would bring him into some hopeless box canyon from which he would have to retreat, with the voices of waterfalls mocking him down the spray-wet walls of the ravines. Instead, he selected a long slope, vaguely like the vast, muscled arm of a giant that extended from the upper mountains down to the plain. Then he went to sleep and dreamed of pretty Charlotte Guernsey; of handsome La Salle with his back at last against the wall and ruin before him, and, lastly, of high-heaped treasures which turned, under the touch, to the dead leaves of counterfeit.

He wakened half drugged, with the sun up, and the desert already dancing with heat waves. The very horses were sluggish, but he began his march at once on the black because he felt that, in case of a pinch, the bay would show a better sprint.

It was bitter labour up the mountain barrier. They began in a cactus belt, and passed into tough chaparral, and from this climbed into a region of those hardy lodgepole pines which grow where almost any other tree will grow. After that were bigger pines, spruce, fir; a cooler air with more life-giving moisture in it; and, finally, the top of the barrier, and his own land of mountains gathered and multiplied before him.

He took off his hat to them instinctively, while his eye touched on familiar peak after peak. He knew them so well that they gave back their names to him, as if with voices. Then he turned and glanced at the desert far beneath him. The hills dropped sheer down to it; it was almost like standing at the top of a wall, and he was staring into a well of dusty atmosphere, distinctly red-tinged by the colour of the desert sands. It seemed to Graem that surely he had covered the bitterest part of this long and hard trail to which he had committed himself.

In the meantime, there was no immediate cause for worry, he felt. If La Salle's men, or the officers of the law were able to trail him even as far as Old Cliff, they would hardly know how he had aimed after that, and even if they guessed this line of march, would they be able to follow him through the mountains?

He gave himself up to the luxury of some days of unforced, quiet travel. If he found good camping grounds at midday, he let the morning march serve for the entire day; and if he hit fresh sign of deer, he paused again to try his luck. Certainly no man ever lived better on mountain fare than he during this part of his journey. He could feel the wretched leanness of the desert fall away; his mind grew more at rest; for now he felt that he was committed to a sea of troubles so vast and so mysteriously clouded at the horizon that he would be a fool to try to predict the next storm. He could merely look out for breakers ahead, and steer his ship steadily forward, letting Luck play her share in the game.

Twice, from loftier mountainsides, he saw villages, one in the pleasant haze of the noonday sun, and the other twinkling at him out of a dark valley as deep and as black as the waters of a well. Otherwise, he never was near a human being. The ranges reared up before him, parted, and re-formed in his rear while other waves of granite and porphyry lifted themselves in his face. So he came at last to the verge of the gentle valley where he had found his way back to life in those dreamy, delightful months of convalescence. He smiled as he looked down upon it, but the smile went out at once. He rubbed his eyes and stared again.

Yonder, certainly, was the same stream of water, or its very brother, along the banks of which he had fished with such success; and these, too, were the hills, or their cousins in close relation. But where the house and the barns and the sheds and the stacks should have risen, there now was nothing except a sort of cloud-shadow resting on the spot. There was no cloud in the sky; and when he fixed his strong glass on the place he had the explanation; all had been burned. All had vanished in clouds of rolling smoke—the comfortable stables; the chicken house to which he had gone so often at Charlie's orders to get the chicken for Sunday dinner; the kitchen where Charlie worked and sang; the dining room where her happy eyes had flashed at him as he told whimsical tales of the range; the bedroom where he had watched the river-system of cracks upon the ceiling, and where Charlie had sat beside him reading, or talking softly, and hushing him when he strove to speak in turn.

Graem closed his eyes, for the sweetness and the sadness of those memories gripped his heart. From a vest pocket he took out a lump of yellow glass that burned and sparkled most wildly in the sun.

Perhaps that was all that was left; perhaps when that fire was lighted—by La Salle's orders, of course—man, woman, and even pretty little Ruth had been shot down as they ran from the flames, and their bodies thrown back into the fire. There were other rumours, too dark to be talked of freely at any camp fire, of La Salle's occasional manner of wiping out and leaving no trace behind to tell the story.

Now, as Graem studied the charred site of the home, he saw that what once had been a stack of straw was still smoking faintly. That might mean that the fire was hardly twenty-four hours old; it might mean that the atrocity had been committed a week before, and that all this time the fire had been smouldering in the roots and bases of the old stack. Now, as he scanned the valley through the glass once more, he saw that what had been missing from the picture even at the first glance was the cattle. They were gone—swept clean away. Not a single dot of colour showed on the hillsides or by the river where, at this time of the day, they were in the habit of wandering down to the water's edge and wallowing in, belly deep, to stand chewing their cuds and letting their odd-shaped reflections float and ripple on the stream.

All was so still, so empty, rather, that the first stir of life focused the attention of the observer at once. A saddled horse darted out from the grove of pines which had furnished fuel to the Guernsey house and a playground for the squirrels and for the tomboy, Ruth.

The horse was instantly pursued by two riders, who worked it in a circle and presently had a rope on it. Then the pair with their captive hurried back to the shelter of the trees.

When he had seen this, Graem settled down in a safe point of vantage behind two rocks and prepared to study the grove carefully. It struck him as odd, indeed, that three men should be in that grove; yet this was not far after the noon hour, and therefore, a travelling trio of punchers, riding across the range from one job to another, might have made a halt here for their lunch. However, when an hour went by and there was not a sign of a rider leaving the trees, his mind ruled out this possibility.

There was neither hunting nor fishing in that grove; there was merely shelter from the sun and from the eye of a watcher, and Graem set his teeth as a possibility rose in his mind. Surely there was more to this than met the eye. Three men in a grove—near the burned house—lurking.

He had no sooner fixed this thought in his mind than he saw two riders issue from the trees and ride straight off up the valley. The third might be delayed with his horse—no, the first two were out of sight around a shoulder of the hills, and still there was no sign of the third horse. It was such an invitation as Graem could not resist. He drifted his two horses cautiously down the slope, keeping them well in cover all the way, only pausing from time to time to sweep the valley and make sure that the third horse had not yet appeared; then at the foot of the slope he tethered the pair and went ahead on foot to complete his stalking.

22

RIDERS IN THE WOOD

NOTHING could have made easier stalking. To one accustomed to work up toward deer on barren mountains, using scant rocks and occasional shrubs for cover, this was the paradise of the hunter, for from the foot of the mountain into the heart of the copse there was a scattering growth of big trees, and he needed hardly a precaution except to make sure that his footfall caused no noise. Like an Indian he went, swiftly and steadily, with only a pause now and then, falling upon one knee, his ear close to the ground.

Twice in those pauses he heard a heavy, dull sound, like the stamping of a horse not far away; but as he went onward, he had a different noise to listen to, and that was an occasional murmuring like water—but there was no water in this grove!

The noise dissolved, presently, into the voices of two men speaking from time to time, and at this he paused. He had planned on finding one rider in the midst of this wood; two made a quite different story.

However, he had gone on so far that he could not well withdraw until he had learned something more about these lurking fellows. He doubled his precautions and slipped onward like a shadow, crouching behind the trees, peering here and there, and steadily drawing closer to the talkers until at last he came to that central opening where several trees had been felled and where Ruth, even on rainy days, could conduct her play-world in comparative shelter and in that thrilling loneliness which delights a child. Now, with a broad-browed stump before him, he could see what lay in the clearing well enough. There were two men, and he who faced him was none other than his old acquaintance of the handsome, brutal face—Bud Crogan!

The other, an older and slighter figure, had his back turned, and they were playing seven-up on a saddle blanket. On the edge of the clearing two saddle horses were tethered—two fine-limbed, proud-headed creatures such as La Salle's emissaries always bestrode. And the black suspicion deepened in the mind of Graem.

"Try two," said Crogan.

"No good, kid."

"What is it?"

"This is it, old son!"

"Look out there, Dick, what're you doing to the cards?"

Dick removed the stakes with a chuckle.

"This here game takes brains, kid. Real brains. You watch me and you'll learn."

"It's a queer game," Crogan informed him.

"You want to quit?"

"No, not while I got a penny. I never stand up from any game while I still have a cent in my belt. Go on and deal!"

"That's a good kid," said Dick with cunning encouragement. "Here you are. I'll shoot the moon, Bud."

"You'll not!" groaned Bud Crogan. "I had a perfect layout, too."

The cards were played swiftly but earnestly.

Dick again collected.

"Take a rest," advised the winner. "Take a rest, because it'll clear your head out; a gent gets tangled, staying with a game too long."

"Except Graem," answered Crogan.

"Him? The old man is simply giving him rope and will gather him in when he wants to. That's easy."

"*You* never tried Graem," said Crogan aggressively.

"Me? Oh, I'm no bronc-peeler and I'm no hero-buster. It's La Salle that I'm talking about, and I say that he always gathers in when he wants them. Look at here, for instance. Who could be stowed away more safe and careful than Guernsey? But when La Salle wanted him, he snapped his fingers. There you are."

The eyes of Crogan glistened with a venomous admiration.

"Think of having power like that!"

"All you got to do is to be La Salle, and you can have it."

"What'll he do with Guernsey?"

"Keep him in the shack for a while, make him wish that he was dead, and then bump him off. What would *you* do?"

"It's hard on his kids."

"*He* should've thought of that before he told La Salle to go to thunder."

Crogan's companion stood up and stretched, turning a little as he did so and showing a face of middle age, a stern fighter's jaw, and a keen eye.

"You should've got Guernsey when he run out of the house," suggested Crogan. "That was stupid."

"He run like a teal flies; and except that he was trying to carry the little kid, we never would have caught him. I never seen such a fast man and strong on his legs."

"If I'd been you——" began Crogan, and then ended with a gasp and reached for his gun.

It came out in a clean and flashing draw that might have been in time were it not that his centred and startled look a moment before had warned Graem. He started up, firing from the hip as he rose, and Crogan dropped on his face, writhing.

As for Dick, he had leaped sideways at the explosion of the gun and now stood in a ridiculously unbalanced posture, his right hand clutching at the Colt at his hip but apparently unable to draw it. For he was fairly and securely covered.

"Turn your back," said Graem, "and hoist your hands. Move slow, say your prayers, and be a good boy."

Dick, like an automaton, turned as directed, and cautiously pushed his hands above his head, while a tree squirrel, frightened by the explosion, now ran out on an overhanging branch and scolded the men vigorously. In the meantime, Graem got from Dick one revolver and a bowie knife of ancient and formidable pattern.

"Now, you take a look at the other rat," he ordered, and sat down on the stump which recently had sheltered him.

There was an oath and groan from Crogan as he was turned on his back, but the examination of his wound continued under the ruthless hands of Dick, who presently reported:

"Through the shoulder and out below the shoulder blade. Dead if it's touched the lung; pretty sick for a few weeks, anyway."

"Oh! to've had a fair chance at him," moaned Crogan, "the sneakin' vermin!"

"Tie that up and leave it tied," said Dick. "You can't make

trouble for yourself no more, Graem being a white man; but you may make trouble for me."

"Tear up his shirt," said Graem, "and make a bandage of it. Work fast. How long before your pals come back?"

"Sunset," said Crogan, "and I'll be a dead man before that. Graem, are you gunna leave me here to pass out like a dog?"

"You are a dog, Crogan," said Graem, "a murdering, useless, poison-toothed dog. Dick, tie him up, will you, and don't go beyond ten minutes. I'm a busy man."

Dick, willingly enough, worked furiously at the bandage. His touch was ungentle enough to bring a storm of curses from Crogan, but the work was done neatly in the end.

"There's not much bleeding now," announced Dick. "That'll hold him. I had it in the same place eight year back and I remember that the doc handled me just this way."

"You killed him for it when you got on your feet, then," suggested Crogan.

"Let him lie," said Graem. "Hold on. Put a canteen near him and fold that saddle blanket to put under his head. It's better than you deserve, Crogan. Now you, take the horse yonder that belongs to you, and come along."

"Come where?" asked the other, turning pale.

"I'll tell you that later."

For a moment Dick hesitated, as though desperate plans of resistance were forming in his mind; but resistance would come too late; this game lay obviously in the hands of his captor, and, therefore, he obeyed with a sullen look and downcast head. He mounted a strongly made brown mare and, under the direction of Graem, walked the horses on in front, going back through the trees in the direction from which the latter had come.

They moved on without a halt until they reached the spot where the bay and the black were tethered. At the sight of them there, Dick exclaimed loudly.

"You've killed Lowndes!" he cried. "You've killed Lowndes, Graem, and if you can manage that, you'll be killing the chief himself, one of these days!"

"What chief?" asked Graem.

The other was silent, regarding his captor from under lowering brows.

"Nobody," he said with a boyish stupidity.

"Listen to me," said Graem, "I know a little bit about you, friend, and I intend to know a lot more. You're a shade better than Crogan——"

"I hope to tell a man!"

"But not much. Dick, you were with the gang that burned out Guernsey. Is that right?"

It seemed to have passed from the mind of Dick that he had been talking on that very theme only a few moments before; now he stared wildly at the inquisitor.

"Who told you that?" he asked.

"Is it a fact?" shouted Graem in a fury that was only half pretended.

"No—no! It ain't true!" groaned Dick.

"You lie," said Graem. "You were lying out working your rifle at him, when Guernsey broke for his life out of the house, carrying his little girl."

Dick made no answer. But his little animal eyes flicked from side to side and his jaw began to sag.

"I wouldn't call you a murderer," said Graem. "Murder is clean compared with what you tried to do that night. A child, by heaven—a baby!"

"I didn't hardly see what he was carrying—and I only aimed for his legs——" began Dick.

The long arm of Graem reached out and his hand fastened on the throat of his victim; like a dog shaking a rat he shook Dick, and, like a rat, Dick shuddered in that grasp.

When he was released he staggered helplessly, his hands fumbling at his bruised neck.

"Are you gunna kill me, Graem?" he whined huskily. "Are you gunna murder me, man?"

"You've been lying to me," said Graem. "I tell you, if I have another lie out of you, or anything that ain't the whole truth and the bare truth, I'll shoot the head off you and leave you here for the crows to pick at and the buzzards to wolf down. But if you talk up fair and square and answer what I ask you, you'll have your life in exchange."

The relief of Dick at this news was so great that a sort of ghastly smile came on his lips and he stretched out his shaking hand.

"It's a bargain, Graem," he stammered. "I swear I'll tell you everything just as it happened."

Graem struck down the proffered hand with loathing.

"Sit down on that log. Pull yourself together. Then you can talk later. Remember, I know enough to spot the lies. Now, you start right in at the beginning."

"The beginning of what?"

"The beginning of the evil that you worked down here in the valley."

Dick drew in his breath loudly, as a man weak with illness draws it in. He licked his unsteady lips.

"I'll go right back to the beginning," he said.

"What's your name?"

"Richard Sampson Wendell."

"Go on. How long with La Salle?"

"Three year, going on four."

"Get ahead with this business."

"I never liked it from the first——"

"You lie. It's the sort of a job that you loved. To lie there in the dark and shoot at a man by the light of his burning house—why, that was nuts for you!"

The hand of Wendell shook as he glanced anxiously at the armed hand of his captor.

"I mean—I never volunteered or nothing. I was just sent for and told what I would have to do. Why, Mr. Graem, it ain't any use saying that you don't want to do a job, once you're in the gang of La Salle. You know that!"

"Go on. Tell your story."

Wendell picked up a dead stick, and with this he made designs on the sand; now and again he looked up, but when he could not endure the eye of Graem, he stared down again, and punched a pattern of holes in the ground.

"Dan Benjamin had the job in charge."

"I know that man. I'll remember him, too!"

"He had the picking of his men for the work. He took me, and 'Pudge' Harkey, and Little Joe."

"That's the Canuck, ain't it?"

"Yes, that's him."

"I have an old score against him already," said Graem, touching a white scar which ran from his wrist upwards and disappeared under the cuff of his coat. "Go ahead, will you? That was the hand-picked party, was it? But how did four swine like you dare to tackle a man like Guernsey?"

This question the other met with a feeble attempt at a smile. His eyes wandered, and his face was so pale that Graem had to say: "I won't bother you any more. Tell your story. Make it straight, and no matter what you did you'll be safe from me."

"Oh, bless you," stammered the gangster, and he cleared his throat to begin.

23

STORY OF FOUR HAWKS

"WELL, we rode down in the morning," continued Dick Wendell, "because we planned to come to the place by night, but we missed our calculations in the mountains. It would take a hawk, you see, to find the way to this lost valley and not have any trouble over it. And we weren't hawks."

Nevertheless, like four hawks they seemed to Graem, four terrible creatures winging their way through the upper ravines and hurrying in search of their prey—the comfortable old farmhouse where Guernsey, and little Ruth, and beautiful Charlotte were sleeping.

"We got lost," ran on the tale. "It was dark as pitch. We got tangled up in brush and rocks and ravines; there were clouds and we couldn't steer by the stars. Finally Pudge Harkey said we'd better sit down and wait for the dawn. He played a mouth organ to us for hours, sitting there in the rocks. We didn't dare to light a fire, and it was too cold for sleeping. We sat around in a bunch and listened to that mouth organ moanin'. Dawn came. We were right over the valley. You remember the story in school about the wishing-gate? That's what we'd done—gone to sleep under the wishing-gate, I mean. So we worked down lower. Benjamin had a glass and with it we studied the valley, which looked like a pretty neat place for one ma.. to own, and too good for anybody like Guernsey."

Here a peculiar sound like the growl of a dog came from Graem, and the narrator winced and paused; but he went hastily on again.

"We saw Guernsey start out in the morning to ride up the valley and I wanted to lay for him on the way and finish him up so, but Benjamin wouldn't have that. He kept saying something that I suppose he'd heard from the chief: 'Root and branch! Root and branch!'

"It was a pretty miserable job waiting there in the rocks all the day, shivering in the morning and baking hot in the middle day, and sizzling all through the afternoon. We finished off the water in our canteens and there was water in plain sight not more than a couple of hundred yards away. Here—you can see it across the valley now."

He pointed to a slim thread of silver that was painted on the side of the opposite wall of the valley.

"Benjamin wouldn't let us go to get it. He pretended that if we moved from our good hiding place we might be seen and that would spoil everything, but that wasn't his real reason, the swine!"

"What was his real reason, then?" asked Graem.

"Suppose that you have a dog that you want to have on his toes for guarding your house, what do you do to make him savage? Tie him up a day without food or water. You try the same thing on any one of the best and most law-abidin' men that you ever heard of and see what happens to him. He'll be ready to kill before the day's over. We didn't dare to move, because if we had, Benjamin would have reported us to La Salle; but we lay there hating the fellow, and Pudge says to me: 'Suppose in the middle of the fight that a bullet was to hit Benjamin—from behind, I mean?'

"We felt like that, and Benjamin, he must've known what we were thinking, but he's got the nerve of a man of iron; he just lay in the sun with his hat pulled over his face. Heat would've killed anybody else, but not Benjamin. He lay there and pretended to sleep, but whenever his hat blew off his face, you could see his eyes as bright and as wide awake as a bird's. He was just thinking.

"And then along about evening he pretended to wake up more, and as the sun went down Benjamin sat up and began to groan under his breath, savage, and long-drawn-out. He said that he'd never spent a worse day than that day—which I could agree with him, too. Never had been a worse day or a worse night, and Guernsey would have to pay for it, he would!

"Of course, it was easy to see what he meant, and at first the rest of us just looked at each other and grinned sort of sick grins, but after a while we forgot about knowing Benjamin and seeing through him. We forgot, halfway, that we knew he'd done this just to work us up raging and wild, and as he kept on talking and cursing Guernsey, pretty soon we began to drift along with the same idea.

"Talk helps to let off steam, you understand. I mean to say, if you're miserable it helps to curse a little, and since we couldn't very well curse Benjamin to his face, we cursed Guernsey instead, not meaning it; but after we'd cursed him a while and blamed him for the miserable day that we'd been spending in the hills, starved and sick with the heat, and mad with the thirst, we just talked ourselves into believing what we'd said. We hated Guernsey; I remember feeling that I'd walk twenty miles and swim a river for the sake of taking a shot at him.

"Benjamin wouldn't let us move till we were absolutely in the dark again, and then he led the way to the water. Well, it tasted pretty good and took the misery out of us, but nothing could take the meanness. There wasn't much more talking; everybody was quiet, but we were as hard as the rocks we'd been lying among.

"Then Benjamin rounded us up in the darkness and he made a little speech. He said that Graem might be down there in that house, because he was pretty wild about the girl; he said that Graem had slipped away from the hunt that was after him and that it might very well be that he would be in that house; sooner or later, he was sure to come back there, and if we got him it would be worth making us all rich. La Salle had said so and swore so. But if Graem was there it meant a bad fight, and we'd have to shoot pretty straight at everything that showed itself coming out of the house.

"Then we turned around and started for the house, where the lights were beginning to shine; and, on the way, Benjamin told us the plan: two of us were to set fire to the house at the north-east and the south-west corners and we had along two big cans of kerosene to do the work, and after the fires were lighted we were to lie back, a man for each corner of the house, and start shooting the minute that anything showed."

"Now, wait a minute," broke in Graem, half choked with anger. "Will you tell me why La Salle or any other devil would want to kill a girl hardly more'n a baby and another girl that was like—like——"

"He didn't want to kill 'em," continued Wendell. "I could swear to that. No more did anybody else in the gang. Only, if there was a chance that Graem was in that house, and Guernsey, everything had to be fired on that showed itself. You've done some tricks, Graem. Coming out dressed up like a girl, that wouldn't be anything for you to do. We didn't dare to take any chances with you. Man, I'm afraid to go on talking."

"I'll do you no harm," said Graem. "I'll do you no harm. Go on and talk."

"Benjamin and Pudge Harkey done the lighting of the fires. They worked some kindling and dead leaves under the two corners of the house and soaked everything with kerosene. Then they lighted the oil and scuttled for cover. It might have been pretty dangerous if the folks on the inside had been on the lookout, but both the boys got into cover without drawing a shot, and there were the flames licking up the walls of the house.

"The point was that they were making a good deal of noise inside, because it was after their dinner, and the piano was rattling, and the voice of the girl was ringing and singing along. It stopped, finally, and then there was a woman screaming for a minute—I suppose that was your girl, Graem."

Graem, fingering a smooth, white bit of stone, kept his eyes steadfastly upon it and made no answer, no comment.

"Then we had a long silence. The flames they eat out the two corners of the house like nothing at all. You could begin to look into the inside of the house, and every minute we grabbed our guns harder, waiting for the break. It looked like Graem must be in the house, because otherwise Guernsey would just've surrendered at once.

"And then something busted out of the ground right under my nose!"

He paused and stared with amazement even in thinking about this shock of surprise.

"Oh, we seen afterwards how it happened! All Guernsey's stores were kept down below in a cellar. He'd worked that cellar deep and big because it's sandstone that cuts like chalk; and he'd come down into the far corner of that cellar and then popped out at us through the trapdoor that was simply covered over with sand and pebbles and such. You know, Guernsey was down in the Apache country when he was a kid, and he could remember some of the tricks that they had to play there, the ranchers, I mean.

"Anyway, I seen a shadow jump out of the ground and it scared me a good deal. I put in a couple of shots, but my eyes must've been pretty near closed, for he got past me; and I could see the flutter of a bundle of cloth, it looked like, in his arms, and then I seen the scared, white face of the girl, saying nothing and hanging on her daddy's neck."

Graem groaned.

"It was hard to nail him," said Dick Wendell, sitting straighter, and with a sort of detached excitement now. "He dodged like a flying teal—wonderful to see how he shifted himself around! I kept blazing away and missing. There was three rifles after him. Then he tripped, fell, and got up without a gun and run on again. He wouldn't drop the little girl. That was where he was a fool; we wouldn't've touched her.

"'Take him alive!' sings out Benjamin.

"We done it easy. No man can carry a bundle in his arms and run very far.

"While he was dodging that way, out of the other side of the house slipped the other girl. Pudge Harkey caught her, and she fainted, and he lugged her around to the rest of us.

"And when I seen the little girl crying and hanging on to her sister, and asking if she was dead, well, I got to say that I was pretty sick——"

Here he was interrupted by a faint gritting sound, and the sandstone collapsed in the grasp of Graem.

"And that's all," concluded Dick, "except that Benjamin and Little Joe took the family up into the hills, and we got reinforced and stayed on here to try to bag you, and that's the whole truth, Graem, I swear to you."

24

MYSTERY HERE

THERE was in the attitude of Dick Wendell something of the schoolboy who, having recited, waits for the approbation of his teacher; but there was neither praise nor blame from Graem—only one burst of wonder: "There was no one killed, man?"

"Not yet," said Wendell.

"And will you tell me one thing: What made La Salle so set on the murder of Guernsey?"

"He ain't the only one that's worked for La Salle in the old days and wanted to bust loose. Suppose that I wanted to be shut of La Salle. 'All right,' he'd say. 'Here's some money to help you get started. I wish you luck. Only, in a pinch I may send for you and, to the end of your days, you're my friend and you hate my enemies.' Well, that's fair, considering. But Guernsey took in the worst enemy that La Salle has and gave back his life to him, after La Salle had fixed him for dying. You see for yourself how the chief figures things? Besides, he hoped to get you and Guernsey together."

After all, it was clear enough; and the wisdom of La Salle seemed impeccable in the eyes of Graem.

"Where's the place Guernsey is hid?"

"I dunno."

"Wendell, look me in the eye and say that again."

Dick Wendell closed his eyes with a groan. "I'm in the fire!" he said. "You'll wring the life out of me before you're finished."

"Is is a long ride?"

"Not five hours'."

"Push on," commanded Graem. "When your two partners come back, they may come on to our trail. How many guard Guernsey?"

"Maybe none, by this time."

"Dead?"

"Or reasonable. I dunno. I'll show you the way. Am I free after that?"

"Take me straight to him, and I'm through with you. Are the two girls there?"

"No. They're at another place."

"What place?"

"Over on a farm that an old codger has back on the Channing River. You know that valley?"

"I've been up it once."

"There's a side branch that comes jump down out of the hills. Full of white water."

"I remember seeing it. A wild-looking sort of a ravine."

"Full of good grazing land, those hills are. That's where the house is that holds them."

"What's the name of the man?"

"By the name of Larribee."

"Martin Larribee?"

"You know him, eh?"

"I've heard of him."

"Nobody knows him," muttered Dick Wendell.

A wave of helplessness beset Graem, such as had passed over him whenever his thoughts recurred to the old man of the red desert. A shack there in the hot southland, a house there in the northern hills. What else was he connected with? Apparently with La Salle.

But about this, Dick Wendell, as he guided Graem through the mountains, would not talk. He said plainly that he knew little of Larribee, and cared to know no more; he already understood too much of the little old man to be happy in his understanding. What he meant to La Salle or La Salle to him Wendell either could not or would not say, though it was apparent that there was a connection from the fact that La Salle had lodged the two girls with him.

It was patent, above all, that Dick Wendell was almost as much in awe of the old man as he was of La Salle; and he spoke of Larribee with a peculiar intonation and a look of mingled fear and disgust and horror. So that Graem, unwilling to press his captive too far, dismissed the subject from their talk, and kept the figure of Larribee far back in his mind.

It was a comparatively easy ride. They kept to the high lands, but they rode at almost one level, winding in and out along the side of the range; and such was the pace which their horses were able to maintain that it was no four-hour journey. In three, while the sun was yet up, they came to the shack, sitting in a tangle of brush through which a narrow path was beaten to the door.

Halting in the edge of the nearest trees, Graem sent Wendell on to the door of the cabin, to call out whoever was within. In the meantime, Graem's rifle would cover Wendell, and unless he were very foolish indeed, he would not attempt to leave the straight and narrow path of his mission.

The door, accordingly, was seen to open, and on the threshold appeared the tall form of Guernsey. With a great burst of joy and affection, Graem recognized him; and, a moment later, Wendell turned and beckoned toward the trees. It was apparent that Guernsey was alone; otherwise he himself, no matter at what risk, certainly would have warned back any advancing friend, yet he made no signal as Graem rode out of cover.

Wendell turned back from the house and, pale with eagerness, met him at the mouth of the walk through the shrubbery.

"I'm finished, Blondy?" he asked anxiously.

"You're finished," said Graem. "You can go back and take care of your friend Crogan."

Wendell smiled faintly and his eyes wandered.

"Or go to the nearest headquarters of La Salle and his hired hands and tell them that I'm here; or else hang around in the edge of the trees and try to drop me when I come out of the shack. That's fair enough for you."

Wendell attempted a laugh which shook and broke off; then he sidled his horse toward the woods, waved at Graem, and finally swung the head of his mount around and bolted into the shadows among the trunks like one who fears a bullet may fly after him.

It seemed to Graem most unlikely that this man would level a gun at him for some days to come; for the nerve had been poisoned in Dick Wendell, and his nightmares through life were apt to be filled with the face and the voice of Blondy Tucker Graem.

That, however, was not worth considering. What mattered was Guernsey standing on the threshold of the hut. It occurred to Graem, at first, that his friend had almost lost the use of his eyes, for he was not advancing, though he was free to do so. Instead, he remained on the threshold shading his eyes and peering at Graem as though he never had seen him before. The brightness of the westering sun might account for that.

At any rate, slinging himself out of the saddle, Graem rushed up the path, with his hand stretched out and a loud welcome on his lips.

Silence greeted him; the hand which he took returned no pressure; the eye of Guernsey was as dead as that of a man dying of slow posion—and realizing his death clearly before it came to him.

Yet Graem forced back this horrible suspicion and maintained an air of cheerfulness with a great effort, running on: "If you haven't a horse, I have a spare one, and it's yours. Climb into the saddle, old fellow. You're free; you're off with me, man! D'you hear me?"

"I hear you," said Guernsey, and paused.

Graem became silent, also. He could not disguise from himself the patent truth that he was not over-welcome here.

Then Guernsey, tardily remembering, stepped back from the door and waved his guest inside. "Come in. Set yourself down. You'll be hungry, I suppose?"

Graem strode in, but there was no thought of hunger in him; mystery and horror overwhelmed him.

"Are you sick?" he asked.

"I'm as right as can be," answered Guernsey. "You won't eat?"

"No."

He sat down, for he was beginning to turn so weak, of a sudden, that standing was uncomfortable. And still the silence continued between them, while Guernsey, resting one hand on the edge of the log table, looked away past his guest and out of the door and over the blue mountains with hollow eyes.

"Guernsey!" cried Blondy Graem at last. "You *are* sick, man! They've given you some secret dope or other. They're killin' you by degrees. Listen to me—I'm here to take you away, Guernsey—I'm——"

Guernsey lifted his hand.

"I'm staying here," said he.

"Aye, you've given your word to La Salle, but what does your word count when you pledge it to a skunk?"

"I haven't given my word. I—I like it here."

Graem caught his breath, and in lifeless tones the other explained:

"What more d'you need? Plenty chuck—house—bunk—gun—everything a man wants."

"Your children——" murmured Graem.

"Woods full of game," went on Guernsey, apparently not hearing. "What more does a man want?"

Graem raised his voice.

"Ruth and Charlie?" he asked sharply.

"Even reading matter," said Guernsey, and waved toward a shelf loaded with old magazines. "What more could a man want?"

Graem stood up; he was beginning to shake with weakness and with fear of something which he could not name, and still Guernsey stared past him, and out the door, and over the deep mists of the valley.

Wendell had fled from this, too, lest he should be forced to stay and give an explanation.

Graem made one last effort:

"Account of me the trouble hit you, partner, and I'm here to pay back the harm I done, as far as I can. I want to take you away with me—I know where the girls are—d'you hear? I know where they are!"

There was no answer. The sun had set and the hut was growing cold and dark.

"Guernsey," murmured the younger man in a broken voice, "I'm only asking you one thing: can you forgive me?"

He waited.

"If you got to be going, good-bye," said Guernsey.

25

GRAVE ENOUGH

THAT evil hard-mindedness of Larribee's had seemed to Graem a wall of steel against which he could make no impression, yet it was as nothing compared with the solemn despair of Guernsey. The thousand protestations, the inquiries which he wished to make concerning Charlotte, all these died on the tongue of Graem, and he left the shack with a downward head. When he reached the horses he turned, half determined to rush back and make a final appeal; but the door had been closed, and only the blank, unbroken wall of the hut confronted him.

Still, he turned back, and at the door he said: "Guernsey, I'm going to try to get to Charlotte and Ruth. If you've got any message to send by me, will you tell me what it is?"

He had no answer, and stepping closer to the door, he looked through one of many yawning cracks and saw his friend bowed over the table, his head fallen in his hands.

Softly, like an eavesdropper, Graem went to the horses, mounted, and rode north down the slope. Never had he been so sick of heart, and he felt as though he were sinking into the troubles around him, and the waters were closing over his head. But he pointed the black horse steadily to the north to find Channing River fifty miles away.

That evening he went deep into the darkness, riding up the side of a winding river, with the glimmer of the stars here and there in the still water at the edges of the stream. He was wasting many miles, as he knew, by this sinuous course, but he could not compose himself to make camp. Not until late did he halt at a forking of the river, and on the bank he rolled himself in a blanket and slept with the roar of the waters in his ears.

In the morning he wakened before dawn was well begun, but the mountains stood vast and black against the sky, and above him he could see the dark branches of the trees, so that an odd calm spread over the spirit of Graem. He lay for a time in his blanket—a thing he had not done for years—and the roar of the river moved far off, returned, and carried him forward through life without volition of his own, past many wonderful and terrible images on the banks. Life indeed, was like that. He had found gold on the Las Vegas, and through that the full weight of La Salle's power dropped upon him and almost crushed him, but he was carried to Guernsey's house, and saved by purest chance, which in turn seemed to have destroyed Guernsey, while he, himself, voyaged into another great tangle which, the longer he contemplated it, the greater it grew and the more inconceivable. Murder, counterfeiting, and now the nameless riddle of the dead man: "Council house mystery man river."

Those were the five words which had drawn poor Jerry to his death because he had found their meaning, or a part of their meaning, no doubt. And there was a fatal presentiment in Graem that if he solved the problem it would destroy him also.

He had a quick breakfast, saddled, and found his horses still in excellent condition for the trail. They were a bit thin, especially along the back, but such thinness meant hardness of muscle and absence of fat rather than exhaustion. In case of need, if he could not crush La Salle, he was fairly confident of being able to run away from him.

So he faced the north, and there before him arose two mountains under which he had stolen without knowing, the night before; they were tall, slender summits, sloping away from one another, and looking oddly like a pair of donkey's ears, flopped down in weariness at the end of a day's labour.

Donkey's ears—mule's ears!

It jumped into his mind with dizzy suddenness that this was the very clue for which he had determined to hunt. Here was the thing before him—aye, and the rounded knoll between them like the bump of the mule's head.

There was no doubt about it. This was the landmark by which Jerry had been guided in his journey to the south which had carried him into the influence of the five words and the ruin that attended them. He was on the verge of swinging his horses around; but then he remembered Charlotte, and he pushed resolutely up the valley.

He reached the Channing River before noon, climbing over a small divide to gain a ravine that dropped into the main stream. After that, the going was easy enough. There was a broad trail which travelled close to the water, a trail over which a wagon could have passed, though by no means could it have been called a good road. This trail he followed for the sake of speed, for speed, he guessed, was shrewdly needed.

There had been that in the eye of Dick, on parting, which meant definite mischief; and it might well be that, even if Dick were not able to make better time across country, at least he could have telegraphed or telephoned a warning to the house in the Channing valley.

So long ago might the warning have been given that even now the ambush might lie across the road waiting for him!

Graem kept a bold heart in spite of that thought, for boldness alone could save him.

The trail left the side of the river, which passed through a sharp-walled canyon, and as he came down the slope of the hill higher up, winging in toward the river again as the valley opened, he thought he heard behind him a sound like the cough of a horse, but faintly, and more than half covered by the distant sound of the stream.

He turned in the saddle and stared back. There was not a breath of wind, and yet he saw the top of a young poplar sapling tremble and stir a little; certainly he saw a bush top sway in the opposite direction; and he was sure that he was followed!

He could be sure that Larribee would give him no protection against pursuers, no matter how much information might fall from the lips of that wicked old man; and if he wished to see Charlotte with any safety, he must stop the man or the men who rode up the stream behind him.

He rode straight on, without quickening the pace of the bay, which he was now riding; but where the trail turned a little to the left, he rode into a thicket of willows and waited, rifle at the ready.

For a long twenty minutes he remained there, but though the birds which he had disturbed came back to settle in the trees, there was no sign of any pursuer coming up the trail. He grew impatient. The time had gone for quiet patience, he felt, and action was now required; guns were needed to help him through. And still not a sign of the cunning pursuer!

So he went on again, keeping his head continually turned in the hope of catching some sight in the rear that would help him to locate the danger. He even thought of making a wide detour so that, striking in far back on his own trail, he might find and follow that of the hunter as well and so bring this matter to a head. Yet time was short —very short. He had forestalled La Salle and La Salle's men often in the course of this adventure, but now it was time that the tables should be turned, and the fear of the future became cold and grim in the heart of Graem.

He pressed on rapidly, therefore, and presently he came to the mouth of the tributary valley down which, in the distance, he could see the streak of white water of which Wendell had spoken. Here should be the house where Larribee kept the girls, if Dick had spoken the truth, so Graem turned into the place and presently found a narrow bridle path, winding back and forth through a dense thicket. He could not leave that path without entering such brush that his coming would be heard a mile away; and so long as he followed the trail there would be the sign of his progress printed plainly for all who cared to read.

So he went on.

He felt that he was playing the part of a fool, certainly an unworthy part in the game which he must attempt to win against La Salle, but there was no wit in him to think of a better thing. The shrubbery, at last, gave way to a fairly open growth of small pines, second-growth stuff, for all the region had been well forested thirty years before and closely cut. He sighed with relief, and, turning sharply to the left, he continued until he was under the very wall of the ravine where the noises of the little river struck and rebounded in humming echoes.

Then he worked his way higher in the canyon, taking what care he could to keep to firm footing where the trail would be as little legible as possible.

In this manner he reached a spot at which the trees ended abruptly, and he found himself looking out into a strange pocket in the canyon, where the walls fell back on either side and left a sweep of meadow land half a mile across and nearly twice as long. The creek itself was loftily arched by a stone bridge; by the river on either side were ploughed lands; and at the farther end of the meadows, where the valley wall descended in low, round-headed hills, he saw a relic of virgin forest standing, and between the massive trunks, dimly, the outline of a house. Undoubtedly that was the place where Larribee held the girls.

There was a neat problem offered, at once, in the difficulty of crossing that very considerable stretch of open land without shelter of any sort. Graem tethered the horses and went scouting to the edge of the water, hoping that he might be able to slip up under shelter of the bank, but when he reached the place he found that the slope of the river bank was everywhere so steep that it would be impossible for a horse to maintain a footing upon it.

He climbed up from that observation point with a good deal of difficulty, and he was spread out like a bear, as it were, hands grasping at a bush above him, feet scrambling for a toehold in the yielding bank, when he heard a hoarse voice above him calling: "Graem! Graem! Look up!"

He looked up, and there he saw a horseman looking larger than human on a lofty horse, with a rifle pressed against his shoulder, and a steady bead drawn on him.

"Stand where you are, old-timer," said the husky rider. "You're just right to take a tumble into the water, and that'll be grace enough for you."

Graem, staring upward, was unable to recognize this man. He had the typical appearance of a puncher, an unshaven, lean-faced fellow, with perfect assuredness in his glance and in his whole bearing.

"Just steady yourself a minute," continued the stranger. "They sent a long way for me, and I wanted to look you over before I finish you off."

26

A MAN FROM ARIZONA

SOME men, when death stands before them, see the past in a chain of lightning pictures; but only one thought went through the mind of Graem—that since he had been foredoomed to defeat, it was as well to have the thing over with now.

He was able to judge a man with some accuracy; had the avenger been another, he would have tried throwing himself backward into the stream and taking the chance of a broken neck in order to be swept out of view by the spinning current; but when he looked up at that hairy face and those keen eyes he knew that here was a man who could not miss.

He simply answered calmly: "Well, partner, take your look."

"They been telling me yarns," said the other, "that made me figure that you were some great guns, Graem. I would have laid that on the trail you'd be as handy a man as ever rode a horse, and I figured that a big life insurance would be a useful thing to carry when I went after you. They sent a long distance for me, Graem; but here I've got you at the end of the first try. Doggone me if it don't make me think you breed a small kind of man around these here parts."

"You come from down Arizona way," suggested Graem respectfully.

"Now, how might you know that?"

"By the dusty look under your eyes and by the hang of your bandanna; they ain't worn for looks only in Arizona. They breed men down that way, I got to admit."

"I don't mind saying that I was born and bred there," said the stranger.

"What might your name be?"

"What good will it be to you to take that name along with you?"

"Because I can keep asking after you; and you might wind up in my corner after all."

The man from Arizona chuckled.

"I'm Rex Dobie," said he. "Maybe you've heard the name before?"

"Dobie? But you ain't *the* Dobie!" exclaimed Graem.

"I dunno," said the other. "There ain't so many of the name down in Arizona."

"What I mean to say—you ain't the Dobie that——"

He stopped short, staring.

"Aw! you mean the job at Pancras?"

Graem nodded.

"That was nothing," said the man from Arizona.

"Dropping five gunmen—you call that nothing?" exclaimed Graem.

"Five?" cried Rex Dobie. "Well—how'd the yarn come to you?"

"I heard it straight from a man that was in those parts. I hand you the branding iron, Dobie; only I didn't know that you was the kind that worked for pay."

"Now what d'you mean by that?" asked Dobie.

"I mean to say," answered Graem, "that I thought you was a sort of a lone-rider and a long-rider, old son; and I didn't know that you hired out your guns for pay. I've always sort of looked up to you, Dobie."

"You," said Dobie savagely, "being the kind that would be above hiring yourself out?"

"I'd fight for a friend or for fun," answered Graem, "but I thank my stars that I was never no man's hired bloodhound. I'd be above it! And I should think that a famous gent like Rex Dobie would've been above it, too."

"You would, would you?" cried Dobie, purple with anger, and then, the desire to defend himself getting the upper hand, he added: "How d'you know that I'm in this for money? How d'you know that it ain't just friendship?"

"Why, maybe it is," said Graem. "Friendship it might be; only I don't see how."

"Me and La Salle are old pals."

"Ah," murmured Graem, "I begin to understand you now."

"How d'you understand me?"

The rage of Dobie worked in so neatly with his furious vanity that Graem began to feel that he was gaining a hold upon this man. He had a mere glimpse of hope, like the glimpse of blue that glimmered through the overhanging boughs of the trees above.

"You're one of the highfliers, Dobie. You move with the big men."

"Well, I dunno."

"You're modest, of course. But I begin to understand you. La Salle wanted your help to corner me and you just said that you'd take on the job out of friendship to him."

"Kid," said the other, satisfied, "that's about right."

In spite of his peril, Graem felt a smile rising to his lips; he fought it away.

"But I still don't understand," said he, in the rôle of the humble man, "how you were able to work out my trail so fast."

"You thought it was pretty well hid, didn't you?"

"I did," lied Graem.

"Maybe it would've come over some of the trailers in this part of the range, but I'll tell you, Graem, that in my part of the country they'd be ashamed to send out a ten-year-old kid on a dark night without a lantern to work out a trail like yours; they'd leave the job to the women and the babies."

"You're a hard man," said Graem. "But you seem to've made a good deal of a fool of me."

"What I wish," snarled Dobie, "is that I could've had you where others could see the play. The game and the finish of the game."

"You mean the fight?" echoed Graem.

"I mean that."

"This is your idea of a fight, is it—butchering a man who has both hands full?"

"Results is what count," said the man from Arizona.

"I see how it is," said Graem. "You've been filled full of lead a couple of times?"

"I've had my share of it."

"And it's broke your nerve?"

"What?" shouted Dobie.

"I mean, you prefer to take your men from behind, now. I don't suppose that you've got a stand-up face-to-face fight left in you."

"You lie!" cried Dobie. "I never heard a worse lie."

"Maybe you didn't. I'm just saying what it looks like to me. If you wanted the fun of following a trail, then you had it. If you wanted the fun of a fight, then you turned your back on it. Why didn't you sing out behind me, and then come at me man to man and fair and square?"

There was a pause. Mr. Dobie had grown pale.

"Might you be meaning," he asked in his hoarse voice, "that I could be afraid of you, Graem?"

"Come, come," answered the other. "I ain't a fool. I give you credit for having been a good man in your day; but if you've been shot up often enough to lose your nerve, that ain't your fault."

Dobie drew a great rasping breath. He had no words with which to answer.

The position of Graem was becoming more and more uncomfortable, for his feet were slipping; nevertheless, he kept the majority of his weight hanging on his left hand, for he was beginning to hope that the right, in the end, might be put to some better service.

"I remember Budge Meyers down in Carson City," went on Graem. "He had a great name and he'd done great things. They jailed him for a year, and when he came out again, any Chinaman in town could make him take water. I suppose that your nerve has gone the same way."

"What I hate worse'n a skunk is a fool," roared husky Mr. Dobie. "And what I hate worse than a fool is a darn fool. And that's what you are, Graem."

"Aye," said Graem thoughtfully. "That was the way with poor Budge. I seen him get a man down one day by chance—after his nerve was gone. Once he had the man helpless, he wanted to carve his heart out. He was that way, terrible brave when his man was down."

"Darn you," groaned Dobie, shaking with fury, "there never was a time when I wasn't a better man than you, Graem. On foot or in the saddle, night or day, with guns, hands, or knives, I can lick you, Graem, and I always could!"

"Bah!" answered Graem. "I've heard that kind of chatter before. I ain't a fool. If you'd wanted a square fight, you'd have called to me to hear you; why don't you confess that it turned you sick, just the idea of having to face me?"

"Oh, Lord," gasped Dobie. "How'm I gunna stand it? But I *won't* stand for it. Climb up that bank, you ornery, rootin' vermin. Climb up, and then I'll show you how a shooting is done in Arizona."

"D'you mean that you have the grit to stand to me, Dobie?"

"And ten like you! I'll eat you, m' son!"

He dismounted, still covering his man, but allowed Graem to climb from his precarious position to the upper edge of the bank.

Then he actually cast his rifle away and stood stiff, his hands at his sides. They faced each other with an absolutely even break. And Graem, still panting from his climb, at last allowed a grim smile to touch his lips.

"Doggone me 'if it ain't like something out of a fairy-book," he said. "There I was, spread out and helpless—and now I may have to kill you, partner."

"Make your move, you dirty rat," said Dobie. "I'll give you that advantage."

"There's a crow been cawing over in the field," said Graem. "Next time we hear it, we'll make our play. Now, steady down and calm yourself, kid. You been a fool. I hope you live to get better sense, but I got to have my doubt. I heard about you in that bar-room fight—but it wasn't anything favourable. You shot from behind a corner of the bar, flat on your belly. It was one man you dropped, and not five. This here is going to be the end of you, you poor wooden-head."

The fury of Dobie departed; for one instant his eyes wavered. Then he grew pale, and his glance fixed upon Graem. It was plain enough that he saw he had been tricked from an admirable chance for a murder into the most dangerous of fair fights. Now the creek roared in the upper falls, the wind sighed in the trees, but there was no signal from the crow. If no other advantage could be stolen, at least a vital fifth of a second could be seized from Graem, and Dobie went for his gun with a convulsive twitch of elbow and wrist. Never was a cleaner draw; at the hip the gun flashed, and the bark of the explosion rang neatly and evenly with the noise of Graem's revolver. The hat was lifted from Graem's head, but Dobie, clutching his body with both arms, whirled wildly around, staggered on the edge of the creek bank, and pitched headlong. He was seized as if by a hundred hands. Very glad was Graem, standing horrified on the bank, that he had not trusted himself to the current, for he saw Dobie broken like a dead stick against a sharply projecting rock, and then as a log is hurled down a river in flood, so poor Dobie was hurtled out of sight. The creek did its work well.

27

THE DIAMOND AGAIN

GRAEM followed down the edge of the stream for a short distance, but he saw it was useless to attempt to recover Dobie. The little river ran like a mill-race and, immediately below this point, there was a long, smooth slide over which the water leaped to a new shark-mouth of projecting stones. There was a red froth on this place; no other sign of the dead body—so he turned back. He took the mustang from which Dobie had dismounted for the fight, and led it back to the canyon wall where the other pair were waiting.

Three horses were too much for such a business as this; two in fact were a handful, but he could think of no manner in which he could get rid of the mustang except by putting a knife through its ribs to the heart. And Graem never yet had killed horse, dog, or cattle in cold blood.

Now, Graem, instead of meditating upon the shortness of this life and the sudden alterations of fortune—since Rex Dobie had dropped from victory to death at one turn of the wheel—contented himself with lighting a cigarette and sitting on his heels against a stump while he blew the smoke upwards in pale drifts through the branches of a young straight-armed spruce.

After a moment he took out and cleaned the revolver which had sent home the fatal bullet, reloaded it, and then began with the file-blade of his pocket-knife to make a notch on the handle. It was an uncivilized proceeding, but in certain ways Graem was an uncivilized fellow, and took a number of his customs from originators no more cultured than the Indians of the plains.

When he had prepared his gun and shrugged from his strong shoulders the strain of that last encounter, he calmly took out stale, hard pone and cold fried bacon and made a meal of them with the greatest relish. Another cigarette topped off the ceremony, and then he stretched himself in the shade with his hat over his face and dropped into a sound slumber.

Perhaps it was not so rash a thing as it appeared, for if an enemy came that way there was more than a reasonable chance that one of the horses might give warning; besides, he felt he was approaching a consummation of great peril, and it was highly necessary that he should be as fit as possible in muscles and nerves when that test should be made.

His eyes remained closed hardly ten minutes when he was up again, considering the work before him.

Close to the left wall of the canyon, as he looked up toward the more southerly mountains, there was a scattered growth of trees, but considering that any watcher from the house would not have a broadside view of the growth, it was more than probable that he could get his horses up the ravine without being noticed. At any rate, he could not afford to waste further time in the ravine.

He dismounted, for the sake of lowering the general level of his little cortege, and so he proceeded, hugging the canyon cliff closely. It was rough going, for he was constantly among broken rock, or forcing his way through dense shrubbery. However, his progress was constant; the dark, tall grove which sheltered the house drew nearer; and presently he stopped, for the time had come for closer reconnoitring.

The sun was westering fast, and from the opposite valley wall a shadow lengthened; already it had reached the stream and, higher up the ravine, the white cataract was turning blue; but still on his side of the canyon the sun was bright, and the cliff reflected the heat almost too intensely for comfort. Graem had decided that he must wait when something moved beneath the great trees near the house, and then a small girl ran into the field with a white bull terrier frisking about her.

He knew it was Ruth Guernsey with his first glance; no other little girl in the entire world had that same fiery freedom of action, like a young colt enjoying the air; then her familiar voice floated to him as she shouted.

He pressed to the verge of the screen of shrubbery which protected him here and rejoiced as she drew nearer and nearer. One touch of reflection banished his pleasure, for if she found him, what would she do? Go back to the house, of course, and tell the whole story with her first breath; and that would make the canyon about as healthy for him as a foxearth for a gander.

No sooner had that thought come to him than an imp of the perverse, of course, possessed the child and turned her straight toward him. He looked frantically around him. If he attempted to retreat, she was now so near that she was sure to detect the movement in the brush; and before he could decide what should be done she was fairly upon him.

He stood up.

The bull terrier saw him first and, following the instinct of his kind, he went at the apparition with bared teeth. Then: "Mike! Get back!" shrilled the child, and the dog swerved to the side. "Oh, Blondy darlin'!" she cried and ran at Graem with her arms stretched wide.

She was half stifled with laughter, with panting, with surprise and with joy; but before she could speak she reached into his vest pocket and brought out—the yellow diamond, as huge, as flaring, and florid as ever.

"I knew you wouldn't sell it," said she, "and I knew you wouldn't lose it!"

With the child still in his arms, Blondy Graem sat down on a convenient rock—sat down with some care, for the white terrier was by no means settled in his mind about the stranger, and moved around making battle-noises deep in the hollow of his throat.

Ruth seized him by the tail to make sure of him.

"I know what happened to your home," said Graem.

She closed her eyes. There was at least one mature emotion of horror and sadness in that childish heart.

"After that, we just waked up," said Ruth, "and it was pretty sad, Blondy, waking up without a home. But we came here, after a while, and daddy will be with us before long, you know."

"Of course he will," said Graem.

She searched his face.

"He *will* be with us," she insisted.

"He will," said Graem with a more assured tone. "Are you happy here—you and Charlotte? Are they nice to you, Ruth?"

"*I* don't like it," declared Ruth. "I hate it, and I hate him!"

"Who?"

"The old one, I mean."

She looked toward the house with a shiver, and he knew at once that she meant Larribee.

"Charlie?" he asked suddenly, for he could keep from the question no longer.

Ruth grew suddenly absent-minded; she even relaxed her grip on the terrier's tail, and he promptly curled up at Graem's feet.

"Blondy——" she said.

"Aye?"

"No matter what happened I would always love you, Blondy."

"Thank you, honey."

"More'n anybody, except daddy, of course."

"Of course."

"But he's different, isn't he?"

"Yes, he is."

"You got to have a best one of everything, Blondy. I mean, you got to have a horse you like best, and a dog you like best, and a daddy you like best, and a man you like best."

"I guess you do," said he.

"Well," went on the girl, "you're that way, I suppose?"

"I am," said Graem.

"You love me more'n any other *little* girl, Blondy?"

"Heaps!" said he.

"And Charlie, you love her more'n any big one?"

"A thousand times more," said he, with such a voice that all at once she turned sharply toward him and looked long into his face. And then tears suddenly filled her eyes.

"Honey," said Graem, growing cold with misery, "has anything happened to Charlie?"

"Not being sick or getting hurt—nothing has happened that way, but I mean, she ain't like you and me, Blondy!"

"She's like nobody but herself!" said Blondy Graem. "God bless her, how could she be?"

She wiped the tears out of her eyes and sniffed.

"I would feel a lot better if I could cry," said Ruth.

He could not imagine what was coming, but he knew that he felt very dizzy and weak with fear and foreboding.

"You take your time, honey," he said with a shaken voice. "You just take your time, and tell me in the best sort of words that come along handy. All I've heard you say is that she ain't sick and she ain't been hurt."

"No, she hasn't been. There's worst things, Blondy!"

He gasped, but still he was totally at sea.

It seemed, however, that Ruth was unable to express the thought that was in her mind.

"You remember Pinto, the little colt?" she asked.

"Like myself! He would come when you whistled to him."

"When the house was burning, he—he ran up and whinnied, Blondy. I guess he was looking for me in case I should be in the fire, and when he didn't hear me call, because the fire was roaring so big, he ran right into the fire and never came out."

She paused and gripped both her hands hard.

"I never would love any other horse the way I loved Pinto," she said when she was able to speak. "But Charlie, she's not like that!"

"I don't know what you mean, Ruth. I'm trying to follow, but I can't."

"I mean," cried Ruth, in a great burst of denunciation and grief, "that Charlie could love two men just as well as she could love one!"

As if a knife had pricked him, Graem winced and shrank.

"Oh, aye!" he said. "I guess I understand."

"Oh, Blondy, Blondy," sobbed the child, "don't you say it like that, because you just break my heart!"

And she fell on his shoulder in a great passion of tears.

28

YOU'D NEVER GUESS

IT had seemed to Blondy Graem, not long before, that this world was a sufficiently difficult place and that no man's task could be much more strenuous and hard than his, but now he felt that he had been living almost in Eden, so dark and gloomy became his thoughts.

He had to set his teeth to rally himself.

"You'd better speak to Mike," said he. "He thinks I've made you cry, and he'll tear my throat out, pretty soon."

"Bad Mike," said the little girl, and Mike cowered before her and beat the ground with his tail.

"But you're not really thinking about Mike at all," she told Graem over her shoulder.

He told her that everything would turn out well; it could not help but turn out well, because they were such great friends, all three of them; that Charlotte would not do wrong simply because she was so made that she *could* not do wrong; and that the best thing for them both was to go on to the house and find Charlie as soon as possible, so that he could have a chat with her.

To this, Ruth agreed soberly and would have started straight on across the meadow with him, but he was forced to explain in more detail. She herself feared old Mr. Larribee, but not half so much as Graem feared him; for other reasons—so many that she must simply take his word for them—it would be folly for Graem to let himself be seen by the people of the house in the trees. The best plan was for

Ruth herself to go ahead and draw her sister out of the house and bring her to the woods near the canyon wall.

Ruth listened to this scheme with a darkening frown.

"I dunno how I can," she complained. "Charlie and me aren't friends, today. I'm not talking to her; I told her I wouldn't speak to her for a week!"

"Folks change their minds," said he. "You could change yours to please me, honey."

He persuaded her with difficulty to put aside her pride, but finally she promised, and trudged faithfully away across the field with the white dog trotting in subdued fashion at her heels.

Graem watched her out of sight beneath the shadow of the trees; then he continued his slow progress up the canyon wall until he came to the point where the scattered group of trees joined the gigantic woodland surrounding the house. He did not enter that preserve, except far enough to gain a clearer idea of the house itself.

It appeared to be built on a large scale and something in the style of those mansions which pleased the hearts of the Southern planters in the before-war days. He saw the glimmering of the white columns of the front porch, standing out in a noble semicircle from the façade, and he was aware of a long stretch of house and outbuilding, once white as well, though somewhat weather-stained and a dingy grey.

If this were Larribee's own house, Graem's opinion of the old fellow had to be revised again; for it might be that he actually was a last scion, though a degraded one, of some famous and ancient stock. When he had made that observation, he retreated a little to the spot where he had left the horses, and from a hedge of shrubbery, he kept close watch to see Charlotte coming.

Chiefly he kept looking for the figure of little Ruth scampering along among the shadows; but no Ruth came, and it was Charlie herself whom at last he saw, half running and half walking, and sometimes pausing sharply and looking all about her with a half frightened and half happy air of expectancy. His heart grew warm and confident at once. So he would have dreamed of her coming to meet him, full of diffidence, but full of love. With such grace, with this very smile, he had seen her in his dreams.

He hardly could keep from starting out from his hiding place with a shout, but he restrained himself until she was much closer, and came down between the monster trunks of two old, sky-towering pines which had grown so close together that their branches were jammed and interwoven.

Then he stepped through the screen of shrubbery and stood before her.

She neither shrank back from him nor started forward with joy; but she looked at him from dazed eyes, with a hand thrown up to her face, as if for protection; then she stammered his name: "Blondy, Blondy!" as though trying to assure herself that he was not a vision.

He had been arming himself with indifference, and hardening his nerves so as to be prepared for just such a moment, but his first sight of her had caused him to forget all the cautionings of Ruth and now he suffered mutely and terribly. She saw that suffering, and the pain was reflected in her gentle face as she cried out softly: "Oh, Blondy, oh, Blondy dear!"

With that she came toward him with her hands stretched out, as though she would have taken him in her arms; and her face was tipped up a little to kiss him and receive his kisses; but it reminded Blondy Graem of a good child going to welcome an unwanted play-mate.

He took both her hands; he had made himself smile down steadily at her at a cost of perspiration on his forehead and dizziness in his brain. All that the child Ruth had said was bitterly true, he saw, and yet he swore to himself that it could not be; and if he and Charlie had exchanged no pledges or promises, nevertheless he vowed that she was bound eternally to him, and, being what she was, how could he be wronged? Tested and proved gold cannot tarnish; the sun cannot go out!

He was tormented, and he was baffled as well.

He could not help but see, too, the relief she felt when he greeted her in the more formal manner; for now she met his eyes only by flashes, as though she wished to make herself believe the good cheer of his smile, and all the while she talked breathlessly—how unlike the Charlie Guernsey of that happy valley!

Did he know everything? Ruth had told him, of course, about the fire, and the wonderful escape, and how as they came through the mountains under guard, Oliver Landon had scattered the men of La Salle and set them free, and carried them here to the happy haven of old Mr. Larribee's house.

"I suppose that you've heard of Oliver Landon?" said she, and she flushed wonderfully and tenderly as she spoke the name.

"I think I've heard of him," said poor Graem, and he knew that that was the man.

"He—he—I supposed that everybody would know about him," went on Charlie, "except us in our silent little valley where we slept."

"Did he drive off La Salle's men?" asked Graem.

"There were three of them," said the girl, like one who chants a battle hymn, "and all I can tell you is a crashing of guns, Blondy, and then Oliver plunging through the smoke. Oh, they didn't dare wait for him, and I saw one of them shot from his horse and tumbling head over heels down the slope—so he swept us away! He was simply laughing!"

She laughed at the memory, softly, with a brooding joy.

"Then he got us here to Mr. Larribee's house and told us that daddy was safe and free. He'd done that, too; but he wouldn't talk about it. I never would have known from him, except that we got a letter, at last!"

She took it from her bosom and held it out to him.

"Because I want you to know; because I want you to come and meet Oliver!" said she. "But read it, Blondy, because you'd never guess, just seeing him!"

She waited, hushed with delighted expectancy; with what cruel ease she had forgotten the happy days in the valley—sleepy days, had she called them?—and now praised this other man! He began to nod as he took out the paper and held it before him, acting as though everything were patently clear at once, but as a matter of fact, he hardly could read the words because of the blur that swept across his eyes.

He had been hearing unprecedented things. In those old days of Wild Bill and the rest of the heroes, one gunman would beat three; but such things no longer happened; and certainly in his generation no one person defeated three men such as those handpicked warriors who rode to execute the orders of La Salle. And, granted all the effect of ambush and surprise, those men of La Salle's were not the sort who turned and fled before one of their number was bowled over by a shot. Apparently they had run from the fusillade of Oliver Landon; it was most strange indeed.

He concentrated on the letter, and made out the cramped and heavy hand of Guernsey.

Dear Charlie: The trouble is over; I am free from La Salle's men by a sort of miracle. Call the miracle by a name, and it's a young fellow named Oliver Landon. He has sent word to me that he has you safe in Mr. Larribee's house. He has been the saving of all of us, and I send back this word by his messenger.

There were two men guarding me into the mountains; they were a pair of La Salle's best fighting men, but the other day a young fellow rode out in their faces and with a couple of shots he scattered them, yelling that Landon was after them. They seemed to know about him, and what they knew made them want to get to cover.

Landon took me into the hills and showed me a safe place for shelter, and here I'm lying low until he's handled the rest of La Salle's cut-throats and brought the man himself to justice. In the meantime, he's going to see that everything goes well with you.

I thank God you are with Larribee. Trust everything to him. He's a wise man, and, if I know anything, a good man.

Good-bye, my darling. Before many days I'll be with you.

Such was the letter, and Blondy Tucker Graem read it slowly through a second time. Undoubtedly something was wrong, and very wrong. The very day before he had seen in poor Guernsey such blank despair as he never before had found in a man's eyes; and yet here was his letter talking of hope and a cheerful future!

Odd language, too, for an unlettered puncher like Guernsey!

"Handled the rest of La Salle's cut-throats and brought the man himself to justice."

How was it that Guernsey used such phrases instead of saying: "Until La Salle's gang is rounded up and shot"?

"Brought to justice"? He could not find such a phrase in his memory of Guernsey and Guernsey's speech.

Other peculiarities stared in the face of Graem. Above all, it fairly passed the miraculous that for a second time this extraordinary hero, Landon, had routed a division of La Salle's expert gunmen—once more driven them in headlong flight!

Yet Graem knew that wonderful things may be accomplished by a truly magnificent fighting personality, and brightly across his mind came a picture of his younger days in a Canadian logging camp when one bold, wild fellow had stepped into the murderous tangle made by half a dozen men fighting with knives and kicked and beaten and hammered them into submission without a murder done. This Landon might be such a man, as bright as a sun compared to the dim, starry light which ordinary mortals show to their fellows.

Slowly Graem raised his head from the reading of the letter.

"Charlie," he said, "can I see this man?"

"Why, he's in the house now!" she exclaimed.

"I'd rather see him," said Graem, "than anybody in this wide world!"

"Dear old Blondy!" cried the girl. "I knew how you'd feel about it. Oh, I knew!"

"Can you bring him out here?" he asked.

"But why? It's growing damp and chilly, Blondy."

"Is Mr. Larribee at home?" Graem asked.

"No."

"You're sure?"

"Why, what a strange way you talk, Blondy! No, he's not at home!"

"Nobody but you and Ruth and Landon?"

"That's all. The old Chinaman who cooks doesn't count!"

"Then let's go inside," said Blondy Graem, and stepped on with the girl.

29

WHEREIN GREEK MEETS GREEK

SHE was childishly grateful for the way in which he had taken her change of heart without any direct admissions or confessions on her part, and as she walked on with him, she looked sideways up to him and smiled in the thickening shadows. He dared not be too fully aware of her, for the ache in his heart could grow in one instant into a sickening pang.

They passed through a mighty portal formed of two giant silver spruce, and so came out into the clearing just before the house. Seen close at hand, it was not nearly so large as he had been led to expect by the glimpses he had had from the distance. Like most colonial houses, its style was more imposing than its actual dimensions; nevertheless, it was a spacious residence, ridiculously and monumentally out of place in this wild and isolated spot.

The western sky was turning crimson when Charlotte Guernsey pushed open the front door, and showed Graem into a lofty hall with a fine stairway rising from it and circling through a high, dark well to the top of the building. Hunting trophies bristled dimly on the walls.

"Charlie!" called a pleasant voice from an adjoining room. "What did Ruth want of you? Was the little rascal whispering treason against me again?"

"No, no—Oliver," she panted with her excitement. Then to Graem, in a whisper, "Quick, Blondy, right behind me! Oliver, I've brought you somebody!"

She ran joyously into the room, with Graem gliding behind her.

"He's come back, Oliver. My best friend—Blondy Graem!"

So, like an enchantress after a master touch, she danced back to the side and held out her hands as though to lead them together. But they made no hasty movement toward one another. Graem stood right in the doorway and tensed for sudden and desperate action as he never had been prepared in his life before, for yonder fellow rising slowly from the chair—with a hand at his hip—yonder Oliver Landon who twice had routed the gunmen most heroically, was no less a person than La Salle himself!

Never had he seemed to Graem so beautiful as at this moment, rising among the shadows of the big room with the dull crimson of the western sun coming through the windows against him; and, half blinded by that light, straining his eyes against it, he was delivered, surely, into the hands of his most mortal enemy.

By a thread of silk those hands were tied; explanations never could do away such a deed in the eyes of Charlotte if her hero was shot down before her.

"Do you know each other already?" the girl was crying. "Are you old friends, after all?"

"We've known each other for years," said Graem hoarsely. "I don't know a man in the world better than I know him."

And he advanced with a rather slow, stiff step toward La Salle.

If that master of crime had hesitated at first, with a cold certainty of death sliding like a knife into his soul, he recovered himself now and went rapidly to meet Graem. Their hands met, or seemed to meet.

Then they stepped back; Graem's back was turned to the girl, and the whole burden of the acting was laid upon the shoulders of La Salle. Magnificently he endured the load, for his face shone with gladness and cheerfulness as he exclaimed:

"It's Tucker Graem! By heaven, it's Tucker Graem! And how do you come here, old man?"

"But you never told me!" exclaimed the girl. "You never told me when I mentioned his name!"

"How could I ever dream that it was my old friend?" said La Salle with most convincing amazement.

"I'll make Chang hurry up supper," cried Charlotte. "We've got to sit down all around a table and talk about everything. It's the happiest day in my life. To think that you should be old friends!"

She came beside Graem and rested a hand on his strong shoulder.

"But I could almost have guessed it; you'd just have to be friends!"

With that she was off toward the kitchen.

"That's woman's instinct for you," said La Salle quietly. "Inner knowledge—extra sense—that sort of thing, you know."

"You poison-faced snake in the grass!" said Graem. "You lying buzzard and coyote!"

La Salle moved a little to the side, so that the light was more equalized and a shadow instead of an overwhelming brilliance struck against his eyes.

"You haven't improved your vocabulary, Blondy," said he. "But sit down and we'll have a chat. Charlotte won't be back for a while. She'll stay in the kitchen to plan some surprises for us, and let us get over hugging each other and doing the friendship dance. Thoughtful kid, isn't she?"

He set the example by taking a chair; though, to be sure, he sat rather forward on the edge of it.

"There's a fine lot of sunset left outside," said Graem. "Step out with me, man, and there'll be a little accident, and one of us will die."

La Salle flung himself suddenly back in his chair.

"If you shoot me here, you're a cold-blooded murderer," said he. "And as for giving you a chance at me outside the house, you forget, old fellow, that I never throw chances away; I play every game to win. Sit down and be reasonable. I'm astonished to find you here."

"You had me dead, eh?"

"I never thought you'd get out of the desert. However, you've always surprised me, Blondy. I've always beaten you, but I never can knock you out."

A cold, strange pleasure began to grow in Graem. He never had been in such a situation before; he never would be in such another again, and certainly La Salle was right. If the girl meant anything to Graem, he dared not push a quarrel with her hero.

"I've never had a chance to get my hands on you," responded

Graem, as he sank cautiously into an opposite chair. "But now I have my chance, and somehow I'll manage to work it through. I don't think you'll leave this house alive."

"Perhaps not," answered La Salle, with perfect good humour. "I enjoy this, Graem. I enjoy sitting here and studying your face. Haven't had a chance at that for a good many years! Not at any length since——"

He paused, thoughtful.

"Since you stole the horse, fifteen years ago, and left me to choke in the desert," supplied Graem.

"Don't be ugly," answered La Salle. "This is a great occasion, Blondy, and we ought to act in the grand manner if we can."

"I never had the education that you got," replied Graem. "All I got the heart to feel is that I hate your innards, La Salle, and the only words I got is enough to say that much."

La Salle regarded him with a sort of quiet wonder.

"There are a few others like you, I suppose," he said. "Fellows much greater in action than in reflection; but when I hear you talk, Blondy, actually you seem a child. No imagination. Nothing to rise to the occasion. And yet here we are! Blondy Graem, who has done me more harm than any other hundred men, who has split through my lines, made fools of my best agents, put my back against the wall more times than I care to think about; and here am I, who have turned a comfortable part of your life into hell, I take it, made you out a horse thief and a murderer, shut every door against you except Bergen's, dumped the whole weight of the law against you—why, Blondy, we ought to meet in a more cordial manner! This is epic, and we ought to take it in the epic manner instead of snarling like a pair of starved wolves. I propose a truce. Until tomorrow morning our hands are tied——"

"And by that time you'll have half a hundred of your gang around you?"

"Don't underrate me," answered the other sharply. "I'm capable of being generous to my workers, and I'm also capable of playing fair—inside time limits—with a really great enemy like you. Shall we sit down at the supper table, talk like old friends, chat through the evening, and enjoy one another? Or is it poison and guns and knives from the start?"

For a long moment Graem studied him.

"I'm one man," he said at last. "You know that you could trust me, besides, if I gave you my word. I know that I can't trust you, but there's one reason that makes me want to do it. You know what that reason is."

"I don't suppose we shake on this agreement?" said La Salle, smiling.

"I don't suppose we do," answered Graem.

30

WHAT WILL HAPPEN?

THE reason which made Graem so willing to accept the unspeakable danger of remaining in that house through the night on apparently friendly terms with his enemy was simply his desire to see Charlie Guernsey for a few more hours, for doubtless they would be the last hours in which he would have a chance to hear her voice. And he could not help appreciating the instant tact of the other in understanding.

No sooner had they come to this agreement than La Salle apparently proved that he accepted the terms at their face value, for he rose and sauntered to the windows, turning his back fairly upon the other.

The voice of Graem followed him as he was remarking on the grand effect of the sunset.

"What will happen, La Salle, when she finds out your name?"

La Salle turned; he did not seem pained or shocked by the suggestion, but rather troubled and puzzled.

"No one can tell," said he. "It will be a great shock to her, and perhaps it will finish me like a bullet through the head. But I have a pair of hopes against one doubt."

Graem waited. He could feel the bitter edge of his hostility to this man gradually dying away, even though he struggled to resurrect it. A more brutal criminal might really have been more forgivable, but the smooth intellectualism of La Salle removed friction, beyond a doubt.

He did not need to be questioned now, but went on softly, musingly, thinking aloud.

"I'm established in her eyes as a hero and a generous soul, also very modest."

"All of which is faked."

"Not the modesty, Blondy. I'm not vain. The only reason I used the hero play in front of the girl was because she had to be taken from the three boys in some way, and also because you had set the fashion with her. She'd grown to connect worth-while men with gun plays, since you came into her horizon with three holes in you. How the devil you managed to ride through the hills with those wounds and get through the weather, luck alone can tell!"

"I'm being saved," said Graem slowly. "I'm being saved to be used on you."

"Perhaps you are," admitted the other calmly as ever. "But let's continue with Charlie. Of course, I worry over the thing night and day. If she learns who I am, then it follows that I appear for a flash as a sneak, a hypocrite, and so forth. But also I remain the fellow who made the grand gesture; I was kind to her, I humoured her little devil of a sister, and I parted her father from his troubles."

"I saw him dying of a broken heart," commented Graem.

"He deserved to die," said La Salle earnestly.

"You dictated the letter he wrote to Charlie?"

"Of course. And you spotted it, old fellow? You've improved since I last chatted with you."

His admiration was open and sincere.

"Ah, grand work you've been doing!" he continued. "But, to go back to Charlie, I think that there are two chances out of three that I'll win. The great matter with all girls is the breaking of the soil, so to speak. One has to get their attention, focus it, win the sympathy, wake up the heart, enter the dreams—excuse me for growing a little poetic, Blondy—but after that's done, I think it's rather hard for them to transfer the emotion from one subject to another."

There was something like a growl from Graem.

"I beg your pardon," broke in La Salle with real pain. "Of course, you are a glaring example to the contrary, but do let me try to explain a little more clearly what happened in your case. You came as the wounded hero; you left before you had a chance to show her that you were a dashing one. You built up the market for gun fighters and such, so to speak. Very well; then you foolishly stepped off, I stepped on, and in the rôle which you hadn't a chance to play. I was the dashing one; I played every card in turn—saved her and her sister; saved her father; beat off hordes of villains——"

He stopped to chuckle, as though his own craftiness mightily amazed him.

"You see, I continued in your rôle so long that she began to accept me in the part; but still she has us jumbled up together. She doesn't divide us in her mind, actually. She knows that we wear different faces; she is a bit more for me because I'm most recently with her; but, after all, my old friend, she's only been touched by a passing fancy. Can I ripen it and expand and throw fuel on until there's a real fire? I don't know; I hope so. There you have my mind on the matter!"

It was impossible for Graem to doubt that he had heard the truth; still, as he lighted a cigarette, La Salle stared heavily before him.

In that moment, therefore, when the bars were down, with all his force Graem strove, leaning forward, to break through the mask and come at the naked truth about this man, but it was impossible. There was no line of remorse and none of savagery; there was no subtle sneer of malice, and there was no meanness of deceit. He was five years older than Graem in fact, and a thousand years older in evil; but he looked five years his junior.

If there was justice anywhere some of the evil in this fellow should have showed. There was no cruelty of which he had not been guilty, there was no villainous, crafty trick which he had not tried, from marked cards to murder he had had his hand in the planning or the execution of every species of knavery; and yet he looked like a handsome, clean-souled boy, weather-browned from a vacation in the wilderness and ready to return to a home of culture.

Fear came back on Graem with a wave, and he could not help a tightness in the throat that made him swallow hard. One other man in all the world had had the same effect upon him; now every moment he half expected to turn and see old Larribee appearing among the shadows.

"I want to ask you one question," he said suddenly.

"By all means—by all means, and I trust that I'll be free to answer it."

"Larribee——" began Graem, and stopped in spite of himself, so vividly did the pronouncing of the name bring the terrible old man back before his eyes.

"Old Larribee told you a good deal in the desert, didn't he?" murmured the criminal.

"Has he always been one of you?"

"I don't follow that."

"One of your men, I mean."

The astonishment of La Salle could hardly have been all assumed.

"One of my men?" he exclaimed. "Larribee?"

"Well?" murmured a voice from the door.

And there stood Larribee.

He had come in silently as a cat, as Graem knew that he would do; now he stood there in the shadows, and Graem merely saw the glint of his teeth as he smiled.

"Is the little one in here?" asked Larribee sharply.

"Who? Little Ruth?"

"Who else but that brat?"

"No, she's not here."

"I'll come in, then," said Larribee.

But first he looked keenly around him, as though he half expected that Ruth might be hidden somewhere, and, if she were, he would flee at once; it was the very last quality that Graem would have expected in this old monster.

Near the door Larribee remained, therefore, until he had completed his examination; afterwards he advanced until he stood in front of Graem. He was dressed fully as wretchedly as he had been in the desert, when he sat at the entrance to the ragged shack and smoked his pipe. The same pipe was between his teeth.

"Am I one of the kid's men, you ask?" said he. "You better answer that, La Salle."

La Salle, however, merely chuckled.

"Well," said Larribee, turning and moving noisily toward the ashes on the hearth, "I'll be hanged if I ever heard such a thing!"

"But you buy back his horses cheap for him," commented Graem, struggling vainly with this problem.

"La Salle!" barked the old man suddenly.

"Well?"

"Those two hosses that I picked up from this young fool for a hundred dollars——"

"I know them."

"You know them, but have you seen 'em since?"

"I haven't."

"Have any of your cheap, two-for-a-dime gunmen seen 'em?"

"I'm afraid not."

"Are you or any of 'em apt to see that span again?"

"They're gone, I suppose," sighed the younger man. "Two thousand dollars' worth of horseflesh snuffed out, as far as I'm concerned."

Larribee turned to Graem.

"Have you got your answer?" said he.

"I suppose I have," muttered Graem.

"Thick," said Larribee. "He's thick in the head. He's a muddler. He'd work a cleaned-out mine. He'd try to round up goats. That's what he'd try to do."

These remarks were levelled in a grim voice at Graem, who accepted them without remonstrance.

"I suppose," said Graem, "that La Salle only *happened* to bring the girls here?"

"You keep thinking and studying," said Larribee, "but you'll never hit it. La Salle!"

"Well?"

"When are you going to ship that brat away from this house?"

"Before long."

"You hurry, or I'll do the job myself."

It left Graem totally bewildered, for Larribee seemed to regard little Ruth as a gun levelled at his head, and certainly La Salle had no fondness for her.

"Supper!" called the voice of Charlie down the hall, and the echo prolonged it, like the note of a bell.

31

REVOLT

In the hall, La Salle drew back beside Graem.

"You have two horses somewhere near the house, I suppose," he said.

"I have three, now," answered Graem, and looked straight into the eyes of the other.

"Three?" muttered La Salle. "You'll be picking up a herd as you travel!"

"That seems to depend on you," said Graem, and the face of La Salle turned grim.

"Who gave you this last one?" he asked.

"A killer you brought from a great distance. Rex Dobie."

They had fallen quite a distance behind; now La Salle stopped and exclaimed impatiently.

"Did that fool show himself on your trail?" asked he.

"He came up and covered me with a rifle, man; but I persuaded

him that he ought to make himself famous by trimming me in a fair
fight."

La Salle threw back his head with a groan.

"He had you under a rifle—and let you stand up for a—oh, what
an opportunity!"

Graem stared. There was such open rage and regret in the voice
and face of La Salle that it was very like the passion of a child; and
indeed he began to wonder if there was not a considerable portion of
child in this celebrated and evil man.

They went into the dining room, where La Salle gave directions
to the cook's boy to bring in Graem's horses, after the latter had
described the spot where they were located. Then they sat round the
table. Charlotte Guernsey was at one end; Larribee in his rags faced
her; Ruth was beside Graem, and La Salle opposite. Two voices
maintained the conversation, those of Charlie and La Salle; but
Larribee neither talked nor ate. He drank one cup of black coffee
after another, and from beneath white shaggy brows his eyes glit-
tered from face to face until he came to little Ruth. Then he looked
sharply away, and often with a frown. It seemed more than odd to
Graem, and so was the behaviour of the child. She had been a great
chatterer in the happy valley, but now she said not a word and ate
with downward eyes, and only when she had finished did she raise
her head.

Then her calm and gloomy observation passed slowly from face to
face, beginning with old Larribee, and bringing a positive snarl to
his face; then passing on to La Salle, who was the only one able to
endure the search with any degree of composure, and finally resting
on her elder sister. That dispassionate and most unsisterly gaze
reduced Charlie to confusion and a changed colour at once.

Very odd! thought Graem. He began to grow afraid of this child
himself, but when she turned her head and looked up to him there
was a deep well of love and trust in her eyes.

They nearly had ended the meal when a chorus of neighing broke
out just down the valley below the house, seeming to come from at
least half a dozen horses. Graem looked straight across the table
at La Salle, but the latter covertly shrugged his shoulders, as much
as to give signal that he knew nothing of who the riders could be.

Conversation was lagging at the table when confusion and much
noise broke out in the kitchen. The door leading from that to the
dining room was opened, loud voices rang; it was jerked shut again
with a slam, and still the argument seemed to rage.

"You'd better have a word with your cook, Mr. Larribee," suggested La Salle.

"Let the cook be," said the old man. "He's got some of his friends in, and maybe they've had a little liquor. Don't you worry, honey," he added to Charlotte.

Here the door from the kitchen opened a second time, and the cook was heard saying loudly: "Keep out of there or you'll never stop bein' sorry you went in."

"If he's there, I want to see him—I'm *gunna* see him," shouted another.

"And me!" said a second, and suddenly several men burst into the room, lunging forward as if about to deliver an attack. The excited cook gibbered Chinese and pidgin English in the background.

"What the devil's the meaning of this!" exclaimed Larribee, springing to his feet.

Charlotte slipped from her chair and gathered Ruth into her protecting arms.

"You'd better go out with your sister, Charlie," said La Salle.

Instantly she left the room, with one terrified backward glance, and hardly had she departed than the storm was breaking.

"By gravy," exclaimed the leader of the party, "there he is, as big as life or bigger, and sitting at the table with the chief—they're working hand in glove! And we're murdered by a plan between 'em!"

Old Larribee reached up and took from the wall a blunt-nosed heavy instrument of destruction—a sawed-off shotgun, one of those old weapons either barrel of which would hold a whole handful of slugs. Charged with a vast load of powder, it was rather a cannon loaded with grapeshot than a hand gun.

He did not raise his voice, but his snarl gave his words an incisive edge.

"Get these barking dogs out of this here house, La Salle," he commanded. "I've given 'em a warning, and if they don't get, I'll wash the whole gang of 'em into eternity. And I'm talkin' what I mean!"

"And who are you?" asked the foremost of the men.

He strode toward Larribee, but paused suddenly.

"Take a good look," said Larribee grimly. "Maybe you'll see something worth remembering."

Whatever it was that the other saw, he recoiled suddenly among his fellows; his violence left him.

"I didn't know——" he began, and then turned on La Salle.

"We got a right to know about this," he declared, and he pointed at Graem. La Salle did not rise. He merely turned his chair, so that he was half facing his men.

"Back up against the wall," he commanded. "You, Lowndes, this is the second time I've had trouble with you, and it'll be about the last. Back up, all of you. Charlie Moon, you're making a boob of yourself! Larson, take your hand from that gun. Every one of you knows that in this house there's no gun play allowed. You're going to pay for this, my friends!"

Graem, a gun resting on either knee beneath the table, waited and listened with gleaming eyes; these were the three, according to Larribee, who had chased him in the desert. Now they were back in the mountains and bent on mischief with the most determined air.

Lowndes, a great, stark wolf of a man, now made himself spokesman.

"We want no trouble with you, chief," said he. "The point is, we been riding our horses to death and working overtime to get this gent, and at the end of the trail, where do we find him? Sitting pretty at your own table——"

"My table!" broke in terrible old Larribee.

Lowndes gave a side glance at the old man and shuddered.

Then he added: "We've been in hell, chief. If we went a bit too far, we had a reason for it. I seen my black horse in the stable behind the house; and when I see it, the pony of Rex Dobie was standing alongside. We know what's become of him; but it didn't seem no ways possible that we'd find—that—in here!"

He pointed at Graem as he spoke. There was no word, apparently, sufficiently powerful to be used in the naming of Graem.

"I hear you," answered La Salle quietly. "Go on, Lowndes. What's the trouble with you?"

"D'you know what's happened to Crogan?" asked Lowndes suddenly.

"Well, you can tell me."

"He's done."

"Dead?"

"Worse. He's ruined. Right shoulder fixed so he'll pull no gun again so long as he lives."

"The clumsy fool never knew how to pull a gun," answered La Salle. "Besides, it may make an honest man of him. He didn't have sufficient brains to be a long-rider. What else? Was Crogan a great friend of yours?"

"He was one of the boys," said Lowndes firmly. "We've all rode together and fought together and stood together. And now we lack Crogan, but that ain't all. D'you know where Rex Dobie lies?"

"Tell me that, too."

"Down yonder in the creek, jammed between two rocks, all battered out of shape so's you hardly would know him. There's where he lies, and who did it, I want to know. It was Graem! There's hardly a man in the range that would've dared to stand up to Dobie except Graem. He's murdered Dobie for us. And Dobie was my partner down South. I tell you, I'm gunna have revenge for it!"

He waved to the others.

"And the rest of the boys, they agree with me. We want revenge for it, chief, and we got to get it. Besides, he's made fools of us, and he's made a fool of you!"

"There's a lot of sense in that talk," put in the nasal voice of Larribee. "He's made a fool of the lot of you. He rode where he felt like riding; he took your horses away from you, and he's laughed in your faces. He's shot down your best men, and he's slipped through your lines. What d'you say about it, La Salle, you that are so smart?"

He turned to the younger man with a leering grin of challenge.

"I say that we'll go to bed," answered La Salle, rising. "It's nearly my hour. And I don't want to be disturbed. As for my friend Graem, he's not far from his last day, and I chose to have a quiet chat with him before he disappeared. Mind you, I don't want to be disturbed tonight. You hear me? Furthermore, I've let you act like a tribe of wolves or pigs. Now get out of the room and don't let me have to look at your faces again before the morning."

They backed through the door as though he had struck them across the face with a whiplash.

"I hope that settles that," said La Salle, as the kitchen door closed.

"I don't though," said Larribee. "It don't settle it at all; and your boys are getting out of hand, La Salle. They're getting out of hand, at last!"

32

THE SINKING SHIP

As he spoke, the old man began to rub his dry, gnarled hands together, and he nodded with a venomous satisfaction over his words.

"I always told you that the time would come," said he. "I always told you that when your luck changed they'd begin to leave you. But to think of you, La Salle—to think of you hittin' a reef that's only one man, and wrecking on it! To think of that!"

He began to chuckle with an absolutely devilish pleasure as he taunted the younger man, and Graem was astonished to see the other turn white with emotion.

"D'you think I'm wrecked?" he asked of the old fellow in great excitement. "I tell you——"

"You can tell me that you got a fine strong ship. But I tell you that it's the beginnin' of the end. You've got a leaky hull under you, and I'm glad of it, and the rats are pretty near ready to leave the sinking ship. And why, La Salle? Because there's one man that you can't handle, and there he sits!"

He leaned back in his chair and waved genially toward Graem.

La Salle, following that gesture, regarded Graem with a consideration almost as profound as hypnosis. He was still white, and moisture gleamed on his forehead.

"I've heard enough of this nonsense," he declared.

"You'll hear more, though," croaked Larribee. "I'm gunna tell you more. I see it comin', and I'm gunna tell you more——"

"I'm going to bed," said La Salle.

Still his fascinated eyes could not leave the face of Graem.

"You can't budge out of your chair till I'm through with you," answered the old man, compressing his lips with terrible satisfaction. "Chang, you rascal, you! Chang, come here!"

The kitchen door opened, and the frightened, withered face of the old Chinese cook appeared.

"You blatherskite, you long-haired ape, you slant-eyed thief," said Mr. Larribee, "why ain't you brought in some hot coffee before this? Bring in the pot so fast that you burn the slippers off your feet!"

Chang grinned in a faint effort at sympathetic understanding; he reappeared almost at once with the coffee pot, and he placed it near the tyrant.

Still Larribee delayed in his prophecy until he had filled his coffee cup, and began to sip. The pipe was in one hand and the cup was in the other; between puffs and sips he gave forth his words slowly. They did not seem very impressive—only very strange—to Graem. What made them remarkable was the manner in which La Salle received them, as if they were the handwriting on the wall.

"Look at him," said Larribee at last, and he waved at Graem.

There was no need to invite a closer attention, for La Salle was poring over the face of Graem as though over the book of his own destiny.

"What do you see?" said Larribee. "Puncher. Plain puncher. Common or garden puncher."

"You lie!" said La Salle. "You know you lie!"

"I'm tellin' you the facts, young man, and gimme another word back like that, and I'll tell you not another word. You hear?"

La Salle was silent.

A peculiar excitement began to rise in Graem himself. He was by no means nervous or imaginative, but now the scene began to eat like acid into his mind. Everything took on a new significance—the glimmering plates, the silver splashes of light on forks and knives, the white, strained face of La Salle, and the flame in the circular burner of the lamp, rising and falling mysteriously under the influence of some imperceptible draught. But above all, an air of wizardry clothed old Larribee as he sat with his coffee cup poised, and, through the fumes of the pipe, his narrowed eyes glittering.

"Common cow-puncher," he continued at the last. "Common, ordinary, range-growed product, long-horned and skinny-ribbed. And what are you? What are you?"

La Salle moistened his bloodless lips. It seemed horrible to Graem that the man should stare so at him, while it was Larribee who was speaking. A hard stare to endure, but Graem fixed his own glance in response, for he felt that if his eyes wavered it would be a peculiarly important victory to La Salle.

"You might've been the same thing," said Larribee, "but it wasn't good enough for you. There was a hope that you might be turned into something extra special and fine. A handsome kid, that young La Salle! And so there was blood spent to give you your chance; blood spent, La Salle, to give you books and teaching and every way to make yourself a big man. Am I right?"

La Salle closed his eyes and kept them closed. It seemed to Graem, though he could not be sure, that a tremor possessed the criminal.

"Away you went; got your book learning; got to be a fine smooth article of a man. Everything done for you. But what happened? I tell you, La Salle, something can't be made out of nothing. It can't be done! You done your work left-handed. You climbed pretty high; you had a grand machine workin' for you. And then what happened?"

He turned and pointed to Graem.

"Common puncher. Range-raised and bred. Nothing but a common cow-puncher!"

His voice had altered ever so slightly, and Graem, looking askance at the old man and away from the closed eyes of La Salle, saw that the grin remained on the lips of Larribee, but now it was a grin of plain agony. Agony, too, was in the voice, so that all at once a whirl of confusion seized the mind of Graem. Who was this old man? What actual wizardry and devilishness possessed him and yet left him human enough to suffer in this fashion.

"What can he do? I ask you," old Larribee went on bitterly. "Nothing but what he learned out of the books of the range—shoot straight and shoot fast; read a trail; sit on a pitching bronc. That's all he can do."

The voice of the old man lowered a little. "And his word is as straight as the gun he shoots with, and he sticks to his friends like he sticks to the bronc he's peelin'."

He raised his tone again.

"Well, you bump into this here common cow-puncher, and what happens? You get him cornered, you shoot him full of holes, you turn loose the law on him, you send twenty fightin' men to run him down, and the law is ridin' beside you to help—but, La Salle, you ain't got a chance. You're beat, you're broke, you're finished, you're a dead man! One honest man has smashed you like this!"

And, draining the cup at a swallow, he dashed it on the floor, where it crashed into a thousand scattered shards. At that, La Salle stumbled to his feet, staggered, and then went blindly for the door, cast it wide open, and rushed into the hall.

Graem rose also. He felt that he could not endure the atmosphere in that room for another moment, but he lingered an instant over Larribee.

The old man had slumped down in the chair, so that his head

rested against the back of it, and he looked at Graem out of eyes that seemed half dead, and saw him not. The same grin was on his lips— a grin of mortal anguish.

"Are you sick?" asked Graem as gently as he could. "Is there anything that I can do for you?"

"You?" snarled the other in a voice which was barely stronger than a whisper. "Yes—get out of my sight!"

So Graem left, gladly. He shut the door behind him, and leaned against it, breathing deep, his eyes closed.

Then a small, cold hand closed on his.

He looked down to Ruth.

"Come along!" she whispered.

He followed her, glad that she would lead him, and she took him down a side hall and out through a narrow door. They stood among dead, whirling leaves, for the wind had risen somewhat, and was mourning down the canyon and through the trees which sighed and swayed above them.

"You know, Blondy," said the girl, pressing close to him. "Charlie can't understand, but you know, don't you?"

He patted her head, and she went on: "You don't have to say anything. It's pretty hard to talk about, ain't it? *I* can't hardly talk about it, though I been here a lot longer than you have. But oh, Blondy, Blondy!"

She leaned her head against his breast and began to sob, stifling the sound so that it reached the ear of Graem only as a soft moaning.

"Steady, honey," said he. "We understand; we'll work it out, I guess."

But he did not understand. It seemed to him that the confusion of the end of the world hardly could be greater than the darkness which swirled in his mind. It was no longer La Salle who obsessed him. It was old Larribee with the face of a satyr and the nature of a devil, and yet with something terribly human and terribly sad joined in his soul.

"I won't cry, Blondy," gasped the girl. "I gotta talk—I won't cry!"

She was hard at work for a moment trying to control herself, but then she was able to speak with a trembling voice.

"Blondy——"

"Well, honey?"

"What're we gunna do about Charlie? *What* are we gonna do about her?"

"I'm tryin' to think."

"If you can't save her, nobody can save her, Blondy."

And then hastily she added: "Do you want to try?"

"I do."

"But do you, really? Do you still like her a little?"

"I do."

"Then what will you do, Blondy?"

"I don't know. I'll only try to do what I can, because—listen to me while I whisper a secret to you, Ruth."

"I'm listening, Blondy dear."

"Just in your ear for only you to know, honey: I love her more now than ever I did before."

There was a faint gasp from the child. Then she found one of his hands and pressed it.

At length she whispered: "I know, Blondy darlin'. You never know how much you like a thing till you've given it away—like the yellow diamond, Blondy!"

33

TRAITOR

He had to take Ruth inside at once, for tears were becoming uncontrollable with her; and in the hall they met Charlotte, who had just run laughing and singing down the stairs. There was such a great happiness in her that even at the sight of Ruth in tears she was not instantly sobered. Then she hurried to the child, and would have taken her up to bed, but Ruth, with hanging head, defended herself, and pushed sullenly past, then scampered up the stairs, and from above could be heard one explosive sob as she ran for her room.

It left Charlotte wide-eyed with trouble and wonder.

"What *is* wrong with her?" she asked Graem.

"She's homesick, maybe," he suggested, looking down at the floor. "And she misses her father a good deal, I suppose."

Charlie sighed, and at that he met her eye and found it very sad.

"I thought you'd understand—and—and—when you met Oliver, I mean," said she.

"Oh, I understand," said Graem miserably, and wished with all his might that he could run past with a hanging head, like Ruth, and burst away for his room.

She threw out her arms in a gesture of despair.

"I don't know what it is!" she cried. "I know it's something, or you and Ruth wouldn't feel the same way about it!'

"Well," he said as gently as he could, "maybe we have different reasons. Ruth doesn't want to lose you, Charlie."

"She never cared at all when"—here she stopped short, and then she forced herself slowly and gallantly ahead—"when she thought that you and I—Blondy, I'd like to cry!"

"Now, don't you be worrying," he tried to reassure her. "I'm not gunna die; I'll wait ten years for Ruth, you see, and I'll get rich in the meantime, and we'll all be happy ever after."

She shook her head.

"There's something else than that in your mind," said she.

At that, he made himself smile at her, and he answered: "I'm mighty jealous, Charlie. You can't want me to throw up my hat. You can't just expect me to cheer, honey."

"But you and Oliver are such old friends, it turns out."

She said it in a rather complaining and wondering tone.

"Nobody's got a friend, when it comes to a girl," he explained.

"Only, Blondy——" began Charlie, and stepped closer.

He held her hands gently, and waited.

"You don't despise me, Blondy?"

"I?"

"And you don't hate me, Blondy darling?"

"Look at me!" said Graem.

"If I do," said the girl, "I'll just begin to cry!"

"Look at me, Charlie."

She managed it, and trembled as she did so.

"There's nothing that you could do in your life," he said solemnly, "that ever would be wrong to me. Will you believe that now?"

"Dear, dear Blondy. Will you kiss me?"

He took her carefully in his arms.

"I won't break, you know," said Charlotte, trying to laugh.

He could not touch the lips which were raised to him, but he kissed her forehead, saying: "Good-bye, Charlie."

"Oh!" she breathed.

And then he went past her, and into the living room, where La Salle and the old man were sitting by the fire, talking cheerfully of odds and ends as though, not long before, they had not been talking most terribly, most strangely not twenty steps from that spot.

He, from the door, regarded them with profound interest. He had felt, when he first talked with Larribee in the desert, that no other man in the world could be compared with La Salle except that withered and lean old hermit. Now that he turned out to be no hermit at all, but simply a desperately shrewd and eccentric frontiersman, the comparison between them was still more interesting. The sight of them together, conversing quietly and cheerfully in this manner, was an excellent antidote for the great gloom which had descended upon him, and the bitterness of his soul as he left the girl in the hallway. For if she was a transparent spirit of light, here were two opaque souls, he could be sure. They were iron men, truly, and softly as they spoke with one another, it seemed to Graem that he heard the distant clashing of swords.

La Salle greeted him with attention and kindness; old Larribee gave him not so much as a side glance. He was holding forth on his favourite theme—the differences between the men of other days and this fallen generation of luxury lovers—where man flesh and horse-flesh had fallen, fallen from the old ideal.

Graem listened only a moment, summoned a yawn, and said that he must turn in; so La Salle went out to show him to his room.

"I don't know where Charlie is to say good-night to you," he said as they passed down the hall.

"I've said good-night to her already."

At this La Salle could not help turning with one keen, stabbing glance, but Graem shook his head, and La Salle dropped a hand on his shoulder.

"You're playing the game—a grand game," was all he said.

He took Graem up one floor, and led him to a corner room.

"There's a little noise here from the creek," he explained, "but there's no window within reach, and this door, you can see, is extra strong. You see, there are four bolts. The old man used to sleep here, and he likes to shut out the ghosts."

"You mean Larribee?"

"Yes, of course. He's—a little strange, eh?"

But Graem returned no answer, and it was plain from the manner in which the other hurried on that no answer was wanted.

"I think you'll be comfortable here, Blondy."

"I'll do fine," replied Graem. "I expect to sleep hard."

"D'you mean that?"

"I mean it."

"Thanks," said La Salle, and flushed a little. "I'll say good-night, then."

He went to the door and there paused for a moment.

"Look here, Blondy."

"Well?"

"Dare I ask you a favour?"

"Certainly."

"Then tell me what makes the little girl hate Larribee and me so thoroughly?"

"I'd tell you if I knew."

"Nothing but instinct," murmured La Salle.

Then he added suddenly: "I'm going too far. I can't help it. I know that I've cut your throat in nearly all possible ways, Tucker. At the same time, I want to point out that I can have you squared with the law, put you on your feet as a flourishing rancher, with everything that a man could ask for in the way of layout and stock of cattle and all the rest. I'd do those things and a thousand other things as well, if we could call things square between us."

Now, leaning against the jamb of the door, with his fine eyes dark with an apparent sincerity, he seemed to Graem the very sum and picture of all that was graceful, strong, brave, and beautiful in man. Like a picture Graem regarded the speaker and then he answered slowly: "If I have five minutes of life, I'll spend it trying to finish you, La Salle; if I live to fifty, I'll spend that time the same way. If you want it put stronger, I'll try different words."

"No," sighed La Salle, "I have to expect that. It wouldn't be you, otherwise—always Homeric!"

He mixed a smile and a touch of a sneer with these last words, and then turned swiftly and disappeared down the hall, shutting the door softly behind him.

Graem, left alone, began to go thoroughly over the walls and the floors of the chamber, tapping here and there, but presently he stood erect and flushed, although he was alone. For he realized that La Salle was capable of a great many sorts of falsehoods, but such a lie as this was a bit beyond even La Salle's range.

He went to the window, next, and examined the surroundings. All was as La Salle had said—no other window near, and the pleasant, sad music of the creek in the distance, with a screen of great trees to shut off all sight of the water. The moon was well up by this time. It cast on the ground great thick shadows, or varied patterning of leaf shapes; it turned the outer foliage to silver; and somehow it made the fragrance of pines and moist, cool earth more enticing, more delightfully unreal.

He stepped back quickly from the window and faced the comparatively stuffy atmosphere of the room. Downstairs, La Salle and Charlie Guernsey, by this time, would be walking out, no doubt, to watch that moon sail through the upper branches, or plunge along racks of translucent clouds, like a white ship throwing up gigantic spray in silence throughout the night.

Well, there had been a time when he had been able to stand at her side, but now that he looked back upon the days in the happy valley, he felt that he had thrown his time away. Certainly he had rarely so much as touched her hand, and how seldom had he told her that he loved her in order to have back her answer like a golden echo!

In these things, La Salle was the wiser!

He went to bed after blowing out the lamp. The smell of kerosene and the smoking wick died away; and the pure night air came in with the moonlight and filled the chamber with sad fragrance. He was right, he felt, in acting as he had acted, for if he had attempted to betray the secret of La Salle to Charlie, she could hardly have believed him; at any rate it would have precipitated a crisis the end of which most probably would have been to cast her definitely and irretrievably into the arms of La Salle.

So he fell asleep and dropped into vast and troubled dreams in which he found himself striving to row a boat up the face of a cataract, and again he was climbing an endless mountain of pale ice. He woke suddenly.

The silver hand of the moon was on the wall just above his bed, but a ray of another sort of light, he knew, had been a moment before playing on his face!

34

THREE TO ONE

Had it not been for La Salle, Graem would have lain like a wolf, with wide-open eyes and ears as he slipped his revolver from under his pillow. But he could not help remembering, at this juncture, the assurance which that arch-criminal had given him. Therefore, he sat up boldly and suddenly in bed, looking toward the window. A head and shoulders were framed there against the white of the moonlit tree outside; and inside the window two forms crouched close to the floor. He snatched at his revolver, but, as he did so, there was a cutting whisper through the air and a rope jerked home around his neck with such violence that he was flung from the bed and hurled with a crash to the floor.

He who has had to take many a fall from a pitching horse learns how to fall so as to accept the shock most easily; he lets his body go limp and rolls with the impact, and so Graem did now, twisting over and over on the floor, while the revolver, skidding before him, exploded with a flash and roar.

He saw the gleam of a poised knife as he landed, but the roll which he managed saved him, and the thrust which was meant for his breast lodged in the pine boards of the flooring instead.

"Hold the knives! Guns, boys!" said the voice of Lowndes.

Still in motion, his impetus allowed Graem to pitch to his feet, and he lunged at the man who held the end of the rope that was choking him. A gun spat fire fairly in his face, and then his reaching fist went home against a heavy body and there was a sharp curse in response.

The strain on the rope ended. Slipping his fingers inside the noose, Graem worked it free and jerked it over his head with one motion, then pitched for the floor as two guns thundered. The echoes were chasing each other in a maddened dance; heavy feet stamped on the floor, and the pungent odour of burned powder now filled the room, but by the grace of fortune and ceaseless movement he had avoided any injury except the rope-scald on his neck.

Things could not go on as well as this, however. He had no weapon, now, except the chair on which his hands fell as he smote the floor the second time, diving out of the gunfire.

The man of the window was in, now, a gun in either hand, and both guns speaking, but all work had to be more or less at random, for the moon lighted the chamber only partially, at the best, and where the shadows stood they were as thick as starless midnight. Moreover, these three bent on murder had danger from one another to consider, and now there was a yell of pain and: "Harry, look out! You nicked me then!"

That form by the window, crouching, its two guns working, was the target for Graem, and at this mark he cast the chair with all his might. It struck with a splintering shock that drew a yell of pain, and the third comer toppled in the corner fairly on top of him who was apparently Harry Lowndes.

Now all these things were clear to Graem. His nerves were strained to such a pitch that his vision thrust through the shadows like a ray of light, and, to his speeding thoughts, all movement was absurdly retarded, like a slow-moving picture.

Thus, he marked the flung chair in the midst of its flight—it turned once before striking. And he saw the man before the window throw out a hand, vainly striving to guard himself—saw that hand beaten in, and watched the form of the victim falling, so that it seemed to hesitate in mid-air; leaning at a sharp angle, and then lurched down into the shadows and rolled in confusion with Lowndes.

Now for a gun, now for a gun! One bullet would drive through both bodies! One bullet would save him.

The third man, driven to despair by this accident, was shouting: "Get up, you fools! We'll catch it in a second if we don't polish him off!"

And he lurched across the floor, firing as he came.

Slowly, slowly he moved, as it seemed to the feverish brain of the assaulted man, and whole ages came between each explosion of the levelled guns. But Graem's own body seemed paralysed; it hardly reacted to the demands of his jumping nerves; he felt like a boxer, wanting to fight back, eager to drive home a telling blow, but with the portion of the brain that governs motor activities stunned and half helpless.

He rolled under the little table by the wall, caught it with one hand, and cast it in the way of the charge. In mid-air the top of the table split across—a bullet had cracked through the board, but the two pieces crashed at the feet of the third man and he stumbled to his knees.

Now for a gun, if there was any fortune in this world!

Graem cast himself from hands and knees and straining bare toes, like a leaping cat. His shoulder smote into the face of his enemy and then the weight of his body crunched on the other; they rolled together, over and over, but with one hand Graem had clutched a gun, and now he beat the barrel against the head of the twisting, snarling, fighting fellow.

Let that blow settle him!

But he was far from settled. No African skull ever was more thickly armour-plated than this, it seemed. The sombrero which had shadowed his face now toppled off with the stroke and exposed a vast mop of curly hair and the features of Ed Larson, locked and twisted in fierce effort. He flung himself in with outspread arms and locked them tight around the body of Graem.

Graem had his left hand free, but the right, holding the Colt, was fixed against his body and almost breaking under the tremendous pressure of Larson.

"Help, boys!" gasped Larson. "He's got one of my guns. Smash his head in quick!"

All of this, of course, had happened in a bitter half-second or so, and in the corner Graem could see the two fallen men disentangling themselves from one another and rising gradually, as it appeared, to their feet. One of them staggered; both seemed to take infinite time and deliberation.

If he could drop Larson, then let the two take care of themselves when once his gun began to blaze! But he could not drop Larson. He poised his left hand and selected his mark. A famous left hand was this. Whether in Canadian lumber camps, or all down the mountains and the deserts of the range, men knew the sharp-shooting accuracy of that hard fist, and tales were told of smashed noses and of cracked jaws when it went home. With that left alone, thrusting like a rapid piston, he had cleaved a way through a fighting crowd. Now he poised it confidently and selected for a target the yielding and soft bone beneath and behind the ear of Larson.

Straight to the mark he struck, and waited to shake himself free from the crumbling form of the other. But Larson merely snarled like a wounded dog, and, dropping his head on his shoulder to guard against another such blow, ground his shoulder into the ribs of Graem and increased the strangling pressure of his grasp.

On the side and on the back, Graem smote; his fist fairly re-bounded from the cushions of muscles which covered the body of this very powerful fighter.

And here were the two advancing upon him with lurching steps from the corner, with the keen voice of Lowndes barking orders:

"Charlie—take him from the right—club your Colt; look out for Larson! Hold him, Ed, good boy! Now you, Graem, this is gunna be the end of you!"

Aye, the end indeed, most inevitably!

Sweat blinded Graem, yet despair made him cold; and in the midst of that passion he could not keep back a half-drunken laughter that rang terribly through the room. For it seemed stupid folly and utterly senseless chance that ended him in this room, where the shield of La Salle's protection should have extended over him!

The side of Larson's head was sheltered by being dropped on his shoulder, but not perfectly shielded. A driving uppercut grazed the side of Ed's forehead and snapped his head upright. Before it could be brought back to shelter a second blow sank home fairly on the temple, and at last the work was done. The mighty arms grew nerveless and relaxed; the knees buckled; the head rolled back on the shoulders, with mouth fallen open.

So it was done, and done too late, for Lowndes and Charlie Moon were speeding in from either side, and in the window a fourth form was appearing.

A voice clanged through the uproar of cursing, panting, groaning.

"Lowndes! Get back from him! You devils!"

It checked the upraised hand of Lowndes, and never again would he have a chance of lifting head or finger's weight, for from the window a gun spoke, and Harry Lowndes toppled off balance to the side. He looked ridiculously like a Russian dancer in an odd position. He seemed to paw and beat to get back on both feet, and then pitched heavily on his side.

Charlie Moon could have struck the decisive blow, after all. He was close enough, but the fall of his companion and leader sapped the strength of Charlie Moon at the root. And as Larson fell inert at the feet of Graem, Moon shrank back against the wall, shouting: "Don't shoot! Don't kill me, chief! I was dragged into it—I didn't want to bear a hand!"

La Salle was stepping through the window, with his guns already put up. He lighted the lamp, and as its flame jumped Graem saw that he was pale and strained, but with the flaring nostrils of a fighter.

He raised the lamp; iron was in his voice as he asked: "Graem?"

"I'm not hurt."

"Now—thank God!"

"That's Lowndes, isn't it, on the floor?"

"You shot him through the head; he'll never move again."

"And who's the other? Larson, of course?"

"Yes, it's Larson. He's only stunned."

"Moon," continued the leader, in the same precise, hard voice, "get out of this; take your horse, and ride for Carey. Report to him. I'll let you know later what's to happen to you!"

Moon shrank without a word for the window; and the two then turned to Lowndes. He was dead.

Larson was still in a swoon. When they rolled him over, they saw three bleeding places on the side of his head where the iron knuckles of Graem had bit through flesh to bone. "Game! Dead game!" murmured Graem.

"Blondy!" shrilled the voice of Charlie from the hall. "Blondy! Blondy!"

La Salle turned on his companion.

"You know I had no hand in it?" he asked in a strained voice. "The murderers!"

And he said it with a wonderful, honest indignation!

35

THE BEGINNING OF THE END

WHEN Graem opened the door he found Charlotte half in hysterics, and little Ruth beside her, with great round eyes like an owl, but making not a sound.

"There's been trouble," said Graem. "Three fellows tackled me. With Oliver Landon's help, I drove them off. That's all. Now you'd better go back to bed."

"Oliver!" exclaimed the girl with joy suddenly flooding her face. "Of course, he's everywhere!"

She went, and turning in the hall after a step, seemed about to come back, but changed her mind and went on again, leaving with Graem the picture of a pale face trying to smile, a blue bathrobe, and hair on which the lamplight glistened like fire.

Ruth had not offered a word, but simply had looked gloomily up to Graem after one flashing smile of welcome and joy when he first opened the door.

Then he went back to La Salle and found the latter at work rapidly bundling the dead body.

Ed Larson, silent and doubly pale because of his fear, assisted his chief, and poor Lowndes was rolled in a blanket and then lowered by the lariat through the window.

"You know what to do with that," said the chief to Larson. "Afterwards, go to Carey and tell him I sent you. That's all."

Ed Larson climbed out the window and put his feet on the top rung of the ladder up which the three had come to the attack of Graem. He paused there to bend one final glance upon Graem, and couldn't help snarling: "Brass knuckles!"

After that he disappeared below the sill of the window, while La

Salle interrupted quietly: "That's the trouble with these fellows, No imagination, Graem. That man never was hit as hard as you hit him; he never was cut as your knuckles cut him, and so he puts it down to brass knuckles. And the odd thing, Blondy, is that while he was doing a murder, he was outraged at being struck with an unfair weapon. And there you have them all—children!"

He seemed quite good-natured, but there was such a shadow in his eyes that Graem knew trouble lay somewhere in the offiing.

He went on to explain what had happened. He had slept until a puff of wind blew in the open shutter of his window, and the change from light to dark roused him. He got up to secure the shutter, and, looking out the window, he saw three men going softly around the corner of the house in single file.

They might be some of his men returning to the house; they might be the worst sort of danger stalking the place. At any rate, he slipped down the stairs in time to see the three put a ladder against the wall and disappear through Graem's window. Guns began to crash before he could get to the scene, and the long and dangerous fight which, in the mind of Graem, seemed to have occupied endless minutes really endured only so long as it took La Salle to get to the ladder and climb to the top of it.

In conclusion, he said: "I never dreamed that they'd dare to try such a thing outside of orders; and after the trouble I had with them last night! But they'll be taught their limits, Blondy. I'll promise you that!"

How they would be taught, Graem did not ask; he was almost afraid to learn. In the meantime, he had dressed and buckled on his guns and put his hat on.

"You've got to leave now?" asked La Salle.

"Not that I don't trust you," Graem assured him. "But it's for another reason. I've got a long trail before me, I suppose."

La Salle did not smile, but nodded gravely.

"You're working me out, I suppose?" he asked politely.

"Yes, I'm working you out."

"I can't wish you good luck. I suppose this is the last time we meet, Graem."

"You'd like to have it that way," responded the other. "But the trouble is, La Salle, that I'll never leave your sign until one of us goes down."

"I've tried to be courteous," said La Salle with a sharp change of tone. "I've tried to make some amends, because in every phase of the game I've always beaten you from the beginning. And I always shall to the end. I would like to warn you that if you get out of this range and mind your own affairs, I'll never let harm come at you from my men. But if you don't the end has come, Graem, and you'll live to see very few more sunrises!"

Only one answer came to the mind of Graem, and he was not ashamed to use it.

"Larribee don't agree with you," said he.

La Salle snapped erect like a soldier at a challenge.

"Good-bye," he said shortly.

"So long," answered Graem. "You can tell Charlie that I was called away in the middle of the night, and didn't want to disturb her by saying good-bye." Then he added, with a touch of grim pleasure: "You may manage for a while with Charlie, La Salle, but you can't manage long. Ruth understands you. And that's the beginning of the end."

Then, as he closed the door and so shut out the sight of the burning eyes of La Salle, it occurred to him that he had made a small repayment to a man who, after all, really had saved his life on this night.

Conscience did not prick him very deep.

His own last Parthian shaft was one in which he had no faith; certainly he saw no grounds upon which Larribee could base his feeling that failure lay before La Salle, for it appeared to Graem just as the latter said, that from the beginning he had won in all respects in all of the games which they played against one another.

The dark house creaked softly and secretly as he went down to the lower storey; he passed the open door of the living room, inside which the red eye of a dying ember glared at him from the hearth; and he was a happy man when he stood once more outside the building.

He turned at once past the corner of the house and at a dog-trot he went to the stable. There might be some danger there for him, but he was reasonably sure that it would not come at the hands either of Larson or Charlie Moon. In fact, he found no one at all in the old, capacious barn. He found the bay asleep and Lowndes' black horse in the adjoining stall. So he could leave the house of Larribee as well equipped for the trail as he had been when he came.

It was still a good hour before sunrise, and the ideal moment to begin a march such as he had before him when, after saddling the pair and looking at his pack—where all was in good condition—he came out before the barn, and, by the dying moonshine, high and huge to the north, he saw the twin mountains, like the ears of a mule, and the round lump between them.

He started at the sight, remembering what poor Jerry Tyndal had told him on that other day of the interview with La Salle "at his place" under a tree, and how he had ridden three days to the south with the mountains in view behind him.

Graem had intended to retrace his steps to the mouth of the canyon and ride down Channing Valley; now he instantly made up his mind to push straight up the canyon as fast as he could, for he had no doubt that this very house was the place where Jerry had seen his chief at that last important interview.

Up the ravine, therefore, he rode, taking care always to maintain a brisk pace.

"Ride like hell for three days and kill your horse with work on the last day," had been the instruction of La Salle to Jerry Tyndal on that day.

A pace which would kill off one horse would only be a brisk gait for two; to that pace, therefore, Graem decided he would cling, shifting every two hours or so from one saddle to the other. The ravine rapidly climbed and narrowed. He went past the cataract of thundering white on a trail hardly a yard wide, and, as he rode through that narrow pass, it seemed to him that the foaming dashing masses of water were like the power of La Salle, irresistible to all normal human force but totally overwhelming to a single man like himself.

When he came to the wild and broken ground at the head of the canyon, he checked the horses and looked uncertainly back. It seemed that he was turning his back upon the root and source of his great enemy's power. Yonder in Larribee's house he should wait, or near it, to strike his blow.

But what could come of that, seeing that such numbers and such strength were listed against him? There, too, was Charlie Guernsey, waiting; and was her heart to be broken? If he could only see the end of the trail!

So he rode on again, not at all content. Some great thing, he felt sure, lay at the end of this trail, and doubtless it had to do with the arch-criminal. If he solved the problem, it might mean the definite undoing of young La Salle; if he failed, he had lost all touch with that great man.

Time pressed. No doubt La Salle would urge the girl toward a marriage now that Graem had come and gone and forgiven her for her change of heart. And it was three long days of riding to come to the solution of that riddle of the five words.

"Council house mystery man river."

It never had ceased going backward and forward in his imagination even in Larribee's house; and it rang like five changing notes of a peal through his thoughts as he pressed south. The twin mountains were his guide. He must see them from every rise, bearing behind, and so he could sight his course forward for a considerable distance, always correcting it when he was once more in view of the peaks.

That day was rough work for the horses. How easily Jerry Tyndal had passed over in a sentence a grim piece of riding! He found a good camping place late in the afternoon and there, though he was on fire to go on, he paused. Fresh horses at the end of that long grind were what he would be apt to need. He cared for them with scrupulous diligence. He made of them a working ground on which he used his thought and his energy, loosening girths at every pause, conserving them and yet using them, and acting as though a pursuit were flaming along in his rear.

No doubt it was, if the men of La Salle were able to pick up the trail which he had left, and the best hunting brains in the world would be concentrated on the task of tracking Blondy Tucker Graem, he could be sure.

36

BAD NEWS

BEFORE dawn the next morning, Graem was in the saddle again. There is no march so swift or so long as the early morning march, and swiftly the hills drifted up before his face and faded away again on either side. Throughout that day he pushed relentlessly on until he came to the head of a valley which rapidly widened before him. It was dotted with houses, and in broad daylight it could hardly have been safe for a man wanted by the law to venture through a passage where so many eyes were apt to fall upon him. However, it was not dusk, camping time. He resolved to keep straight on down the valley until he had ridden out of this farming region and come to the safer wilderness beyond.

So he jogged along through the thickening dusk; cattle lowed here and there; several rattling buckboards went past him, half seen on the road; and the smell of freshly ploughed ground came to him again and again.

He was not surprised when, topping a small rise, he saw before him the lights of a town. A desert village is closely bunched as though for mutual protection from the fierce sandstorms and the fury of the sun. But this was a spreading village, in a country where it was worth while to have a large garden and a capacious yard. By the space between the lights he knew that this was such a village, and he began to sigh for a glimpse of it; he could smell the freshness of the lawns, as it were, even at that distance, and hear the whir of the sprinklers at work in the evening.

He closed his eyes for a moment and mapped the country in his mind. After all, it was very far from any district where he had shown himself before, and it would be odd, indeed, if he encountered any man who knew his face. As for identifying him by a description, that is a hard business. Few men look like criminals until they are detected at work. Furthermore, he was urged on by a desire for one more touch of adventure; and, in short, he made up his mind that he would straightway ride into yonder town and put his knees under a supper table that night.

When he had made up his mind to this end, he rode vigorously on. First he cast a compass around the village, and on the farther side he found what he wanted—a secure and snug little grove of poplars which spread across both banks of a creek so shallow that it could be forded with the greatest carelessness. In the centre of that grove and near the water he tethered the horses, removed their saddles, rubbed them down with care, and left them to drink, pick at the good grass around the tree trunks, and lie down when they chose. Perhaps, in the town, he would be able to buy a feed of grain for them.

It was the thickest night when he walked in, congratulating himself that he was approaching from a direction opposite to that in which he might have been expected, if anyone was on the lookout for him in the place. The village was all that he had hoped. Prosperity cried out to him even through the darkness, for here were the typical American lawns, the wide street, the houses set back behind capacious gardens, the rows of trees on the outer edges of the sidewalks.

He breathed deeply of this air of well-being. But as he passed through the shafts of light from open windows and open doors—for the night was still and warm—and as he heard the happy sound of voices and heard the busy clamour of kitchens hurrying the supper preparations, a great loneliness grew up in Graem again. He never would come to such an end as this; rather it would be in the bleakness of the mountains or the barren heat of the desert that a bullet would strike him and turn him limp in the saddle. But for Charlie? Well, let Fate take care of her and bring her to something even better than this. To Graem, it seemed like a taste of Paradise.

He came to the central section of the town. The street was paved here, and there were stores on either side, sometimes office buildings of four and five storeys. This contented him greatly, for in so large and populous a place it was very unlikely that he could be spotted. The bigger the flock, the better the chance for the wolf!

The hotel was a relic of earlier days. This appeared to be a town of homemakers, and as for the entertainment of transients, little emphasis apparently was laid upon it, for the hostelry was a rambling wooden shack, large enough in proportions, but hopelessly reeking of "early West," from the high false front to the long veranda with its slender, square, wooden supporting columns.

The steps creaked unpleasantly under his tread when he mounted to the entrance. In the lobby he was relieved to find a humming crowd of fifteen or twenty men and women. The dinner hour had just come and, after washing, Graem went into the dining room with the rest.

He would have been glad to find all the guests seated around one long table, after the rough fashion of the West, but instead there had been a concession to privacy and comfort, for there were a number of little square tables along the walls. He was at least glad to have a vacant one, so he settled himself at it, had the waiter bring him a paper, and, while he waited for soup, unfurled the journal and found—himself!

Aye, and spread across the front page in large, commanding type:

· "MORE GRAEM COUNTERFEIT MONEY PASSED IN BOSTON."

In Boston! Graem! Counterfeit!

He read that headline thrice. Then he plunged into the article.

He mastered the situation by degrees, though he was so startled that he had to read the article through several times. Its gist was about as follows: bills of large denomination had been presented in quantity at many of the banks in large Eastern cities. Staggering sums already had been realized in this fashion, for the counterfeiting was so skilfully done that only an expert—and perhaps an expert with a glass—could detect the difference between the false and the true currency. It was called the "Graem" counterfeit because the first bill of this sort had been passed in a small Western town by a miscreant named Tucker Graem, wanted for the brutal murder of Jeremy Tyndal in a little hotel by the wayside, also wanted because of this flood of false currency which was appearing.

There was one note of relief in the article. The money had been passed in bills of large denomination, and now that these were under suspicion it should be a comparatively simple thing for careful cashiers of banks to stop the flood of counterfeit. Already three men had been arrested. Of these, two had proved that they came by the money honestly, having accepted it in the course of business transactions; the third under the third degree refused to divulge the source of the money, but doubtless the police would be able to trace it through other trails to its source, which was suspected to be somewhere in the South-east, perhaps in the mountains of Kentucky. Evidently the distribution of the counterfeit was being attempted on a large scale, for there had been simultaneous presentation of it in the West and in the East, at a hundred banks.

If money as accurately made as this, however, had been manufactured in bills of small denomination, then the detectives and the police would be called upon for a gigantic effort, for small bills might rapidly be passed by the most astute cashier without wakening his suspicion.

There was a further article appended by a different pen. It described the hard chase after Graem, and how that worthy had disappeared in the direction of the desert, where doubtless the officers of the law soon would round him up——

"This chair taken, sir?"

The reader looked up at a man with a round, red, kindly face and round eyes obscured by heavy glasses.

"Take it!" said Graem, and smiled in welcome. He could not have asked for a better neighbour at the table on such an evening as this.

"Terrible, terrible!" said the fat little man as he settled to his soup and his newspaper in ambidextrous fashion.

"Terrible," he expanded, "that counterfeiting. Will they get the scoundrels that are producing the money?"

"Of course," said Graem with conviction. "They're bound to get them. This sort of a thing, it always goes bust pretty quick. Somebody squeals. That's the finish."

The fat man looked up over his glasses.

"You think so? You're rather young! It's the police, my friend. A stupid lot. Stupid everywhere. Here's a land full of criminals, wandering everywhere, and the police are blind to them. I'm half minded to lend our sheriff my glasses!"

He chuckled.

"I'm in from a long trip," said Graem, "just passing through. What's wrong around here?"

"Arrested somebody here the other night. Charged him with being Graem, the murderer. Of course, it was the wrong man!"

"Graem, the murderer." It was an ugly title. The very sound of it made Blondy choke a little and finger his throat.

"What you got there?" asked the little man. "*Standard*?"

"Aye."

"The *News* is the only paper in this town. More to it, and better worked up."

He shook out his *News* and turned to an inner page, while Graem proceeded to interview a thick steak, which lay oozing rich juices in the midst of piled fried potatoes, and fried slices of tomato. He ate with comfort, and with long-drawn relish.

He became aware that the little man was no longer opposite him; instead, his round, retreating back was even now passing away down the dining room, and the working of his shoulders showed that he was making haste.

He had seen a friend, no doubt.

In the meantime, there was the abandoned *News* lying on the floor, and Graem reached down for more information.

He had it at once—it stared up at him from the inner page of the journal which his late neighbour had been reading—nothing in print, but a six-inch photograph of himself printed with wonderful clearness, and recognizable, he thought, by any child!

37

FLIGHT

HE thought, at first, of following the fat man straight out of the room, but after a moment he realized that such a thing would be folly. Instead, he slipped from his chair, and, walking to the front of the room, pushed up a window.

"Hey!" exclaimed a burly cow-puncher at a corner table. "Walk outside, if you need more air, will you? I got a cold!"

"Half a minute, partner," murmured Graem amiably. "I just want a snootful of air, and then I'll close it up," and, so saying, he sat down on the window sill and glanced down and out. There was no more than a five-foot drop, to a path which circled around the hotel.

The spur was given him that instant, for a hushed voice gasped at the back of the dining room, and he heard hurrying footsteps. One glance showed him the fat man rushing into the room again, pointing excitedly with a stubby arm, while a pair of rangy, brown-faced men strode behind him, determination written large in their faces.

That was enough for Graem. He swung his legs through the window as a voice said: "Hands up, Graem, or we'll——"

A pistol shot finished that sentence, and a crash just above his head sent a tinkling shower of glass over him. Then he was outside running as hard as he could dash for the corner of the building. The moment he was around it, he dived for the high board fence which ran down the side of the hotel grounds. Well would it have been for Graem if he could have cleared it at the first spring, but the ground from which he took off was a little soft, and the fence was a shade higher than he had anticipated. The result was a heavy shock and a recoil. As he caught the top of it to vault over, half a dozen men spilled round the corner of the hotel. They did not wait to send in challenges. They simply opened fire with chattering guns. Not wild fire, either, for the slugs sang perilously close around the ears of Graem, and he heard the soft chugging as the bullets bit holes in the boards. He gritted his teeth and swung over, and he began to run for his life.

He had jumped into a backyard; if he ran straight ahead there were other fences, more or less high, but if he veered to the right he would come out into the street, where he could hear the pounding of galloping horses already. Certainly this town seemed to live on a hair-trigger, ready for an alarm!

He had some trust in his speed of foot. In his school days he had been able to laugh at his playmates, and at hare and hounds he had baffled the chase many and many a time, yet as he plunged ahead through the night, vaulting the fences, he soon made out that he was losing ground. He had the reason for it almost instantly, for, casting a frightened glance over his shoulder as he sped across a narrow yard, he had a view of two men silhouetted against the stars as they flew in hurdle style over a fence not much under five feet in height.

Athletes, these—trained athletes home for a vacation from some college, no doubt, thought Graem and groaned inwardly. He thought of his guns, which weighed him down, but no weapons had gleamed in the hands of these youngsters. To them, no doubt, it was no more than a game—another version of a race over different obstacles than the conventional hurdles, with other footing than the smooth surface of a cinder path. And Graem, panting, swung over the next fence with his brain in a swirl.

He could not shoot down these young idiots; it would be murder. Perhaps, however, he could frighten them off, so as he saw them rising like steeplechasers over the fence, he flung two bullets perilously close to their heads.

Frighten them? They merely shouted with a joyous excitement and, reaching the footing of the yard, lunged fiercely in at him. Football players, too, perhaps, to judge by the manner in which they hurled themselves forward for the tackle!

He clipped one over the head with the barrel of a Colt and sent him rolling in the dust; the second man, a stride behind, he strove to dodge. It was like trying to swerve from a hunting dog, and with a crash the other smote him.

Down went Graem, with a shoulder of iron driven fairly through his midriff as he fell. The wind was gone from him; red-dotted black heaved before his eyes; and his gun hand was held with a mighty grasp that burned into the flesh and sinews of his wrist.

"Give up, you beggar!" grasped the husky boy. "Give up, or I'll whang you one!"

It brought something like laughter swelling into the throat of Graem. A threat of being struck—a fair caution from a lad too sporting to hit another who was down! Then despair gave Graem an added leverage. He twisted violently, and rolled with his captor, and as he rolled his free left hand was working; it cut into soft flesh, it shocked against bone. Then the constraining arms relaxed, and he was free to rise—and face the rush of half a dozen groaning, winded, gasping men who were swarming over the fence.

There was no escape by further flight in this direction, he saw; but who was it that had said, "the best defence is strong attack"?

He gathered his strength and sprinted straight into the teeth of that attack. A gun flamed before him, but heaving chest and dizzy head do not lead to good marksmanship, and the bullet missed. Not another shot was so much as attempted, while Graem swerved past two pairs of reaching hands and made at the fence. There was no time to vault it; if he could hurdle it in his stride he still had a fighting chance of escape, otherwise he would instantly be buried under a human avalanche. So he rose at it with all his might. It seemed to rise with him, black and sharp-edged, but his right leg skimmed over —his left struck at the knee and pitched him straight forward in a dive which carried him into the capacious chest of a giant who was labouring up in the rear of the advance guard.

He made a serviceable cushion to break the force of the fall, and, rolling to his feet, Graem plunged past the house and ran into the open street, as a fox, beaten from cover, may rush out into the dangers that swarm in the open daylight.

Wisps of thin clouds of dust hung everywhere up and down the street as the horsemen hurried here and there; just to his right a rider was at that moment putting his foot in stirrup. Him Graem struck like an avalanche, beat him staggering away, and whipped into the saddle.

Never was the feel of a horse beneath him so welcome as when that little mustang gathered way and was off like a shot down the dusty street. A roar of voices and of guns behind him, but he angled across the thoroughfare and drove into the dark mouth of the first alley. It wound sinuously between houses, then reached another street parallel with the main one of the town. Here he turned to the left and sank the spurs into the bronco; only a moment's start was granted to him, however, for he heard plainly the roar of the horsemen behind, like the thundering of a cataract in a canyon's throat.

The bronco answered the sting of the spurs with a squeal and a buck and then its best burst of speed, but Graem groaned in despair. No doubt it was a good and game horse, excellent for a long ride, capable of enduring heat and thirst in the desert, but it had not the spring and forward thrust of a long-striding thoroughbred such as he had grown accustomed to backing. Labouring furiously, the mustang seemed to Graem to be standing still.

Yet if it could serve to get him to the poplars just a little ahead of the pursuit, so that he could fling himself on the back of the bay——

For that he rode, and as he shot down the street he heard the pursuit crash out of the alley's mouth and swing in after him. So he issued from the town, and had the blessing of the dim starlight before him—a little more and there was the tall shadow of the poplars. He crashed in among them and leaped to the ground.

Here were the black and the bay—the bay for him, since he could not venture to hope for enough time to take both horses—but as he flung saddle and bridle, with stumbling fingers, on the good bay, it seemed to him, unless his memory played him quite false, that the two animals were reversed from the positions in which he had left them.

That was a mere flash of intuition, rather than actual knowledge. Then, leaving his pack on the ground, the throatlatch unbuckled, one girth swinging loose, he dashed the bay through the ford and smashed through the shrubbery beyond.

He came into the open beyond in time to see the hunt split past the little grove and come boiling down at him from either side. They had no short-legged mustang before them now, however. If the bay were newly in from a long day's journey, still he had rested and fed somewhat, and he had a mighty heart to call upon. Away he flew, and in one minute of glorious sprinting Graem looked back and saw that three-quarters of the hunt were hopelessly out of it already. A mere handful of half a dozen or so hung in front; but these, however, were a different matter. They seemed to ride animals not much inferior to his own and every one of them, of course, was sure to be much fresher.

Before him the valley swept on, widening, growing more spacious and level until it came to the foot of mountains dimly seen against the southern stars; but to the right hand the hills were very near, coming down in great shadowy masses that offered some refuge to the hunted; toward them, accordingly, he veered away, and saw the hunt streamed faintly out behind him. Over the level the bay ran as freshly as the morning, but when they struck the slope his ears went back and his stride laboured. He was even more tired than Graem had feared, and by the time they reached the mouth of the first narrow valley he knew that his mount was nearly done.

The slope increased constantly, and presently the poor gelding was floundering with effort as though it was running in a bog, while up the ravine the pursuit came as if on strong wings. The end was very close, unless something was done at once. And as he turned a sharp elbow bend Graem put his horse at the left wall of the canyon. It was a rough tumble of rocks. He dismounted, and leading his horse he came presently to a low hilltop, littered with great boulders.

38

FOOL'S TRAIL

PLAINLY the bay was done. It stood on braced legs, breathing heavily, head down, ears fallen loosely forward. To ride it another five minutes would be to kill it; to rest here for a short time might mean, perhaps, another fighting chance of escape. He might go ahead on foot, but all this country was strange to him, and to pit himself on foot against an intelligent and mounted pursuit seemed sheer folly. One other factor decided him to remain in this spot, and that was the sound of water near at hand. When he moved a little forward, he found a spring welling up in the centre of a great circle of rocks. It was as though this hiding place were specially intended for him, and, accordingly, here he paused and fell to work rubbing down the bay, after giving it a single mouthful of water.

Again and again he paused as he worked, in order to listen with all his power. The sound of the water shut out small sounds, but plainly he heard the hunt go crashing up the valley, and plainly he heard it come back again.

What would they do now? Nearly the whole night lay ahead, a chill wind was rising, and certainly an ordinary posse might be expected to give up before long and go home, rather than fumble through the black dark after an elusive quarry.

He turned to climb down but, as he did so, he saw in the east a faint glow of light over the mountains, and instantly his heart sank. In another moment the edge of the moon was in view, dazzling bright to the eye of Graem, and rapidly it climbed above the peak and then floated freely into the sky, putting out the stars in hosts. It was almost at the full; the air was crystal clear; and the mountains were flooded with a silver light that seemed almost as revealing as the glare of the sun itself.

Graem concentrated on the horse. Eagerly he worked, but the response was slow, for the bay had been far spent by that strenuous burst coming out of town. He left the bay and climbed again to his lookout. He could see a group of horsemen working up the farther side of the valley; no doubt another group would be exploring in this direction before long, and with every moment the moon ascended higher and higher, and the light grew stronger, the shadows more narrow. He was chiefly sustained by a feeling that it would be too absurd for Tucker Graem, who had surmounted so many dangers, to go down before such a foolish chance as this encounter with the law in a town whose very name he did not know! Certainly he had been a vast fool to venture into the city!

He slipped down from the rock; while his hands were still raised high above his head a voice barked behind him: "Graem, keep those hands up!"

He turned his head, and out of the steep shadow beyond the spring he saw the gleam of a pair of levelled guns.

"Stand fast!" said the voice savagely. "You're just half a step from the end, young feller!"

But Graem whirled about with a cry.

"Lew Bergen!" he gasped. "Lew, old man, how can it be you?"

"Will you stick up those hands and turn back against the rock?" asked the grim voice of Bergen.

"Do you mean it?" echoed Graem. "Man, man, d'you mean it?"

"Do you hear me talking?"

"I hear you, Lew—but it don't sound natural. Answer me one question, and I'll face the rock and welcome. Is it the money, Lew? Is that why you want me? The reward?"

"I want you for murder!" said the sheriff sternly. "And I want you for a counterfeiting hound that's overdue to swing. You've played your game out, Graem. Now face that rock and keep those hands up or I'll break your back. You hear me?"

Not the guns, but utter bewilderment and despair subdued Graem then, and facing the rock he clutched at it dizzily, very sick at heart. The quick, strong step of Bergen came up behind him; his hands were drawn down and lashed securely in the small of his back.

"Lew," said the fugitive. "I'm plain staggered. It don't seem possible—not you!"

"Not me?" cried Bergen in a ringing tone of scorn and anger. "You've made a fool of me once with your lies, but friendship goes out where murder begins. You're gonna hang, Blondy, and you're gonna hang in my county."

There was a sudden murmur of many other voices approaching the rocks, and quickly the hands of the sheriff searched Graem and took away his weapons.

"He's taken!" someone called. "Sheriff Bergen has got him inside the circle of the rocks."

Then a swarm of armed men broke into the enclosure and made it ring with their excitement. It seemed that they could hardly believe in their good fortune.

"His hoss buckled up—look at the bay," said one. "Bergen, we'll get him back to town right away."

"We will," said Bergen. "We'll get him straight back to Loomis as fast as his hoss can carry him."

"Loomis?" cried a dozen voices at once. "After we've run him down, you try to take the name of it away from us—and the reward?"

"It's a plant," said one. "Bergen's a known friend of his. He wants to let him slip."

"That's wrong," said another. "I was close enough to hear Bergen slanging him. No matter what they used to be, there's no love lost between the pair of 'em now."

"Bergen," said still another, "we want that man, and we're gunna have him."

"Keep back, you," snapped Bergen, and he swung two long Colts into readiness. "I follered this trail long enough. I took this here gent with my own guns. Lemme see the men that'll take him away from me?"

"Swarm up that rock," said someone. "Take him from behind. Don't let one man bluff the whole lot of us!"

"Bluff?" said Bergen. "Now, I'll be hanged if there ain't a first-class massacre before you get him away from me! Boys, get sense and think it over. I been panting on this trail for days. I made the capture. All ye kin do won't pry him loose from me!"

They stared grimly at him. Certainly there was sufficient resolution in that great, gaunt form and in that harsh, barking voice.

They swirled here and there, and those to the rear were generally in favour of rushing the sheriff, but those in front held back.

Then an elderly puncher spoke up with the suggestion that the fact of main importance was that Graem should be safely in charge of the law; from his point of view it appeared that in no hands could he be held much safer than in those of Sheriff Lew Bergen. As for the rest of them, they'd better get back to town and finish their night's sleep. After all, nothing could take from them the pleasure they'd had in running down that night's game.

Such persuasion, and the steady, relentless guns of Bergen, began to have weight, and when Bergen commanded them to bear back they obeyed sullenly.

He marched Graem to the bay and made him mount, for the gelding was greatly recovered by this time. The cowpuncher brought up the sheriff's horse, and when he was mounted, with his lariat around the neck of the bay, the gloom of the crowd gave way and they sent the pair off with a cheer.

A very hollow sound had that cheer to the ears of Graem, for he would have preferred a thousandfold to be in the hands of the townsmen, lodged in their jail. With Bergen's grip on him like the grip of a bulldog, it would be hard to shake loose. The hangman's rope seemed perilously close to Graem as they rode down the slope.

But he stared before him as the slow miles were unwound behind them, and the moon floated higher and smaller and filled the mountains with a brighter light.

They came to a small creek, and at the edge of it the sheriff dismounted. For more than an hour he had not spoken. Now he said quietly:

"I reckon you'd better climb down off of that hoss and give it water and grub, Blondy. It looks sort of tuckered out, to me."

And with that he cut the ropes which held his captive's hands!

"Do you—you—why, you old blackguard!" gasped Graem. "You old wall-eyed, knock-kneed, stony-faced pirate!"

"I am all those things," grinned the sheriff, "and I'm worse, too, because I'm turnin' loose a red-handed murderer, and a counterfeiter, and goodness knows what else!"

"D'you hear?" said Graem. "They'll turn you out of your office and doggone near lynch you, for this!"

"They'll never see me in that county again," said Bergen, with an attempt at cheerfulness.

"You're chucking it, Lew?"

"I'm tired of it," said Lew Bergen. "Mighty tired of the faces of the folks and the faces of the hills. I want something new, and I reckon that you and me between us might be able to work up some sort of excitement."

To this Graem listened in despair. It was utter blasting of a career which had started with much promise; and there was the young wife back there at Loomis. He had betrayed her, too.

The sheriff was speaking again in slow explanation.

"After I spotted the hosses," he said, "I hoped——"

"Back in the poplars? Lew, you were there?"

"They'd got tangled up in their ropes, and I had to undo them and tie 'em again."

"But how'd you find them there?"

"Now, how would you think?" grinned Bergen.

"I dunno," said Graem. "I dunno, unless it was the greatest sort of good luck for me that brought you there!"

"Guess again."

"There ain't any guess left, Lew."

"There is, though," said the sheriff. "I've been following you, son, ever since you rode out of Loomis, and of all the fool trails that I ever worked out, yours was the easiest and the worst. A blind baby could've found you. Doggone me, Blondy, I'm so ashamed of you that it makes me blush even to think of it!"

39

LIGHT ON THE SUBJECT

THEY made but a short distance beyond the creek, and, finding a place where grass was plentiful and water near, they camped. From the sheriff's pack, food was provided, and, after they had cooked and eaten dinner, Graem tried his hand at persuasion. If the sheriff would pretend that his captive had slipped through his hand, then, on his return to his county, all men would readily forgive him, since it was known that he and Graem were old and tried friends. And no other blot was chargeable against his record.

At this the sheriff wrapped his enormous hands around his knees and chuckled. "Nobody ever had no job in any county in this here country," he maintained, "without being hated by more'n half the folks that vote. If I go back to Loomis, they'll have me tried in court. After that, my name's gone."

"And show me," said Graem, "how you expect to do any better by travelling with me?"

"I'll show you, son," said the sheriff. "You're on the trail of La Salle, ain't you?"

"That stands to reason, of course."

"Do folks generally know about him?"

"They've heard about him; most people know that he's a great crook, and that nothing can be hung on him."

"Now, Graem, why d'you want to get La Salle?"

"For new reasons since I last seen you, but those old ones were good enough. For one thing, I want to clear myself of a murder charge which you were shouting about pretty loudly this evening, up there in the rocks."

"Well, kid, now listen to this. If you clear yourself, I'm cleared. I mean, who'll be down on me for not jailing a man that didn't deserve to be jailed?"

Graem hesitated. He was beginning to see the light.

"And, on the other hand," said Lew Bergen. "if I can get my hands on anything about La Salle, it'll be a scalp for me, won't it?"

"They'd want to make you president," admitted Graem.

"All right," said Bergen. "There we stand. We got one chance in a million of making good on this trip. I got no chances in a million of making good if I go back to Loomis. Is that all straight with you?"

It ended all argument, as it appeared to them both. They were asleep five minutes later, and wakened the next morning to find the bay gelding still seedy, and his flanks rather sunken. Nevertheless, there was work in him, but, after they had made a wretched breakfast, Graem decided to go ahead on foot, keeping as hard a pace as he could maintain, and so freeing the gelding of that burden.

He had said nothing of his information the night before, but now as they headed south, he walking as briskly as possible, he went over everything that had happened during the crowded days since he last saw Lew Bergen. He arrived at the point where he had met Ruth on the edge of the meadow near Larribee's house, and there he stopped.

"If you followed my trail, Lew, you were near that house, then?"

"Blondy," chuckled Bergen, "I seen you do cruel murder on that short-horned sucker, Rex Dobie."

"You?"

"I slipped up while you was persuading him to get mad; and I thought that if he was fool enough to let you come up the bank, at least he ought to have his chance to fight it out fair and square."

"You were there in the brush?"

"Why, Blondy, I could've followed the sort of a trail that you left by midnight."

"And afterwards?"

"I hung around near the house. When I heard the guns begin to bark, I told myself that you were done for; but afterwards when you come sashaying out, I hoped that maybe you'd polished off somebody worth polishing. Who was in that house?"

"La Salle!"

He waited to see astonishment in the face of his companion, but the sheriff merely nodded, saying: "That's likely."

"What in heaven's name!" cried Graem, "have La Salle and Larribee got to do with each other, because it's easy to see that they don't waste any love on one another?"

"You don't know how they stand?" asked the sheriff curiously.

"I got no idea."

"Well, well!" murmured Bergen. "For a bright young gent you're blind and deaf, son! You've done a grand, fine piece of detective work, and then you fall down on a little thing like that, that ought to stare you jump in the face. You tried to kill La Salle—that was the noise of the guns?"

"I was being killed by three of his boys, but he came in and shot down one of 'em and we handled the other two between us. Then we said good-bye, and I left."

"Steady, son. Don't start in mystifyin' me."

"Why did I go to Larribee's house?"

"To get the Guernsey girls."

"I found 'em, but I didn't bring 'em away. La Salle—La Salle——"

He paused, and the ready sheriff filled in the interval with a soft whistle.

"I forgot that side of him—I've been so used to thinking of La Salle as plain devil. And that's all?"

"That's all."

The sheriff murmured after a time: "You leave right behind you the man that you're hunting. Well, maybe you're right. After all, it's not La Salle that we want—it's some proof of his crooked work."

They determined that one fairly short day's ride would bring them to a distance which, measured from Larribee's house, would fairly well represent the space of three long days' rides to the south. There, according to Graem's first plan, they would cast about for the meaning of the five mysterious words, "council house mystery man river," which apparently had directed Jerry Tyndal to such a secret that he had fled with his knowledge and paid for his flight with his death.

Then, in the late afternoon, they entered a district of low, broken, stone-faced hills, patched with chaparral, here and there, and with some scattered stunted trees. This region extended for many miles in front of them, and, turning, they could see in the blue, vast distance the two twin peaks like the ears of a mule—a similarity much discounted at this remove.

Here they determined to establish headquarters, finding a fairly good camping place in a hollow on the broad breast of a hill, with trees for shade, and grass for the horses and a runlet of water. Graem was left to make the camp, while the sheriff with his fresher horse started out on a circle of investigation.

He came back in the dusk, with the report that, so far as he had been able to ride, nothing was in view except this same bad lands of broken rocks with only occasional patches of grass and other vegetation.

They spent the night at their camp. In the morning Graem would have moved on, but, as Bergen pointed out, they had no clues, and the mystery might be not a mile away, if they knew how to look for it.

Half baked by the heat of the sun in their hollow, not daring to raise a smoke, they chewed hard-tack for lunch and drank lukewarm water from the slow runlet. Afterwards, Graem stretched himself in the shade for a nap, remarking: "We got one thing to thank our luck for—no flies!"

He slept hard, for the fatigue of many days rested heavily on body and soul and mind. He was awakened by a distant sound of voices, and when he looked around him Bergen was not to be seen. His horse and pack also were gone!

Up to the edge of the hollow went Graem, and there he saw beneath him Bergen conversing with an ancient man on a piebald mustang. The conversation had reached its end that very moment, for with a mutual wave of the hand they separated, and, while the rider on the piebald drifted north, the sheriff rode on south and disappeared among the hills.

He was gone.

It did not seem in any degree possible to Graem that Bergen could have left him in the lurch, but nearly an hour passed before there sounded the welcome clicking of shod hoofs over the hard rocks. And presently the sheriff was with him, his horse unsaddled, and a cigarette lighted.

"Where've you been?" asked Graem at last.

A wave of the hand vaguely indicated a considerable section of the horizon.

"Seen anything?"

"Some rocks," answered Bergen.

"Nobody around?"

"A piece of a man," yawned the sheriff.

He seemed on the point of falling asleep, his head was nodding heavily on his breast and his eyes were closed.

At last he opened them.

"Bergen!" exclaimed Graem.

"There's no need shouting," said the sheriff with irritation.

"You've found out something!" insisted Graem. "I know your tricks!"

"Me?" said Bergen innocently. "All I found out was the names of some of the hills, from an old wolf hunter that come by. Sort of interesting, though. Injun names, mostly. Over there, that's Blunt Arrow—that hill without no head. There's Lost Medicine, that scalped-looking one to the north——"

"Oh, let the hills go," said Graem. "Tell me what you've learned!"

"There ain't any patience in you, young fellow," complained the sheriff. "A mean man to be on a trail, I call you. Injun names always have interested me a pile. Now, there's Two Fat Squaws—those three hills bearing west. Except that there's three of 'em, I call those names pretty pat. But accuracy never bothered the Injuns none."

"I'm gonna finish my sleep," declared Graem in a heat.

"Off sou'west," went on the sheriff in his harsh drawl, "that there biggish hill with the long ride along its back, that the Injuns used to call the Council House."

"What?" shouted Graem.

"And around on the south face of it," murmured the sheriff, "there's a trickle of water that dives into the ground and don't come up. They used to call that Mystery Man River."

40

IN THE COUNCIL HOUSE

ALL one portion of the problem disappeared at once.

Poor Jerry Tyndal, out of the knowledge of Indian tongues which had been taught him by the old professor had been able to solve the riddle of the five words with ease, though it had cost Graem so much pain and time to get to the correct answer. But there stood the Council House, looking, now that the clue was given to them, very like an enormous tent with a long ridge-pole. Graem was eager to start at once for the place and make their examination, but the sheriff refused point-blank.

As he showed his hot companion, there was a considerable open sweep of ground all around the big hill, and from the side of Mystery Man River in particular the bluff looked over an ample valley. If they tried to approach they would be apt to fall under observation, and, if La Salle's men were near, that observation doubtless would be fatal to them. What he suggested was that they carefully work their way to the hills facing Mystery Man River, and there wait, searching the rocks with their glass, until dark. Under cover of dark, they would come up to the bluff; and when the moon rose, they would be able to investigate in detail.

This was so sensible that Graem agreed, though the waste of time maddened him. They circled back through the wilderness of rocks, winding in and out among the hills, until they came to a position which was what the sheriff wanted—opposite the southern face of the Council House. Here they took up their quarters, in a sort of crow's nest at the top of the hill where they were sheltered, and, leaving the horses in the hollow behind, they settled down to an afternoon's watch in the frightful heat. Necessarily, they had to choose an enclosed place, and since there was no stir of wind, they fairly melted in the gathering power of the sun. Each man held the glass for a half-hour at a time, scrutinizing the bluff opposite with the greatest care, and then comparing notes with his companion.

The Council House was a hill of several hundred feet; halfway down the southern face of it a spring leaped out and made a white streak among the great boulders, until it disappeared suddenly at the base of the bluff. All that southern face was so seamed and broken and split by erosion and time that a whole regiment could have sheltered in the crevices or behind the big stones with perfect ease.

The two observed the hill; then they mapped it, Graem taking a piece of paper and drawing in the network of the main crevices and minor ravines; he even indicated the greater stones, and the spots at which the Mystery Man River leaped into existence and disappeared again.

Though they lay at a considerable distance, yet the spring was of such volume and fell with such force that, from time to time, they heard a deep, low hum of the reverberations of the water noises among the rocks. So they waited miserably until close to sunset, when several riders came up the valley and turned in at the bluff of Council House. They were lost among the boulders at once.

"Did you spot the hind man of that procession?" asked Graem, who had taken the glass at the last minute, after the sheriff had swept the group of riders.

"I saw him; old fellow, I guessed him."

"By the sag of him in the saddle, you mean. But he ain't so old. That's Guernsey, Lew."

Lew Bergen observed presently: "You'll mark that they ain't showing themselves again?"

"And they won't," said Graem. "Right among those rocks there's something worth seeing, Lew!"

After that, though the sun was growing less and less hot, yet it seemed intolerable to both to endure the passing of the time. Sunset, however, came at last, and as the red disc disappeared and the flaming west was reflected in polished faces of granite among the hills, Graem said for the hundredth time: "What could have brought Guernsey here? La Salle! Why did La Salle send him here? Answer, Lew?"

"A message."

"Wrong, because he has a hundred messengers."

"To get him out of the way."

"Why not kill him at that shack in the hills, then, if he wanted to get him out of the way? Why the trouble of snaking him away down here?"

There was no answer.

But now the dark, so long wished for, gradually came over the hills, and the two started. They rode to a point at the side of the Council House, and then went slowly back across the lower face of the bluff. Moving cautiously, placing their feet with care, they made no more than two shadows, but that first trip among the boulders gave them no return.

They settled down, therefore, among the rocks and waited for the coming of the moon. More than two hours passed in this manner, but the time did not seem long, for their hearts were beating high, now, at the threshold of the adventure. Danger on a vast scale was before them, and how they were to meet and endure it they could not tell. Numbers, certainly, would be against them, if they succeeded in coming face to face with the mystery of the Council House.

When, at last, the moon lightened, they moved up among the rocks, and, at the suggestion of the sheriff, went close to the top of the slope and from that worked down to the place at which the spring issued with a rush. Still further down they went until they came to the point at which the Mystery Man River re-entered the ground. It plunged straight down into a narrow-throated chasm; but behind this, constantly recruited by the showers of spray that fell under it, was a still-standing pool that sloped back under a shelf of rock.

They worked on down to the bottom of the rocks, but the result of their search was an absolute blank; they had found nothing, not even a hole that a pigeon could have crawled through.

They stood together without a word; then the sheriff waved his friend to the right, while he took the left hand, and so they climbed once more toward the top. At the point where the stream of water entered the little gorge, Graem paused again, wondering vaguely if human beings could climb down into that infernal hole. He kneeled at the edge of the pool and stared down at the rush and roar of white water, but after all it appeared totally impossible that any human being could have endured the thrashing of the water for a single moment.

Then, rising to leave the place, his foot slipped, and he was chest-deep in the waters of the pool. He snatched out his revolvers to keep the ammunition from becoming soaked, but as he turned to climb from the icy waters, he saw beneath the rear shelf of stone the faint glimmer of a light.

He stopped and considered. He told himself, at first, that it was no more than the reflected play of the moonlight, thrown into the hollow by the waves which his immersion had started. But moonshine is silver-white, and yonder undoubtedly was a yellow gleam that he had observed!

He set his teeth and pushed on. He ducked his head—his chin

touched the water—and then he was standing erect within a shell-like structure which receded with increasing height and breadth. The water shoaled beneath his feet; and out of the blackness before him, once more there was a play of light—a flash, and then a broad shaft that beat upon the surface of the water and illuminated all the little cave in which he was standing!

He held his breath and ducked low, expecting bullets to follow, in the path of the radiance, but instead, a familiar voice said in the distance—repeated and magnified by echo—"Go outside the water and look around. Be careful, Charlie!"

Apparently a door was closed, for the light diminished at once, and Graem heard a man clear his throat in the near distance. Whoever "Charlie" might be, yonder speaker was well known to him, for it was none other than La Salle himself, and with the feeling that he was almost within gripping distance of that man, the heart of Graem began to race.

In the meantime, by that broad shaft of light, he had seen a sandy incline to the right of the water's edge, and on this he crawled out, on hands and knees, and huddled back against the farther wall. Footsteps were approaching rapidly, and then a shadow went past him. From the pool there was a sudden flash of light, as an electric torch glanced on it, and by that light Graem recognized the profile of Charlie Moon.

With a groan or two, Moon descended into the cold water, and there he paused. Well it was for him, however, that he did not turn around! In another moment he had left the inner portion of the cave and was in the outer pool. Graem heard him splashing out of the water on to the rocks. Then he himself snatched off his wet riding boots, wrung and pressed from his clothes as much water as possible, and went forward again, down a spacious tunnel, as he could make out both walls by the touch of his fingertips, though the top arched above out of his reach.

Going in deeper, presently he saw the least scratch of light before him, and that he took to be the door which had opened a moment before. He came to it and kneeled so as to look through the crack, which was near the door level; and inside he saw a picture which froze the blood in his veins!

A man naked except for a loin-cloth lashed to a wooden cross; in his face an expression of tense and terrible resolution, as though an agony had been braved before, and would be braved again. He was a bearded, swarthy-skinned man, with a lofty intellectual forehead, and a long growth of grey hair. He had the soft, paunchy body that comes of a sedentary life, but though his arms were spindles, and his neck flabby, there was force of spirit in this man.

"That's once," said the voice of La Salle. "Now, what do you have to say to me, Harney? You've had only a touch, my friend. The next time will be a thousandfold worse."

The lips of Harney snarled back beneath his beard.

"You'll be tired first," he answered.

"Is that it?" answered La Salle, and there was a cruel note of satisfaction in his voice. "Well, I'm glad to see that you're a fellow of such calibre; I'd hate to have you give up at the first touch. Take him back, boys. Hold on. I'll go along with you and manage the thing!"

41

DIRTY WORK

HALF a dozen men trooped out, carrying the lashed man; then a door closed, and voices sounded as from behind a second partition.

There were two courses before Graem. He could return to the sheriff and bring him back into the cave; or he could go forward and learn what was possible here. After all, even if the sheriff were with him, it was very little that two men could do against such numbers as were inside the subterranean passages; therefore, with no further hesitation, he pushed at the door, and it yielded instantly to his hand.

He entered a large apartment, more than two-thirds of which was filled with delicately complicated machinery. He looked at it with wonder, and at the system of leather belts by which power was transferred to the machines, apparently. From what source that power came, he could not imagine, unless it were harnessed pounds of falling water, which rumbled and crashed softly in the distance. One smoking lantern lighted this jumbled room; and at the end opposite the door through which Graem had come there was a litter of boxes and rubbish. The floor was half rock and half sand, very damp from the permeation of water through the rock walls. Something else was mixed in with that sand, and, bending, Graem picked up the torn half of a hundred-dollar bill—and a complete, though tattered, note which called upon the Federal treasury to pay the bearer a thousand dollars. Similar bits of paper had been ground under foot everywhere, and it came home to Graeme with a shock that all this had a clear meaning. The source from which the country had been flooded with spurious currency was not the Kentucky Mountains, as the newspapers were surmising, it was the Council House itself! And this was the source from which poor Jerry Tyndal had snatched his supposed fortune! The brain of Graem sang; and his first impulse was one of admiration for La Salle—for the very hugeness of the schemes to which he turned his attention.

That admiration was cut off at the source, so to speak, by a wild shriek of agony from the adjoining room. It drove a pang through Graem; then, as his blood grew hot, he slipped in among the machinery close to the opposite door, through which the cry had come ringing.

He could hear groans, and the voice of La Salle, as cheerful and good-natured as ever.

"Frightfully sorry to do this, Harney. I want to let you out of this easily, but what can I do? Very hard to keep tormenting you, but it's my duty to carry on."

"Duty?" cried the tortured man.

"Duty to my friends and companions here," said La Salle, with a sublime hypocrisy that made Graem set his teeth. "You see, Harney, they have worked a long time, and they have worked very hard. Now they expect a recompense, and you stand in their way!"

"You've taken the money that I had printed," cried Harney. "You've got millions out of that! Isn't it enough for you, you hypocrite and bloodsucker?"

"What a passion you're in," said La Salle softly. "Of course, we got millions of the big denominations, but though you printed them you must have known it wouldn't be long before the counterfeit was discovered. Big denominations kill themselves in counterfeit; they draw too much attention, you know! We passed a little, but hardly enough to pay us for our work. We've had to employ a large and expensive organization by pushing this stuff across, you know. And men have to be well paid to break the law. However, the great fortune is in the little five, ten and twenty dollar bills. Of course you knew that when you organized your very clever scheme, Harney. Now then, I ask you again where we shall find the plates and the rest of the necessary material? We have the paper, at last—and magnificently done paper it is, Harney!"

"You've had out of me," answered Harney, "everything that

you're going to get. You can take the rest of the blood out of me, but you'll take no more of my brains!"

"Patience," said La Salle. "You've had only a taste, poor Harney. I have infinite resources in the matter of giving pain. Now give me your kind attention!"

There was no doubt about it. He was enjoying this fiendish business.

But the next cry was not from the lips of Harney; it was a furious shout which ended under the cool protest of La Salle.

"Guernsey, are you mad?"

"I'll be shot if I stand by and see another moment of this," declared Guernsey. "You're a fiend, La Salle."

"Guernsey," said the leader, "if you'll come back with me into the other room, I'll give you some reasons for the necessity of doing this."

"I want no reasons," said the other. "I have eyes and ears to see the fiendish tricks you're doing!"

Nevertheless, he was persuaded, and presently he came through the doorway at the heels of La Salle. There the latter faced him, with the light of the smoky lantern glimmering faintly and gloomily above him.

"I dunno why you got me down here in the first place," said Guernsey. "Some dirty work, I reckon. You tell me that my girls are here. I think you lie, La Salle!"

"Tush, tush!" said La Salle, but without smiling. "You're rather hard on me, Guernsey."

"The game," said the puncher, "was that you'd have a clear week's trial. I told you you never could persuade Charlie to marry you. You've failed with her, and you've brought me here to tie my hands still. Because you gotta produce her to me sooner or later!"

"I've failed not with Charlie, but with Ruth," admitted the criminal sourly, "and Ruth holds Charlie back. Otherwise, she'd marry me in a minute."

"Your time is up," said Guernsey. "And I'm leaving this place, La Salle!"

"To go back to Larribee's house and take your girls away?"

"Nacherally."

"Ah, man," said La Salle, "d'you dream I'd let you go there? Guernsey, you're not a fool. I brought you down here to keep you safely in hand. Once I'm married to Charlie, you can appear again and say what you please. But in the meantime, if you try too hard to bother me, I'll kill you with as little compunction as I'll kill Graem!"

"Graem? I curse the day that ever I laid eyes on him!"

"If you have sense, you'll bless the day that ever you laid eyes on me! Guernsey, think it over. This fellow Harney undoubtedly has an outfit equipped here for producing counterfeit of small denominations. Once we can print it, we'll flood the country. We'll take in millions, man, and that will be my last crooked job."

"I've heard other folks talk like that," said Guernsey.

"You went straight yourself," said La Salle.

"I never would have gone crooked if you hadn't tempted the heart out of me, and curse you again for that!"

"Steady, steady!" murmured La Salle, stepping back a little, for it seemed as though the other would hurl himself bodily at the leader. "Use your brains—keep your wits alive, old fellow. You're on the verge of wealth. Also, you're on the verge of death. I don't care much which choice you make. I'd like to use you to smooth my way with Charlie to the end; if I can't do that, I'll have none of you. I brought you down here to let you see the inside of me, Guernsey. If I'm willing to torment a man like Harney, an intelligent, really brilliant operator, do you think that I'd hesitate over you? I tell you, Guernsey, I'll have Harney's secret out of him, or I'll tear his heart out with my own hands! Now, judge your own case for yourself!"

"You a husband for Charlie!" groaned Guernsey, and beat his hand against his forehead.

"As good as Graem," said La Salle.

"Who said 'good as Graem'?" asked a harsh voice from the opposite door, and old Larribee stepped into the room, looking more satanic than ever.

"Why are *you* here?" shouted La Salle in a sudden passion.

Larribee raised a forefinger.

"Young feller," said he, "you've never used that tone to me before, and if you ever try it on again I'll make you wish that you could dodge for shelter!"

"I'm sorry," said La Salle, softening and bowing instantly. Graem could hardly believe what his eyes and his ears told him. "I'm sorry, sir, but the fact is you agreed to remove them to——"

"I said that I'd do what I could. It can't be done. The little girl is down with brain fever or something. She is yelling and hollering day and night, begging Charlie to send you away; and Charlie's crying over her and telling her that you *are* away and that you'll never have a chance to come back."

"What!" cried La Salle.

"Not meaning it," admitted Larribee. "Just persuading the kid to get her well again. However, I seen I could do no good there. I come down here to tell you that you'd better get back in that direction."

"I have something more important than women to deal with now," answered La Salle, with a click of his teeth.

"Aye," said the old man. "You have Graem, and I was kind of glad to hear you say that you're a better man than him. Have you got him laid away safe?"

"Graem?" answered the other. "That persevering fool is a hundred miles away."

"The devil he is."

"You overrate him," said La Salle. "You always have. I've handled him like wax. I tell you, Larribee, that the whole game is in my hands; another turn of the screw, and I'll have the secret out of Harney. Then I'm ready to put millions in our pockets. I'll have Charlie when the little brat is well again—or dead. Guernsey here either becomes my man—or never leaves the underground. And poor Graem is floundering through the mountains, with the law chasing him!"

"Chasing him south, I reckon," said Larribee, "because his hoss is just now standin' at the corner of the Council House!"

42

THE SECRET OUT

So profound was the impression made upon La Salle that, for a long moment, his face lost all colour and he breathed hard, like one half stifled.

Then he said jerkily: "Step into the other room and call out all the boys. Hurry!"

Larribee, with a demoniac grin aside, went past the younger man and disappeared through the door. Then Graem—for he saw that this was his one moment—rose from the shadows and said quietly:

"La Salle!"

He had intended to fire as the other whirled. But La Salle did not whirl. He moved like one stunned to face this unexpected enemy.

"Guernsey," snapped Graem. "Drop the bolt of that door and

watch it! La Salle," he added, "I guess this is the last time we meet!"

Guernsey, with a sort of moan of joy, thrust home the heavy bolt. Almost at the same instant the door was shaken from the inside.

"What's up?" snarled the voice of Larribee, faint behind the partition.

Guernsey had leaped to a box and snatched up a rifle that lay on it.

"Larribee," he shouted in response, "we got you boxed and nailed up like fish for market. Try to break through that door, and we'll blow you to pieces."

Utter silence reigned within the other chamber. But now the hand of La Salle jerked back as though a bullet had struck him. Graem risked a glance to the side, and there he saw the mighty form of Sheriff Lew Bergen, with a formidable Colt in either hand.

"Lew!" cried Graem softly.

"I just borrowed some information from a gent by name of Charlie Moon, and come in this way," said the sheriff. "Seems like we have you with the goods on you, La Salle. And a long wait it's been before we could nail you! Be a good lad, now, and hold up your hands!"

"Wait one minute," said Graem. "This is my man, Lew. I've fought and trailed and waited for him. I've got fifteen years to pay him for, and the only reason that I give him a chance for his life is that he played man to me up at old Larribee's house. Lew, him and me fight this out."

"It's right," answered the sheriff instantly. "It ain't more than right and just that you ask, Blondy. La Salle, I stand here, and when I drop my hand it's the signal that you two go for your guns."

He stood at the side. But La Salle returned no answer. Once his eyes wandered in a flash to the side, as though he were seeking for some chance to escape. But then he fixed his gaze upon Graem, a white-faced gaze like that of a hypnotized man, such as Graem had seen before at the table of Larribee.

"Wait a minute," said Graem to the sheriff. "He's not ready. Look here, La Salle. My guns are back inside. You have an even break. Are you ready?"

"Johnnie! Johnnie!" cried the voice of Larribee from within, raised now to a terrible pitch of pain.

"Aye, Father," answered La Salle. "I've reached the end—or the beginning."

He shouted to the sheriff, "Ready!"

And the hand of Lew Bergen instantly dropped in signal.

Very fast was Graem in the draw, and few could vie with him. But now his weapon was hardly out of its holster when the Colt of La Salle flashed from his hip. Chance and chance only saved Graem, for in the very viciousness and energy of his draw, La Salle threw away the advantage of his miraculous speed, his still more miraculous accuracy. The violence of his motion twisted his whole body a little, and one foot slipped wide on a rolling pebble. Even so, the wind of his bullet kissed the cheek of Graem. His shot in return struck that devilishly convulsed face, and La Salle dropped loosely forward.

Silence—the wisps of smoke slowly lifted—and then Guernsey said huskily: "It don't seem no ways possible! He—he's done at last!"

And from beyond the partition the wild voice of the old man cried again: "Johnnie! Johnnie!"

"Unbar that door," said the sheriff to Guernsey. "But then jump back here and help us cover it. How many men are inside?"

"Five, and Harney."

"Who's Harney? Not the counterfeiter?"

"Aye," said Guernsey. "It was Harney that worked up this plant. La Salle got on the trail of it, and he sent word south by Tyndal to Larribee to look for the place here."

With that, he drew the bolt and sprang back, rifle at the shoulder.

"Now, boys," said the sheriff, "you can come through, but one at a time, and Larribee first. And if you try to rush there are three of us covering the doorway. Do what you want!"

Apparently they wanted a chance for life.

Old Larribee came first. Clutching at the door, he looked wildly at the fallen body; then he dropped on his knees beside it.

"It ain't possible!" groaned Graem. "It ain't possible that he's La Salle's father!"

"He is. Shut up. We may have some work here!"

But there was no work.

If there had been any determination to die fighting among La Salle's men, it was taken out of them by the fall of their leader. Out they came, one by one, and, last of all, Graem saw the familiar old face of Crocker, the hotel keeper!

As they came out, each man was searched to the skin, secured, and stood against the wall under the gun of Guernsey. Crocker, coming last, could be examined in more detail, and it was the sheriff who presently said to Graem:

"Blondy, this here ought to interest you a little!"

And he held out a little poniard with a handle not two and a half inches long, and a blade like the bright skeleton of an icicle—a mere ray of slender death.

"You?" shouted Graem, And then he added with a burst of heat: "You hound, it was you that knifed poor Tyndal that night in your own hotel!"

The old man smiled with the utmost self-content.

"Hang it on me if you can," said he. "Hang it on me if you can while *you're* bein' tried for the murder!"

They marched the prisoners out one by one, Guernsey forming the outside guard, and the sheriff conducting each in turn, until he came to Larribee. When he touched that veteran in crime on the shoulder, Larribee, with the head of his son in his lap, did not look up. The sheriff leaned and raised the old man's head. It rolled loosely back upon his shoulders and the glazed eyes stared at Lew Bergen.

43

THE OLD AND THE NEW

THERE was no murder trial of Tucker Graem. For when he and Guernsey and the sheriff reached Loomis, all three were hailed as popular heroes. Already, from a little railroad station, they had telegraphed definite tidings to the East, and marshals and deputy marshals, detectives and secret service agents had swarmed out to examine the seat of the famous counterfeiting. As for Crocker, inquiry into his past revealed that he had accumulated his little fortune in the mines in certain extraordinarily novel ways; usually he went out with a partner and came back without one. These eccentricities formed a bright background against which to place suspicion of the murder of Jerry Tyndal, and finally Crocker himself grew weary of all the talk and cut it short with a note scrawled on his cell floor in the jail. They found him the next morning strangled by his own bandanna which he had knotted to the bars of his door and from which he had then allowed himself to hang, with iron resolution, until he choked to death.

Graem did not wait to see this result. He had been delayed long enough. Guernsey, in the meantime had headed north for the Larribee house; before leaving, he had dispatched several loads of timber and all essentials toward the site of his old home. As for the loss which he had sustained, there was reward money to more than compensate him.

Therefore Graem, when at last he could leave Loomis, after the dreary weeks of examination, witnessing, signing of photographs, much refusal of statements, much dodging of the crowd which insisted on trailing him wherever he went—when he could finally free himself of all his encumbrances, he rode hastily out of Loomis and shot away across country, not for the Larribee house but for the happy valley where he had lain wounded and came back to life and health.

He had, in the meantime, one short note.

"*Ruth is coming on fine; Charlie is just standing it.*"

And the thing haunted him as he pushed the bay remorselessly across the country.

It meant, of course, that her heart was completely broken and that only an iron nerve was sustaining her.

And then, on a day, pushing his horse hard up the last slope, he came in sight of the valley, and hastily glanced down to see where the family tent might have been raised.

But there was no tent in sight——

There was a small house, and a barn beyond, and a tangle of corral fencing, and all seemed to be as it had been before, except that there was one square, black stain on the ground between the house and the barn. That was where the big haystack had stood. What miracle, however, could have happened?

Six weeks had passed since the timber went out from Loomis— ah, well, with a little money and good neighbours, much can be done!

Then down the slope he went like an avalanche, dust smoking up behind, and pebbles rattling and big stones crashing in volleys before him.

The bay staggered as it reached the foot of the slope, and then stretched away across the level.

There were cattle, too, dotting the valley as they had dotted it before, and the heart of Graem began to rise ridiculously high, so homelike did it all appear. Until it seemed that he had been sleeping, and out of bad dreams he was wakened to this.

From the hollow beside the barn appeared a horseman who rode rapidly toward him, slanting at a familiar angle in the saddle—Guernsey!

They greeted each other with a distant shout, and soon they were face to face, gripping hands. The same Guernsey, except that there was a little tightness around the mouth and more grey beneath the hat.

"Ruth?" snapped the newcomer.

"Sassier than ever," said the rancher.

Graem sighed.

"And the house and the cows—what has been happening?"

"Part money, part luck, and part help. I've had fifty men from the big turnouts over here helping. Folks tried to give away cows to me, Graem. They'd hardly take the money that I had until I showed them that it was plenty. Harvesting La Salles is a pretty profitable game. It beats raising cows, son!"

Then his eyes sobered.

"Mostly it was Ruth," he said. "She wanted things fixed up to make you feel sort of at home."

"And Charlie?" muttered Graem.

"I gotta ride down the creek," said the father. "Maybe you can find Charlie for yourself."

So the rancher hurried off, grinning back foolishly over his shoulder. Another thought stopped him, however, and brought him back with a sweep.

"There was a few hard days, old son. I took the bull by the horns and talked facts about La Salle. I began with the way he quit you in the desert and, after that, I branched off a little and I turned loose on the rest of his life, and I wound up, partner, on the things that happened to Harney, with me looking on. I hear they've turned Harney loose, by the way? And a good thing they did. He's had his honey! And when I got through, Blondy, and pointed out that Oliver Landon and La Salle was the same man, I had to put her to bed. She was sort of groggy for a week, son, but after that she was as good as ever. Landon, you see, was a story, something out of a book, a dream, maybe. But he never existed, and things had just left off the day that you rode away from the farmhouse. Savvy?"

He swept off a second time, and now he was gone.

Graem rode slowly on; he crossed the creek by a new little bridge; he journeyed up the old cattle trail, newly worn by heavy wheels, and at last he was dismounting at the familiar hitching rack when a wild young voice cried out, and there was Ruth running.

He swung her higher than his head, and she came down in his arms with tears of laughter and joy.

"Quick, Blondy!" she commanded. "Come here and look at something!"

She slipped to the ground and led him around the corner of the house; in the distance, hurrying toward the grove, was the figure of a girl.

"She saw you coming and said she was taking a little walk," Ruth explained. "But I don't think she'll walk very far. Oh, Blondy, how terribly fortunate we are!"

He, with long, hungry strides, followed after the hastening figure, gaining swiftly. For, though Charlotte strove to hurry, he could see that her steps were faltering. He was close behind her when she reached the grove, but there she stumbled and almost fell; and then, with a cry, she faced around, with one hand steadying herself against the rough trunk of a pine, the other pressed against her heart to control its wild beating. Graem could see that she was not as she had been in the happy valley before, not as she had been in the house of Larribee. Her eyes were darkened, as if by pain; and he went to her slowly, and in silence.

Max Brand® is the best known pen name of Frederick Faust, creator of Dr Kildare™, Destry, and many other fictional characters popular with readers and viewers worldwide. Faust wrote for a variety of audiences in many genres. His enormous output totalling approximately thirty million words or the equivalent of 530 ordinary books, covered nearly every field: crime, fantasy, historical romance, espionage, Westerns, science fiction, adventure, animal stories, love, war, and fashionable society, big business and big medicine. Eighty motion pictures have been based on his work along with many radio and television programs. For good measure he also published four volumes of poetry. Perhaps no other author has reached more people in more different ways.

Born in Seattle in 1892, orphaned early, Faust grew up in the rural San Joaquin Valley of California. At Berkeley he became a student rebel and one-man literary movement, contributing prodigiously to all campus publications. Denied a degree because of unconventional conduct, he embarked on a series of adventures culminating in New York City where, after a period of near starvation, he received simultaneous recognition as a serious poet and successful popular-prose writer. Later, he traveled widely, making his home in New York, then in Florence, and finally in Los Angeles.

Once the United States entered the Second World War, Faust abandoned his lucrative writing career and his work as a screenwriter to serve as a war correspondent with the infantry in Italy, despite his fifty-one years and a bad heart. He was killed during a night attack on a hilltop village held by the German army. New books based on magazine serials or unpublished manuscripts continue to appear. Alive and dead he has averaged a new one every four months for seventy-five years. In the U.S. alone nine publishers issue his work, plus many more in foreign countries. Yet, only recently have the full dimensions of this extraordinarily versatile and prolific writer come to be recognized and his stature as a protean literary figure in the 20th Century acknowledged. His popularity continues to grow throughout the world.